A QUICHE BEFORE DYING

Also by Joanne Pence

Ancient Secrets Series

ANCIENT ECHOES - ANCIENT SHADOWS

ANCIENT ILLUSIONS - ANCIENT DECEPTIONS

The Donnelly Cabin Inn

IF I LOVED YOU - THIS CAN'T BE LOVE

SENTIMENTAL JOURNEY - A CERTAIN SMILE

TIME AFTER TIME

The Rebecca Mayfield Mysteries

ONE O'CLOCK HUSTLE - TWO O'CLOCK HEIST

THREE O'CLOCK SÉANCE - FOUR O'CLOCK SIZZLE

FIVE O'CLOCK TWIST - SIX O'CLOCK SILENCE

SEVEN O'CLOCK TARGET - EIGHT O'CLOCK SPLIT

NINE O'CLOCK RETREAT - THE 13th SANTA (Novella)

The Cook and Inspector Mysteries

DEATH ON A SILVER PLATTER - A QUICHE BEFORE DYING -
THE MARINARA MURDERS

Others

SEEMS LIKE OLD TIMES - DANGEROUS JOURNEY

DANCE WITH A GUNFIGHTER - THE DRAGON'S LADY

THE GHOST OF SQUIRE HOUSE

A QUICHE BEFORE DYING

THE COOK AND INSPECTOR MYSTERIES
BOOK TWO

JOANNE PENCE

QUAIL HILL PUBLISHING

Quail Hill Publishing

Eagle, ID 83616

Visit our website at www.quailhillpublishing.net

First Quail Hill Publishing E-book: February 2024

First Quail Hill Print Book: February 2024

1

San Francisco Homicide Inspector Paavo Smith walked into the homicide bureau for the first time in two-and-a-half months. He had been out recovering from a nearly lethal bullet wound high on the left side of his chest. A tall, rangy man with short brown hair and icy blue eyes, he knew something was up by the way his fellow detectives greeted him. They were happy to see him but at the same time barely able to control their mirth.

And then he saw why. A dozen blue roses sat in the middle of his desk.

They all knew he was the type who would be more at home in the middle of a stake-out than at a desk with flowers. And, he was sure, they all knew the flowers were compliments of Angelina Amalfi. It was her case that had led to the shooting that had nearly killed him.

She had sent the flowers to welcome him on his first day back at work, and would be mortified to learn they had made the others in the squad room snicker. He would have liked to throw them away, but he couldn't do it. She had meant well.

They'd met during his last case. She was wealthy, pampered

and bossy, a pint-sized whirlwind so far out of his league he should have steered clear of her except for one thing. Someone had been trying to kill her. As the case proceeded, when things got tough, she had stuck with him, giving him all her trust. And then, ironically, Angie, the delicate debutante, had saved his life.

He'd fallen for her like a loser in cement shoes going off a pier.

While he'd been in the hospital, she'd stayed near him day and night. When he was released, he went to the tiny apartment of Aulis Kokkonen, the elderly Finnish man who had raised Paavo. Aulis was the only father-figure he had ever known.

Angie stopped by almost daily, bringing big pots and platters of minestrone, cacciatore, lasagna—anything she thought might be interesting, healthy, and filling. By Christmas, Paavo was much stronger, so Angie left to spend the holidays with family at her parents' large winter estate in Scottsdale, Arizona.

Then, as Paavo grew strong and healthy enough to move back to his own house, cold reality had set in. It was time to get on with his life. His real life. A life Angelina Amalfi and her money never would, never could, fit into. Every one of his cop friends had warned him not to get emotionally attached to her —that she was completely wrong for him and the closer he got to her, the worse he would feel when the inevitable break-up happened.

He knew his buddies were right. He'd been a cop for over ten years, and during that time, he'd watched the heavy toll the profession took on relationships. Most women his pals were with were hard as boot-leather themselves—and even those relationships were often train wrecks. There was no way he and Angie could make it work.

When she returned to San Francisco, he held her off a bit, saying he was too busy, or that he was tired and needed to rest.

He couldn't tell her the real reason—how much he'd missed her or that having her in his house, just the two of them, was simply too much temptation for one sensible, practical cop to deal with.

She'd made it clear that she cared a lot about him—maybe even as much as he did her. So he decided to break it off slowly, to see her and talk to her a little less each day, each week, so that, over time she'd realize he was no longer a factor in her life and would open herself up to finding someone else.

He hated the thought, but told himself it was the only "right" thing to do. For both of them.

And now, he found her flowers waiting for him when he arrived at work. They added to the strangeness he felt at being back in the Hall of Justice squad room without his old partner, Matt Kowalski.

He'd gotten used to seeing Matt's prematurely balding head down on his desk, taking yet another nap. That was the other thing that had happened during his last case. Three months earlier, Matt had been shot to death, alone, on the streets... and a part of Paavo had become emptier, colder.

"Mm, sure smells good around here, man." Inspector Luis Calderon, an eighteen-year veteran, tall, heavy-set with slicked back, heavily pomaded hair, stopped in his tracks next to Paavo's desk and lifted his nose in the air. "Am I still at work?" he asked his partner, Inspector Bo Benson, "or is this the perfume counter at Nordstrom?"

"What d'you know about Nordstrom, Luis?" Benson, in his late twenties, black, street-wise and handsome, grinned and jabbed Calderon in the shoulder. "The only perfume you ever smelled was a hooker's."

Calderon widened his eyes in horror. "Don't go using those low-class words around him." He pointed his thumb toward Paavo. "He's gone high society on us."

Paavo folded his arms. "You two'll never make it as comedians. Go solve a murder—maybe your own if you keep up that talk."

"Oooooh, I'm like scared, man," Calderon said, looking at Benson. "How about you?"

"I just want to know what it's like dating a really rich broad." Benson gave him a toothy smile.

"I'm not dating anyone," Paavo said, his teeth gritted.

"Leave him alone." The only woman in Homicide, as well as its newest detective, Inspector Rebecca Mayfield, sauntered up to them. She was a tall woman with long blond hair, a knock-out body, and looked more like she should be wearing well-fitting workout clothes and teaching Zumba classes than chasing hardened killers. She gave Paavo a pleasant smile; but then, she always gave him a pleasant smile. "I think it's sweet his little girlfriend sent him flowers on his first day back. Just because you guys couldn't come up with anything fancier than two dozen Dunkin' Donuts doesn't mean you should put her down."

"Doughnuts are a cop's best friend, Rebecca." Benson said. "How else is Paavo going to know he's really back with us?"

"Believe me, I know it." Paavo rocked on the back legs of his chair. He raised his arms to clasp his hands behind his neck like he used to do, when he felt a spasm in his shoulder and quickly lowered his arms again. If anyone suspected he was less than one-hundred percent recovered from his gunshot wound, he might be sent home. He was tired of resting, tired of too much time to think. He wanted to get down to business and doing what he did best.

He picked up the memos in his In-basket and skimmed through them. Snatches of conversation from his co-workers whirled about him.

"Whaddya mean he doesn't know why he shot him?"

"It's always the bystanders who buy it."

"He blew him away for drugs. So what else is new?"

Listening to the cases the others were dealing with knocked him back into his job with more force than a Canelo Álvarez left-hook.

The ring of his desk phone jarred him. He picked it up. "Smith here."

"Come into my office." It was Lieutenant Ralph Hollins, head of the homicide bureau.

As Paavo hung up the phone and stood, the other inspectors watched with unmasked curiosity. He knew why. He was sure they'd spent the past couple of weeks, since they'd learned the date he would be back at work, speculating on who his new partner would be. The chief had asked none of them to make a switch, although everyone, including Paavo, had heard that Rebecca had volunteered. Her partner, Bill Sutter, was closing in on having the age and time in the job to retire. "Never-Take-A-Chance Bill," they called him, the kind of cop who became so paranoid he wouldn't make it to retirement, he could get a partner killed.

Paavo drew in his breath, dreading this, then squared his shoulders and walked into the chief's office. Hollins and a large man Paavo had never seen before stood as he entered.

"Smith, I'd like you to meet Inspector Toshiro Yoshiwara. He's just transferred down here from Seattle. We're going to try him out for a while. See how he likes us and how we like him."

"Hey there," Yoshiwara said, his big voice filled with friendliness and good cheer as they shook hands. "Good to meet you."

In response, Paavo gave a quick nod of his head. The man was tall, almost reaching Paavo's six-foot-two-inch height, with broad shoulders, a massive chest, and a head big enough to match all that body. His hair was clipped in a short buzz, and he looked like someone who could split a house in two and not raise a sweat.

"Sit down, both of you," Hollins said, then glanced at Yoshiwara. "Smith is one of my best men. If anyone can show you what homicide work is like in this town, it's him." Hollins returned to his chair. "I'd like you two to work together for a while. As a team. Partners."

Although Paavo knew the words would come one day, the finality they gave to Matt's death shook him badly. None of this showed as he firmly stated, "Fine."

Yoshiwara, a big grin on his round face, scooted forward in his chair, looking like a kid at his own birthday party. "Hey, that's great. Paavo Smith, huh? I want you to know I heard of you up in Seattle. This is a real honor for me." He then got up and stretched out his hand to Hollins. When a surprised Hollins took it, Yoshiwara gave it an exuberant shake. "Thank you, Lieutenant Hollins. I appreciate it, I really do."

Hollins stood, and Paavo, too, slowly rose to his feet. "He'll have Matt's old desk," Hollins said. "Show him the ropes, Smith. And do a good job. He got high marks from Seattle."

Paavo opened the door and held it as Yoshiwara passed through. The two of them walked side by side into the middle of the squad room. Calderon, Benson, and Mayfield swooped down on them.

"This is Inspector Yoshiwara," Paavo began. "He's—"

"You can call me 'Yosh,'" Yoshiwara said, grinning from ear to ear, his voice boisterous. "It's Japanese for 'Okay, let's go for it.' Like if I said, 'are you ready?' you'd say, 'Yosh!' How's that for a simple language, huh?"

"You from Japan?" Benson asked.

"Heck, no. I'm from Seattle. Third generation. My grandparents were from the old country. You from around here?"

"Mississippi."

"Yeah? Got a family? Kids?"

"Naw. Too much fun playing the field. I had a steady for a while 'til she wanted to get married. A narrow escape, believe me."

Yosh laughed. "It's a tap-dance, huh?" He glanced at Rebecca. "A woman detective. That takes guts. Good for you!"

Paavo watched Yosh flatter Rebecca, tease Benson, and buddy up with Calderon. He'd never seen anyone work a room the way this guy did. And the other inspectors ate it up like a Hershey bar. Yosh shook hands, shot the bull, and in less than five minutes he knew almost as much about the three detectives' personal lives as Paavo had learned in years.

Paavo's old partner, Matt, had been outgoing and friendly, and Paavo had always been the serious, reserved one. They'd worked well as a team for that reason. But having to work with Mr. Congeniality, here, was another matter altogether. You don't stop bullets with charm.

"Well," Rebecca Mayfield hooked her arms with Calderon and Benson, "we've got to get going. Nice to meet you, Yosh." She all but dragged the other two toward the door.

"Good to meet you, too. I'll bring that *ikebana* book for your daughter, Luis," Yosh said to Calderon. "And you be careful you don't strain your back again, Rebecca. See you guys later."

"Right, Yosh. So long."

The room turned strangely muted. Paavo couldn't remember the last time it had felt so empty. He glanced at his new partner, then he walked to their desks. Yosh followed.

"This one is yours." Paavo's hand lightly touched the desktop, and then he pulled it back as if burned. It was directly to the side of him, some four feet away.

Yosh didn't sit. He could feel Yosh's eyes following him to the FTD display that was his desk.

"You were pretty close to your old partner, I'd imagine." Yosh's voice was soft now.

"Yeah," he answered. He and Matt had started out as rookies at the same time. "We were."

Yosh nodded, and a long moment passed before he added. "It's tough."

"Right." Paavo sat at his desk and looked at Yoshiwara, who was still awkwardly standing, looking over what should be his spot. The desk had been cleaned out, but they both felt the ghost there.

Paavo braced himself. It would be his job to work with this new guy, to protect him, and someday he might even come to rely on him the way he used to rely on Matt Kowalski, although that was hard to imagine. "So," he said, knowing it wasn't Yoshiwara's fault he had to take Matt's place, "what made you decide to move to San Francisco?"

Yoshiwara sat on the edge of Matt's desk. It was a start. "It's because of my wife, actually. She was a student at the University of Washington when we met. But all her family is down here. She missed them. I offered to give it a try. And here I am."

Paavo nodded. "Where's your family?"

"They're all up in Seattle. Without me." Yoshiwara grinned.

Paavo understood perfectly. Since meeting Angelina Amalfi, he understood a lot that wouldn't have made sense to him before. Like how a little woman could keep a big man so firmly under her thumb, especially one that had lilac fingernail polish on it.

The silence in the room grew. Paavo could all but feel Yoshiwara wanting to grill him as he had the other detectives, wanting to ask him if he was fully recovered from the gunshot wound or if he still had any physical limitations or mental traumas that all cops knew went along with a close brush with death. Things like nightmares... like those times he'd wake up in a cold sweat from dreaming about his last case—dreaming he'd walked into a trap, and then dreaming of his own violent death. Or nightmares about Angie, of trying to find her, to save her. But no matter how hard he tried, he couldn't do it, couldn't reach her in time.

But he had no interest in spilling his guts to some stranger, or to anyone, and Yoshiwara had enough intuition—or just plain good sense—to know it.

The phone rang.

Paavo picked it up. "Smith, here."

—Inspector Quan, Missing Persons. We just got an interesting call. Karl Wielund, owner of a fancy restaurant, has gone missing. It hasn't been even 24-hours, so we told his chef it's too early to start an investigation. But the chef insists Wielund would never disappear on his business and staff. I just was wondering if any of you guys are working a John Doe that might fit this Wielund's description.

"I wish I knew," Paavo said, looking around the bureau. Even Lt. Hollins' office was empty. "I'm just back today. The others are out, but as soon as someone shows up, I'll ask and get back to you."

—Thanks. It's a long-shot, but worth a try.

As Paavo hung up, he couldn't help but think it was good that Angie told him she was starting a new job that day. This way, she shouldn't become interested in a missing restaurant owner. Hopefully, he wasn't one of the many people in the city's "culinary scene" that she knew. The last thing he wanted or needed was Angie getting involved in any kind of dangerous case ever again.

2

Angelina Amalfi sat nervously perched on the edge of her chair at San Francisco's local radio station, KYME, scarcely breathing for fear the sound might be picked up and carried over the airwaves. It was her first day at her new job.

Chef Henry LaTour had just finished the opening remarks for his radio show, *Lunch with Henri,* and now hit the button for his audience to call with their cooking questions. For Angie, it was showtime.

KYME was a little-listened to station in the nether regions of the AM dial that blended together in a blur of talk shows, sermons, and classical music. A couple of weeks ago, after hitting the "seek" button on her car radio, Angie stopped it on KYME when she heard a pompous sounding man bumble his way through a simple question about pickling green tomatoes. As she listened with a mixture of amusement and slack-jawed horror at his assault on the San Francisco Bay Area's collective palate, and realized she'd forgotten more about cooking than that man knew, the germ of an idea came to her.

She listened again for the next two days. He needs me, she'd concluded. And, since she was out of work after her last employer, the *Bay Area Cooks* TV show, was cancelled, she had the perfect solution for his predicament.

And for her own.

The thing was, Angie Amalfi needed a job. Not that she *need* needed one—not for the usual reason of lack of money. Her parents had worked hard all their lives, and had built their investments in San Francisco real estate and upscale shoe stores into quite a fortune, especially once Angie's father became even better at investing his money than he'd been at running shoe stores.

Her parents paid for a fine education for Angie, including a stint at Le Cordon Bleu culinary school in Paris. They also helped her pay for a beautiful apartment, clothes, and even a car. But they expected her to do something with all those opportunities.

She kept trying, but so far, her luck seemed to be still on vacation.

So, after a few days of listening to Henry LaTour—or *"Chef Ahnree"* as he called himself on the radio using a cringe-producing French accent—Angie had driven to KYME's small broadcasting studio, located in an old building in San Francisco's South-of-Market area.

There, she had paced the hallway until LaTour, his show completed for the day, stepped out of the station's executive offices.

"I'm exactly what you need, Mr. LaTour," Angie said as she hurried toward him, her hand extended in greeting. He was probably in his early sixties, tall with a "corpulent" body, which seemed nicer than to call him chubby. His snow white hair was thick and styled in a high, stiffly-sprayed pompadour.

As soon as he got over looking startled, his expression turned skeptical. Then, ignoring her outstretched hand, he strutted past her, head high.

"My name's Angelina Amalfi." She chased along beside him

and stuck her business card in front of him. It was from her *Bay Area Cooks* days, which was the only card she had. "I've worked as the chef's assistant on the *Bay Area Cooks* show, where I helped with food preparation, recipes, and whatever was needed. I even worked with the chef on his cookbook. Unfortunately, the cookbook won't be published, but—"

"Isn't that the show where the host was murdered?" LaTour asked.

"It was all quite sad," she murmured, hoping LaTour wouldn't dwell on that unfortunate, let alone scary and deadly, circumstance. "But I've studied at the Cordon Bleu, and I've also written a number of restaurant critiques and even a couple of cooking articles that were posted online, on popular local blogs."

"On blogs?" He stopped walking and gazed down a long ski-slope-shaped nose at her. "Am I supposed to be impressed?"

"I've got a terrific idea," she said, ignoring his put-down. "I'll sit quietly in the studio with a bunch of specialty cookbooks in front of me. As soon as a caller mentions a topic, I'll find the book and look it up. Then, if you get stuck—"

"Tut!" His eyebrows hit his hairline.

Tut? She froze.

"Chef Henri never 'gets stuck,' Miss Amalfi!" He proceeded toward the elevators.

Didn't the man ever listen to himself? She followed. "What I meant was, if the question was a really bizarre one, I'd hand you the book so you could see what the answer was."

"Oh?"

At last, he was paying attention to her. "And then," she continued, her enthusiasm growing with each word, "we could even discuss some special menus or rare foods, which would be really interesting for your listeners."

"*We?*" She got his peering-down-the-ski-slope-nose routine again. "As in, *you* and I? On air?"

"Well, uh, yes. Maybe?"

The elevator doors opened, and he got on, blocking her entry. "I hardly think so."

Her mouth closed and her smile faded as she watched the doors shut in her face.

Three days later, a caller asked Chef Henri about making walnut catsup. His answer ran true to form. That night, he phoned Angie and told her to come see him at KYME the next day, with the proviso that no one—listeners or station—should know that she was "assisting" him with callers' questions. He would introduce her to the staff as his general assistant—one to help him take notes about his excellent answers to his callers' questions, respond to his fan mail, and do any other matter he was simply too busy to handle. "But we can never give the slightest hint of anything that might compromise the image of the great Chef Henri," he'd stated, making Angie shudder.

And so, she had found herself with a job. It wasn't exactly terrific, but it was a start. And in radio, no less.

Now, here she was, in the recording studio.

Henry LaTour sat at his desk with his microphone, headset, and console. Her desk butted against his so they were face to face. She wore a headset so she, too, could hear the caller's questions. A glass window separated them from the radio station's engineering booth—and LaTour had insisted partitions be placed by Angie's desk so the engineers couldn't see what she was doing during the broadcasts. He claimed it was so that she didn't "become distracted," while Angie knew it was so that the engineers didn't see her finding answers to caller's questions.

"Hello," LaTour said into the microphone, speaking to his first caller. "Welcome to *Lunch with Henri*. What can I do for you today?"

"Good afternoon, Chef Henri. I'm Marilyn from San Francisco. First-time caller, long-time listener!" An exuberant female voice pierced through the headphones Angie wore. Wincing with pain, she lifted them off her ears and looked for the volume control. She had none. Luckily, as Marilyn continued talking, her decibels dipped a bit. "Thank you so much for taking my call. I'm a little nervous." She then giggled.

She's nervous, Angie thought, reaching for a glass of water. She pulled back her hand. What if she spilled it? As she tried to ignore the sudden dryness of her throat, she watched LaTour rock his corpulent body closer to the microphone, and half-close his eyelids. "No need to be nervous, my dear." His tone was too sweet, too oily—much like his cooking, Angie thought.

"I love your program so much," Marilyn gushed.

LaTour's jowls jiggled as he nodded appreciatively. Angie breathed a little easier now that LaTour and Marilyn began to converse. She knew LaTour could waste more valuable air time listening to a woman sing his praises than any human being, ever. He was devoted to his own wonderfulness.

"What can I do for you today, Marilyn?" LaTour finally asked.

Angie perked up. Her fingers twitched as they hovered over the row of cookbooks propped up on the desk.

"I have a general question about making sweet breads."

"Ah, sweetbreads. One of my favorite delicacies." LaTour glanced at Angie, giving her a nod as he kept talking. She flipped to the index of his recently released cookbook, *Luscious Licks from LaTour's,* named after his restaurant. LaTour liked to quote himself and plug his restaurant as often as possible on his talk show, given the restaurant's lack of repeat customers.

"... a dry wine, light," LaTour droned, "with a delicate bouquet so as not to overwhelm the subtle flavors..."

Angie madly scanned the index, looking under sweet-breads, organ meats, glands, even innards for a sweetbreads recipe. Nothing. What kind of cookbook was this, anyway? She nearly tossed it aside, but then caught herself in mid-toss. No noise! Gently setting it down, she grabbed at the other books, laying them on the desktop as she dismissed them. A promising one was named *Organ Meats Can Be Fun*. She doubted it. Probably more like "can be awful," not to mention "offal," but she flipped to the index, anyway. Success! Page 127 began a whole series of examples of how to cook the little devils.

Smiling broadly, she quietly handed Henry the cookbook. This wasn't so bad. It was kind of fun, being "behind the scenes," and all.

He beamed at her. "Now, Marilyn. What's your question?"

"Well, the dough doesn't want to rise properly. I'm wondering if it has anything to do with the sugar?"

"Dough? Sugar?" Henry glanced helplessly at the book on organ meats, then at Angie, then the cookbook again. "Ah, sweet *bread*, of course. Now, I see. Yes! Bread... the fruit of all life. 'A jug of wine, a loaf of bread, and thou.'"

He waved his arm frantically, waiting for a cookbook on breads to magically materialize. Angie was too; she had no idea what the question was. Bread... the possibilities were endless. She reached for his book, but it had gotten buried in her rush to find one on the gourmet glands. A book named *Simply Breads* jumped out at her, and she opened it, ready to research the question—whatever it was. She gave him a thumbs up.

Marilyn kept talking. "I used a half cup of honey instead of a whole cup of sugar because it's more natural and all. Do you think it matters? After all, the ancient Egyptians used honey in everything. Pharaohs had it buried in their pyramids, and we all know about the marvels of the Great Pyramid."

"Oh?" Henry said, his eyes a little wild. He was standing now, gesturing for Angie to hurry. Not knowing what else to do, Angie stood, too. But she bumped her desk as she did so, and the recipe books she'd haphazardly piled to look for one that was helpful, began to slide. She managed to throw herself on top of them in time to stop them from falling noisily to the uncarpeted floor. Her sudden skill at tackling rather amazed her.

"Honey, yes," LaTour blathered. "Nectar of the gods. I love it, myself... so smooth, tasty... uh, Egyptians are nice, too." Angie hoped he didn't sound as bumbling to his radio audience as he did to her. Pouring over her materials, her nerves crackling, she found a skinny cookbook called *Healthy Eating*. Putting her finger on the section labelled "Substitutes for Refined Sugar," she leaned over the desk. LaTour's eagerly awaiting hands snatched it from her, making her nearly lose her balance. Her arms gyrating like a windmill, she righted herself just inches above her cookbook library.

Straightening up, her eye caught LaTour's to find him glaring like a foul-tempered librarian, his forefinger pressed against protruding lips and pointed upward toward his nose. His caller chattered on, now asking him about the evils of corn syrup. Angie wished he'd tell her the ancient Egyptians poured corn syrup on the Sphinx. Maybe that'd get her off the air.

Angie collapsed into her chair again... quietly. Where the hell was the commercial break?

After what seemed to Angie like the longest hour the world has ever known, Henry LaTour said to his few listeners, "I hope you enjoyed our little *tête-à-tête* today as much as I did. And remember, tomorrow, same time, same place,"—he took a deep breath then bellowed into the microphone—"*let's do lunch!*"

Angie draped herself over the top of her desk and tugged off the headphones. Two formerly long, formerly silk-wrapped fuchsia-colored fingernails had broken off, her hair felt as if she'd attacked it with an egg-beater, and she was about to be fired. Some days it just wasn't worth getting out of bed.

She sat up, expecting the station manager to walk into the studio any moment to tell her not to come back.

LaTour gave her a quick "goodbye" and left without another word.

She crept into the main part of the KYME office and learned the station manager had gone to lunch. She guessed she was spared to work another day. Somehow, she vowed, the next day would go much better.

As she hurried from the radio station, she decided she needed to treat herself to something special for lunch. She decided to go to Wielund's restaurant, which was quickly gaining a reputation as one of the city's finest.

Wielund's was pricey, but it had valet parking—almost a necessity along Polk Street. Also, she didn't like leaving her Ferrari Portofino parked on the street.

As she pulled up, she gave her keys to the valet and went inside.

The maître d' approached. "Good afternoon. Do you have a reservation?"

"I'm friends with Karl Wielund," she said. "Tell him Angie Amalfi is here and would like a table."

The maître d' looked stricken by her words. She had no idea why, but then he said, "It's not necessary to... to bother Mr. Wielund. We always have a place for a friend of his."

Angie ordered a salad with apples, grapes, cucumbers, walnuts, and prosciutto served with a saffron vinaigrette. When the waiter came over to ask how she was enjoying it, she said, "Very much. And would it be possible for me to see Karl? I'd like to say hello. He's a friend."

The waiter looked as nervous by her mention of his boss as the maître d' had been. He said he'd check, and then rushed off.

A short while later, the restaurant's sous chef, Mark Dustman, came out to see her. She'd met him a couple of times and knew he was actually much more than a "sous chef," but often acted as the head chef since Wielund's was now open six-days a week thanks to its success. "Hello, Miss Amalfi," he said. "I hope you're enjoying your meal."

"Please call me Angie. It's delicious. The vinaigrette makes it special," she said.

"And what are you up to these days? I'm so sorry about what happened to *Bay Area Cooks*."

She nodded. "Yes. It was awful. But the police solved the crime. It's over, and we can rest easy. In fact, I've already found a new job. I'm now working in radio, on Henry LaTour's talk show."

Dustman smiled. "That explains it, then. Today, Henry could actually answer the caller's questions. I always put the show on when I'm working. It used to be good for laughs. I hope that doesn't end completely."

"I hope it does! I'd like to keep my job," she said with a grin. "So, how's Karl? I take it he's not here today."

Dustman took a seat next to her. "He's not. Plus, we had a meeting scheduled for last night and he didn't make it. I'm worried, Angie. No one knows where he is. It's not like Karl at all. I even went to his house last night to see if he was sick or injured, but he was gone. So was his car. I don't get it!"

"Did you call the police?"

"I contacted Missing Persons this morning, but they won't do a thing since it hasn't been twenty-four hours. I insisted Karl would not go off without telling me about it and gave them as much information as I could. Still, they said their hands were tied until the twenty-four hours were up."

"What will you do?"

"If he doesn't show up for the dinner crowd tonight, as soon as the restaurant closes, I'll file an official missing person report. It'll be more than twenty-four hours at that point."

3

A ngie set up her never-used ironing board and dug the iron out of the very back of a shelf in the laundry area. Normally, she never ironed. That's what dry cleaners were for. But the silk dress she planned to wear had gotten crushed in her closet and she wanted it to look perfect when she saw Paavo that evening.

Not only had this been her first day on a new job, it was also his first day back at work after a long recovery. They had lots to celebrate. Or sort of celebrate. Or, at least, to talk about.

Sure, he'd been acting as if he didn't want to see her, but she understood why. They were supposedly "incompatible"—she had a large, wealthy family and had lived a pampered life. Paavo's life had been rough, with hardly any money, and even the person he called his father wasn't really a relative. And during the search for the killer of her former boss, the TV show host, Paavo had lost his best friend and had nearly died himself. No wonder he felt unsettled and troubled.

But she also sensed that he really cared about her, even if he hesitated to put it into words or, so far, into action.

It was late in his work day when she picked up her cellphone and called him. He let it go to voice mail. She phoned again, knowing his curiosity would get the better of him. Sure enough, he answered.

"Angie? Is something wrong?"

"Not exactly. I've got something that belongs to Aulis. I'm hoping you can stop by after work and pick it up. If not, I'll bring it to your house—"

"No," he said quickly. "That's okay. I've got time to stop by tonight... for a minute."

"Great. I'll be here. Thanks."

She hung up with a big smile.

Someday, she'd get past his reserve and caution. Someday he'd open his heart and truly let her in. She was sure they had something between them, something strong.

As she got ready for Paavo's visit, she shimmied her way into the bedroom singing "Walking on Sunshine," in her off-key voice to pick up the clothes hanger holding her wrinkled silk dress. There was a knock at the door.

Now what? she thought. Still holding the dress, she crossed her living room to the door of her Russian Hill apartment. She peered through the peephole. Making sure her short, pink satin robe hadn't fallen loose, she pulled the door open.

"Hi, Stan."

"Hi, Angie." Without waiting for an invitation, Stanfield Bonnette, her neighbor from across the hall, walked in. He had the only other apartment on the twelfth "penthouse" floor. Stan, at age 29, was about five-ten with a lanky build, brown hair, and eyes. He considered himself an up-and-coming bank executive. His father was the bank's president. Angie couldn't pick on him about that too much, however, since only because her father owned the apartment building could she afford to live in it. Still, the more she got to know Stan, the more Angie considered him lucky to have any job at all, family ties or not.

She went back to the laundry room, and he followed. "You busy tonight?" he asked.

She put the dress on the ironing board. "No. I'm ironing a silk dress to sit around and watch 'Married at First Sight.'"

"Guess you got a date?"

She licked her finger and touched the soleplate of the iron. No sizzle. "I'm expecting company soon."

"It's not that cop, is it?"

Hands on hips, she glared at the iron. Now what was she supposed to do? "He's a homicide detective. There's a difference."

"Not much of one, if you ask me."

"I didn't," she muttered. "Stupid iron."

"Time for a change, Angie."

She wasn't listening. "This iron must be broken."

"Drop him."

She touched the soleplate again. It was cold. "It's so maddening."

Stan glanced at her with surprise and approval. "I agree! But still, good for you! I knew I could convince you that he was all wrong for you—"

She scowled at Stan. "What are you talking about?" She yanked the cord from the wall and took the iron into the kitchen. Opened the garbage chute, she dropped the old Proctor-Silex down it. "*Arrivederci*, baby."

"You know, you really should think about recycling—"

A disembodied "Oh!" almost a yelp, yet distinctly human, echoed out from the chute.

"Oh, my God!" Stan cried and threw his arms around Angie, more to seek than to give protection, she was sure. "What was that?"

"Oh, no. It's our neighbor. I'm afraid she's getting worse than ever." Angie wrestled herself free, then opened the chute and stuck her head in. "Mrs. Calamatti," she called loudly, then listened as her voice echoed down the chute. "Is that you down there?"

"Who's that?" The thin, reedy voice sounded like something coming from the center of the earth.

"It's Angie," she hollered.

"Oh, Angie! Someone just tried to kill me!"

Angie glanced back at Stan, shook her head, and shouted, "You aren't actually *inside* the dumpster, are you?"

"Of course, child." The voice was old and quivery. "The Depression, you know. Got to be ready."

Angie put her hand against her forehead. "If there's a Depression," she said quietly to Stan, "she could sell her diamonds and keep living well for forty years!" Angie then stuck her head back in the chute. "What you're doing is too dangerous. You can't get in there ever again. You could get hurt! Now climb out and go back up to your apartment!"

"Be prepared, Angie!"

"*Will you broads shut-up!*" A man's voice from somewhere along the length of the twelve-story building bellowed out at them.

Angie jerked her head out of the chute, her face on fire. "Good night, Mrs. Calamatti," she cried, using the chute one last time.

"Good night, dear."

Angie shut the chute door. "Stan, why don't you go check to be sure Mrs. Calamatti gets back to her apartment in one piece? I can't help but feel some responsibility since my father owns the building."

"Sure thing. I'll just give her some time to get there on her own, first."

"Look at the time! I've got to get dressed." She glanced from Stan to her front door by way of a hint.

Stan remained in the kitchen. "What smells so good in here?"

"It's a pork roast. Don't you dare touch it!" she called heading to her bedroom to find something else to wear.

"I won't. Ah! Left-over lasagna. I love your lasagna, Angie."

"Fine. Take it *home* with you. All of it," she called as she pulled out a cream-colored Chloé sheath and put it on.

As she stepped out of the bedroom, she saw Stan now seated at her mahogany dining room table, a plate of lasagna and a glass of cabernet in front of him.

He turned, as if feeling her stare. "Oh. I forgot to tell you. My microwave is on the fritz."

She glanced at her cellphone. "Oh, no!" she cried.

"It's not that bad, Angie. They're cheap. I'll buy another one soon."

"No, Stan. The time."

"Oh. Are you telling me..." He grimaced. "How much longer until San Francisco's *Law and Order* star arrives?"

"That's just it! He should have been here by now." She began to pace.

"A few minutes is nothing. Don't worry."

"I've got to worry."

"Got to?"

"My grandmother always said if you want to keep someone safe, you worry about that person. It's a way to trick fate, you see. Fate, or karma, likes to surprise you. So, if you worry, it means you *expect* something bad to happen. That way, you can be happily surprised when nothing does. Poor nonna scarcely had time to sleep with all that worrying. It worked, though. She kept her family safe."

"Angie, that makes no sense. Plus, it's just superstition."

She glanced at the clock again, then bit her bottom lip as she clutched her elbows and walked back and forth across the room. "My God, Stan, don't you think I know that? I wasn't born in the Dark Ages."

"Then relax."

"I can't. Don't you see? It might be superstition, but if I stopped worrying, and Paavo got hurt, *again,* I'd never forgive myself."

Stan looked blankly at her, then poured himself another glass of wine.

A half hour later, Angie sat on the yellow silk Hepplewhite antique arm chair. This worrying was exhausting.

A loud knock sounded at the door. She knew that knock. Cops, she thought, hurrying across the room. It always sounded as if they were there to make an arrest. "See, Stan! I told you it'd work!"

She swung the door open. Soft, blue eyes took her breath away and made her heart beat faster. Her gaze raced over his gray sports jacket, black slacks, and a pale blue shirt, the same shade as his eyes, then zeroed in closer for any signs of fatigue after his first day at work.

His face was thin, but then, it was always thin; his nose highly arched; his brows straight, and his eyes intense. Relief, coupled with a pulsating excitement at simply being with him, hammered through her. "You're late!" she cried.

He cocked an eyebrow as he strolled in. The room seemed to shrink in the wake of his presence. His gaze pointedly took in her dressy outfit, then traveled to shapely legs and very high heeled Manolo Blahnik shoes. He shifted his eyes to Stan who was now stood in the living room with a glass of wine, then back to Angie. "I see you have company," he said to her. "Am I'm interrupting the two of you going out or something?"

Her whole world seemed to tilt at the smooth, graceful way he glided into the room, at the cool, arch look he gave her now. God, but she was crazy about him. "He's jealous, Stan," she said, then smiled. "Isn't he cute?"

Stan blanched.

So did Paavo.

"Yeah, a regular, little *fuzz* ball," Stan replied.

"Did you like the roses I sent?" Angie asked Paavo, ignoring Stan.

"They were... thoughtful," Paavo replied.

"The florist said the blue roses were manly," she added.

"Go on, Angie," Stan said. "Everyone knows he's the petunia type."

Paavo turned toward Stan and gave him a sharp glare. "Stan Bonnet... charming as ever."

"Bon*nette*," he squawked. "And I know when I'm not wanted." Still holding onto his wine glass, he left the apartment.

Paavo looked at Angie as if she were crazy. "You have an odd taste in friends."

She smiled. "He says the same thing about you."

Paavo didn't smile, but seemed to stiffen at her words. "Anyway, you have something for me to give Aulis?"

"I do. His pie tin, and it's now holding an apple pie I made for him. Can't return an empty pie tin, after all. But since you're here, I've got a pork roast and spaghetti carbonara cooked and ready to eat. I've just been keeping it warm."

"I don't—"

"I know it was your first day back at work, and you're probably quite tired. I figured you wouldn't feel like cooking or going out to eat, and since you're here anyway..."

"You don't—"

"You don't have other plans, do you?" she asked.

"No, but—"

"Great. Would you pick out some wine while I dish out? Stan said the pork smells delicious."

Paavo swallowed hard. "Yes, it does," he murmured finally, admitting defeat.

As they ate, she told him about her distressing, but exciting day on her new job, and that it was going to be a bit harder than she'd initially thought. Callers' questions were rarely as simply or clearly stated as she had hoped they'd be.

He told her about getting a new partner. She could tell how much it distressed him and said what few words of comfort she could think of. But this was a situation that only time would make less painful for him.

As she served coffee and a chocolate torte for dessert, she decided to completely change the subject. "Paavo, you'll never guess what I heard when I went to lunch today. The restaurant's owner is missing!"

"Missing?"

"Yes! Karl Wielund. He's the city's most popular new restaurant owner and chef. I went to his place for lunch after my radio show and when I asked to see him—we're friends—he wasn't there. His sous chef is quite worried!"

Paavo sat back in the chair, his voice low. "I did hear something about a missing restaurant owner today. No one in homicide has any recent unidentified body or anything like that, so we aren't involved. Your friends are filing a missing person's report, right?"

"Mark Dustman, that's the sous chef, will file one if Wielund isn't at the restaurant tonight. He had to wait twenty-four hours. But this isn't like the Karl I know. His restaurant is everything to him. From what I've heard, if he's not going to be there, he leaves a list of instructions longer than your arm for Dustman and others on the staff. For Wielund to simply not show up makes no sense at all."

"Okay. I'll keep it in mind."

She didn't look happy. "In the meantime, is there anything you can do to get Missing Persons to give this top attention?"

Paavo sighed, and she realized she may have overstepped. "If there's not a body," he said, "homicide doesn't get involved."

Of course she knew that. Her mouth downturned as she said, "There isn't a body. Yet."

4

Angie's second day "on the air" so to speak, was no better than the first. They couldn't work out the sometimes great time lag between the caller's question and Angie finding an answer in the cookbooks in front of her. Henry had to stall. But he was no better at thinking on his feet than he was at answering cooking questions. The only thing he could talk about was himself, which quickly became boring. The station manager looked anguished, no doubt thinking of the radio dials being spun throughout northern California to any station other than KYME. Angie suddenly understood station's call letters. *Why Me?*

As the hour crawled by, with one *faux pas* after the other, Henry's face had turned red and sweaty. Instead of his infamously smooth way with words even if they were wrong, he'd become a man whose mind and mouth had divorced—irreconcilable differences. In a business where elocution meant everything, this was a recipe for disaster.

"And now, friends," Henry said taking a deep breath, "to my surprise, another hour together is almost up. But it brings the moment I know all of you eagerly await. It's time for our helpful hint of the day. Yes, 'Helpful Hints from Henri,' are brought to you each day by Bellweather Automotive Oil, the oil that will keep your engine running smooth as clarified batter... butter!"

Angie cringed. This was, for sure, her last day on the job.

Somehow, she'd get through this... and then, maybe, she'd stop by and see if Karl Wielund was back at his restaurant.

Paavo sat at his desk in Homicide.

Lt. Hollins was taking Paavo's new partner, Inspector Yoshiwara, around the building, introducing him to the Crime Scene Unit, the Assistant District Attorneys, the Medical Examiner, Dr. Ramirez, and her staff, and to others he'll need to work closely with.

But now, Paavo needed a new case, especially after his dinner last night with Angie. It had been too comfortable and way too exciting being with her. The aroma from her kitchen had enveloped him as soon as he'd stepped into her apartment. And he felt stupidly jealous at the sight of her neighbor looking so comfortable in her apartment when he arrived.

But that was nothing compared to the unrelenting joy he'd felt being near her, a joy he knew would keep him going back to her, again and again, if given the slightest excuse. A pie tin for Aulis? Seriously?

It was one thing to tell himself, while in that cold, gray, crisis center otherwise known as the Hall of Justice, or in his quiet house, that she shouldn't be a part of his life, but quite another when he was with her.

And as icing on the cake, her cooking was, as always, outstanding. He'd never been any kind of foodie before. Buying frozen food labelled "gourmet" or "healthy" was about as much care as he gave to what he ate. But Angie had shown him a whole new world of sensory aroma and taste. She was, simply, a terrific cook.

Which made it even harder to contemplate finding a way to forget about her, and somehow manage to not go running when she called.

"Does it feel as if you've never been away, Paav?" Rebecca asked as she leaned against the edge of his desk.

"Almost. Some things'll never be the same, though."

Rebecca's eyes glanced over to Matt's desk, now with a framed photo of Yosh's wife and three children, then she gazed back at Paavo. "We missed you around here, you know. Now, we should be able to get on with solving some of these trickier cases."

Calderon slammed his desk drawer shut and stood, his lips forming a bitter curve. "Nothing tricky about these cases, Rebecca. First, look at the spouse or someone else in the family. If that doesn't work, then look for the dumbest and meanest guy around the corpse. If that one isn't the murderer, then it's the best friend. Always works that way."

She grimaced. "What if you can't find a friend of the corpse? And sometimes you can't find anyone dumb or mean, either."

"Nobody's that empty," Calderon grumped.

"I had one that was," Rebecca murmured as she turned back to Paavo. "Sheila Danning. I'll never forget her."

"What case was that?" Paavo asked.

"Me and Never-Take-A-Chance Bill got it right after you became involved in the murder of that TV host. It didn't get much attention because everyone was interested in the cooking crime."

"I remember that case." Calderon slid his gun into the holster he wore at his back. "She bought it in Golden Gate Park, right? Strangled. The usual stuff."

"Real usual," Paavo sneered, again wondering what was going on with Calderon. He used to be an okay guy, but since

Paavo got back, he had a chip on his shoulder, constantly bickering and putting the ugliest slant on whatever topic came up. His only saving grace was that, so far, he hadn't let his emotions get in the way of his cases.

"What was strange was we couldn't come up with a line on her," Rebecca said, ignoring Calderon. "Seemed no one really knew her. She lived in a studio apartment out on Ingleside and worked as a waitress at Le Maison Rouge in North Beach. We found her parents in Tacoma, but she'd walked out on them and they hadn't heard from her in a couple of years. That was it. We figured she was just an innocent victim. A random thing, wrong place, wrong time. Still, it bothers me that we couldn't come up with more."

"I can imagine," Paavo asked.

Rebecca nodded. "It was the first case I had that required a lot of real detective work. Bill Sutter was the lead, of course, and we worked on it for a month, when he declared we were spinning our wheels, and needed to set it aside until we came across new evidence, if ever. He felt it was basically unsolvable, so moved on to other things. Still, it nags at me."

"There are cases where that happens, and yes, they do nag." Paavo rubbed his chin. He wondered if Sutter hadn't dropped the ball and gave up too soon. Rebecca could be one of the top detectives in the department. It bothered him to think she'd be taught by her partner to give up on a case because it wasn't moving quickly enough. Some cases simply required a lot more work than others. "How old was this Sheila Danning?"

"Twenty-one," Rebecca said. "Hardly more than a kid. She comes to the big city to start a career and ends up dead. I found it all pretty awful."

"That is rough." Paavo grimaced. "How long had she worked at the Maison Rouge?"

"Almost a year, since she first turned twenty-one, in fact."

Paavo gave her a sharp glance. "Almost a year, and none of them could tell you a thing about her?"

Rebecca shook her head. "We came up empty."

That didn't make sense to Paavo. No twenty-one-year-old with the looks and personality to be hired as a waitress in a classy restaurant was that much of a loner, unless there was something very strange going on. "I agree you shouldn't file it away as unsolved yet," Paavo advised. "Something still might fall into your lap, and it'll all tie in together."

"But if it doesn't," Calderon said, his arms folded and his legs wide and rigid, "nobody'll remember for long that you screwed up on a big case, Rebecca. Look at Paavo. He's literally screwing his *last* case."

Paavo's eyes met Calderon's as he slowly lifted himself from his chair. His voice was brittle as chipped ice, and the temperature in the room seemed to drop. "That's not true, but if you want to make something of it, Luis—"

"Knock it off, both of you," Rebecca ordered, then took Paavo's arm, turning him away from Calderon. "He thinks he's being funny. Let's go across the street for coffee."

"Don't waste your time with him, Rebecca," Calderon said as he put on his jacket then tugged at the cuffs of his shirt sleeves. "He don't know a good woman when she's right in front of him. Come on. I'll even buy."

Rebecca looked from Paavo to Calderon and back. Paavo sat down again, and Rebecca took Calderon up on his offer.

The next day, after *Lunch with Henri* ended, LaTour asked Angie to visit him and his wife at their home at four that afternoon to discuss the show. Of course, she accepted, even though it meant she spent the next three hours wondering if she was going to be fired, or would be given some time "on air," or somewhere in between. She had no idea.

Now, Angie double-checked the address. Eleven-forty-nine Pacific Street was the upper story of an old San Francisco flat—a long, narrow apartment that took up an entire floor and was pancaked above another apartment of the exact same size and layout.

The address was about mid-way down the southern slope of Russian Hill, and since Angie lived at the top of the Hill, she walked to the sunny, pleasant neighborhood made up of narrow streets and alleyways, with two- and three-story flats, corner grocery stores, and two cable car lines that meandered up and down its steep hills.

Angie rang the bell to the flat, and in a moment, the door opened by itself. She stuck her head in the doorway. The small, square entry led to a long, uncarpeted stairway that seemed to go straight up to Heaven. "Hello?" she called, her voice echoing up the walls of the narrow staircase.

"Angie!" LaTour bent low so she could see him at the top of the stairs, his hand still on the lever that mechanically opened and shut the door. "Come on up. We're waiting for you."

Her high heels clanged as she hurried up the stairs. Halfway, she slowed down, looked behind her and nearly lost her balance at how long and steep the stairs were. She clutched the railing tighter. Two stories, straight up.

"I guess you don't have to worry about exercise, do you?" She gasped for breath as she reached the top landing.

"Everyone says that. Keeps me young." He gestured for her to follow him down the hall to a small living room in the front of the flat. "Here's something else that keeps me young. I still call her my bride, even though we've been married almost five years. This is my wife, Lacy."

Angie stopped in the doorway. Seated on the sofa in front of the window, Lacy seemed to shimmer in a beam of sunlight. Angie stepped closer to see Lacy better. Immediately, the image shattered.

The first thing Angie couldn't help but notice was her hair, a bright orange color, and piled into a huge, messy bun on the very top of her head. At the same time, her too perfect face, with high, silicon-implant round cheeks, a small, straight, nose with permanently arching nostrils, and highly arched eyebrows, was the sort usually associated with a plastic surgeon's scalpel.

In short, she wasn't at all the type Angie ever expected to be pudgy, white-haired LaTour's wife.

Lacy walked around the coffee table, her hands outstretched in greeting. "Hello, Angie. So nice of you to come to our home." Her Botox-filled face scarcely moved, although she seemed to think she was smiling. Her voice was modulated and accentless, as if she'd gone to a speech coach. Angie wondered if she shouldn't be the radio broadcaster instead of Henry.

Their hands clasped. Covering Lacy's fingernails were three-inch long acrylics with orange-red polish, so sharply curved she could have used them to climb a tree. Angie retrieved her hands. "Thank you, Mrs. LaTour. So happy to meet you."

"Won't you sit down? We were just drinking some Aljuice. It's a scrumptious algae mix—one of my little things to keep my Henry healthy. Would you like a glass?"

Angie eyed the green liquid with little black specks floating in it. "No, thank you. I'm fine."

They all sat, LaTour beside Lacy on the sofa, Angie in a chair facing them. Lacy placed her hand on her husband's chubby knee. "I'm glad you were willing to come here to talk about the show, Angie," she said.

LaTour patted his wife's hand. "I told you she was special."

Angie wondered if he planned to give her a halo. "Well, the radio station doesn't have much room for meetings, anyway."

"Lacy and I were discussing the structure of the show," he said. "We thought it could use some improvement."

"Oh, really?" Angie could think of about five hundred ways to improve it. The first being to let her say at least a few words on the air. She really did know what she'd be talking about, as opposed to the current radio host.

"Not *too* many changes, though," Lacy added, cocking her head toward LaTour and batting her false-eyelashes at him. "Everything Henry does is nearly perfect, already."

Angie hoped this meeting would be short. She didn't think her stomach could take many more outbursts like that one. Besides, watching them sip the green slime reminded her of old monster movies—the ones where a mad scientist would drink a 'potion,' sprout hair on his face and hands, then go on a rampage. And Lacy was a ringer for the bride of Frankenstein.

"I'd be happy to do anything I can to help," she said.

"The problem is," Lacy began, "that Henry doesn't know what the calls are going to be about before he hears them. In such situations, he can easily misunderstand, or he has to just say any old thing until you're able to find an answer for him."

"It really doesn't take that long," Angie said. "And with the commercial breaks and all—"

"It doesn't look good," Lacy insisted, then took Henry's hand. "My Henry needs to have the answer right on the tip of his cute little tongue."

His cute little *green* tongue, Angie wanted to add. And now some of the black flecks were getting caught between his teeth. What were those two slurping?

Henry cleared his throat. "I agree. Chef Henri must be able to respond *tout de suite.*"

Lacy glanced at him. "Henry, dear, you don't need to speak French around us. Right, Angie? My big Pooh Bear is such a show off!"

"Pooh Bear?" Angie regretted it the moment the words passed her lips. Some explanations were better left unspoken.

"That's what I call him. And it'll explain the new theme music we just picked out. Every show should have something very distinctive."

Angie refused the temptation of asking any more about it. "So, about finding the answers for Chef Henri, what does this all mean?" she asked.

"What it means is, we want you to screen the calls before Henry takes them."

Angie stared at her. Some shows, on bigger radio stations, went to the expense of paying a screener to answer every call off the air. The screener made sure it wasn't a wrong number, or a crank caller, or whatever. But not KYME. The radio hosts took their own calls, for better or for worse. "I really don't understand why I would need to—"

"It's just not right that poor Henry has to take these questions cold, with nothing but that silly time delay to bleep them if anyone starts to say obscenities. But how many people swear at cooks?" Lacy formed her mouth into a pout, her eyes darting from Angie to LaTour and back again.

"Well..." Angie decided it'd be best not to reply, but she'd heard plenty of people wanted to swear at him after seeing the size of the bill at LaTour's.

"The problem is," Angie said, "I've got to listen carefully to Henry's calls while they're happening. Many people start out with one question, but before you know it, they've asked about something altogether different."

Lacy jumped to her feet. "But that's not what's important!" Her voice was shrill, yet quivering.

Angie jerked back in her chair, gawking up at the woman in surprise. "Not *important?* It's the main part of what I do."

"Now, dear," Henry jerked on Lacy's arm, trying to get her to sit back down. "Let's not upset Angie about this. Good help is so hard to find, these days."

"Good help?" Angie repeated. She forced herself to be patient with him. She wanted this job; she could be good at this job; and if Henry would ever let her say even one word on the radio, she could prove it. It was more than a little ironic, she thought, that any Tom, Dick or Harry from the greater Bay Area could call and be on the radio, but if she said anything and ruined the illusion that Henry's answers were popping full-blown from his head like Athena, she'd be canned. She bit her tongue and did her best to stay calm.

"Angie," Henry said soothingly, "won't you at least give it a try?"

"But Mr. LaTour," she said, "what happens when I'm busily talking to a future caller and the one who's on the air with you asks a follow-up question?"

"I'll just have to answer it."

"Isn't that what got you in trouble the first time?"

Henry's face flushed red. "Trouble? What trouble?"

"God help us," Angie whispered under her breath.

"Henry can do whatever he wants," Lacy said, twisting her fingers. "And anyway, if he doesn't know the answer, he can simply take a station break. Right, dear heart?"

"Of course, lambikins."

Just then his cellphone rang and Henry stepped into the hallway to answer it.

"So." As soon as Henry left the room, Lacy stood and paced back and forth in front of Angie's chair. "It's all settled."

Angie didn't think so. She folded her arms. "Oh?"

Lacy stood and glared at her. "It'll work. Whatever Henry does always works."

Angie slinked back in her chair. "But—"

"Look, sweetie," Lacy's voice turned hard as she stepped even closer, "I've been around a long time. Girls like you are a dime a dozen around here, all looking for their big break in radio. You come and go, thinking you know best. But I care about Henry and what's best for *him*."

"But every day—"

"I know, I know. He gets one or two tough follow-ups every day or so. But that's nothing. He answers at least four calls on each show. You screen them, and it'll cut down on his misses. I'll take odds like that anytime. Wouldn't you?"

Everything Lacy said left Angie speechless.

"Lacy!" LaTour stood in the doorway, his face white.

Lacy jumped at his voice, his demeanor. "Henry, what's wrong?"

"I just got bad news. Unbelievable news. Karl Wielund is dead!"

"No!" Lacy stared at him.

"Oh, my," Angie said, as she realized Wielund's restaurant was right across the street from LaTour's. Obviously, the owners knew each pretty well, judging from Henry and Lacy's reaction to Wielund's death. "That's horrible. What happened to him?"

"It sounds like some kind of accident," he said. "They found him in his car. Apparently, it went off a cliff up in the Sierras."

Just then, Lacy put her hand to her chest and seemed to be having trouble breathing. "Lacy, are you all right?" LaTour rushed to her side.

"Yes, I—"

"Have her lie down," Angie said. "I'll get a glass of water for her."

"Down the hall—the kitchen," LaTour said, helping Lacy stretch out on the sofa.

Angie, too, felt shock at the news, although given that Wielund's whereabouts had continued to be unknown, she feared something terrible must have happened to him.

As she hurried to the kitchen, she noticed the bedroom at the end of the hall. The door was open, and the wall appeared to be covered with large black-and-white photography portraits. Angie darted down the hall to see them better. Covering an entire wall were photos of a young Lacy in bathing suits and ball gowns. She looked like someone ready to step into a Miss America pageant with a good chance of winning. With light, lustrous, red hair, an amply curved figure, and surprisingly innocent face, she was an all-American dream.

Angie forced herself to stop gawking and moved even faster to the kitchen.

Lacy looked quite a bit better, the color back in her face, after drinking some water.

"I couldn't help but notice your photos as I walked down the hall," Angie said. "They're beautiful."

Haunted eyes lifted to Angie. "Thank you."

"Were you a model?" Angie asked.

She stared thoughtfully at Angie a long moment, and finally murmured softly, "No. I was just a secretary. I didn't do anything much until I met Henry just five years ago. Now, I'm on top of the world."

Angie couldn't help but think she didn't sound like it, but obviously, Karl Wielund's death had hit her hard.

It was time for her to leave the LaTours alone. She said her goodbyes and headed for Wielund's restaurant. She was wondering why Karl Wielund would have gone to the Sierras, some four-to-five hours away from the city, and not tell anyone. And why he'd be there on a day he was supposed to have a meeting with Mark Dustman about his restaurant. It seemed there must be more to the story.

6

Paavo walked into the lobby of Angie's apartment building, and waved at Mr. Belzer, a man of about seventy-five years and retired, who was the building's "security," as he headed for the elevator to the twelfth floor.

Paavo had no idea what the old man could do if anyone truly dangerous showed up, but someone watching the door was better than no one at all. And he could call the police if necessary, hopefully.

On twelve, as he approached Angie's cream-colored door with gold plated letters that read "1201," a beat of anticipation surged through him, a beat that grew stronger rather than weaker as he came to know Angie better.

Paavo recognized why the other detectives distrusted Angie. The police force was like a family. The men, and now one woman, in Homicide probably knew each other better than anyone else knew any of them. They lived in a world separate from other people, saw it differently, and were wary of strangers or anyone else who tried to invade them.

But they were wrong about Angie. She was one of the few

"civilians" he accepted and trusted even though she wasn't a cop and never would be.

He knocked on the door. She had left a message to say she had information about "his case" and didn't want to talk over the phone, that he should come to her place as soon as possible. Since he didn't have a case at the moment, he suspected it might have been a ruse to see him again. To be honest, he'd willingly take any ruse she offered.

She opened the door. He couldn't move as he took in her big, brown, sparkling eyes, and a wide mouth that was curled up in a broad smile for no reason except that she was happy to see him. He was so used to people looking either afraid or angry when he rapped on their door, he was still taken aback by Angie's reaction, even after nearly four months of knowing her—although a lot of that time he'd been in the hospital or at Aulis's apartment, and she was in Scottsdale with her family.

"You're here!" she said, stepping back so that he could enter the apartment.

"As requested."

He took off his jacket, draped it over the back of a dining area chair, and sat on the sofa while Angie went into the kitchen. A moment later she came back out and carefully poured a bottle of Guinness into a pilsner glass for him, creating a perfect creamy foam. "You must be surprised I already know about the death." She placed the glass on a coaster on the coffee table before him. "But he was a chef and you know what a small world that is. Has the department decided to investigate? Frankly, for him to go to the mountains without telling anyone is more than a little suspicious, if you ask me."

He took a sip of the deliciously chilled and refreshing stout and then placed the glass down before looking up at her. "How about you start at the beginning?"

She gaped at him a moment. "Wait a minute. You do know he's dead, right?"

"Who are you talking about?"

She threw up her hands. "Karl Wielund! Who did you think I've been talking about?"

"Possibly Henry LaTour, since he's your boss."

"Henry! It's just his *show* that's dead, not Henry. He's alive and probably in his restaurant giving customers ptomaine poisoning as we speak. I told you Karl Wielund was missing. And now, I've learned he's dead."

Paavo's eyes narrowed. "What happened to him?"

"They say it was an accident in the mountains. But after I heard he'd been found dead, I went to Wielund's restaurant—to give my condolences. They were closing the restaurant out of respect for Karl when I arrived, but I did get a chance to talk to his assistant manager, Eileen Powell. She was in Paris, but flew home when she heard Karl was missing. I told her I used to be a good friend of Karl's... well, not *such* a good friend... but anyway, she said nobody believes Karl went to the mountains because he wanted to go. It just wasn't like him."

"I see." He grimaced. He saw, all right. He'd watched this sort of thing happen before. Someone gets involved in a murder the way Angie did not long ago, and next thing you know, they're seeing murders under every corpse. He gazed at her, at the wary excitement in her face—the thrill of a dangerous chase, so similar to the look he'd seen on the faces of rookies when the dispatcher gave them their first big call. "I'm sorry to hear he was in an accident, Angie. But despite the mild weather and the blue skies of San Francisco, if he was up in the mountains now, in winter, we all know how treacherous the Sierras are this time of year."

"I know that," she said. "I grew up hearing gory tales of the Donner Party eating each other when they got snowed in up there. But that's not what happened. Something more did. I can feel it."

"The Sierras aren't my jurisdiction."

She folded her arms. "But Karl lived in your jurisdiction. Don't you want to make sure his death was a true accident?"

He shook his head. "There's no reason to think otherwise."

"People who know him think otherwise," she added. "At the restaurant, Eileen Powell, Mark Dustman, and even a couple of waiters I don't know, all had suggestions about what happened, including that he was kidnapped!"

That caused an eye roll. "If no one got a ransom note, I doubt that."

"Okay. I get it. I will not interfere. See this?" She began backing up. "This is me going into the kitchen where I've got some delicious food ready to be heated and served. I hope you'll join me for dinner, if you haven't already eaten." At the door of her kitchen, she cocked her head. "What say you?"

He felt conflicted, wanting to stay... "I don't want you cooking for me, Angie."

"Don't be silly. A while back, I made some crab-and-ricotta stuffed manicotti with an Alfredo sauce for company. It's frozen, but will take no time to heat up. Plus, I've got homemade ciabatta bread." She hurried into the kitchen, then called out, "I know how much you like it. While I make us a salad, would you open up a bottle of cabernet sauvignon? There's some in the wine fridge."

He had to admit, he was glad she didn't take "No" for an answer. He knew his refrigerator was empty, which meant stopping at the grocery or a fast-food restaurant if he wanted to eat tonight. He wasn't sure what manicotti was, but being stuffed with crab and ricotta, how bad could it be? Plus, the thought of her cooking had him salivating.

Clearly, his will-power was nil, at least where Angie was concerned. "All right," he called, checking on her wine choices.

She brought bowls of salad out for them to start as the manicotti continued to heat up. "By the way, are you busy Sunday afternoon?"

He lifted an eyebrow. "That depends on what you had in mind." He helped her set the table.

They both sat. "You are so full of yourself sometimes, Inspector. Anyway, Eileen said--"

"By Eileen, you mean the manager of Wielund's, right?"

"Assistant manager. Eileen said she and the sous chef, Mark Dustman, will hold a memorial service at Karl's restaurant Sunday afternoon. I'm sure it won't last much over an hour. But all his friends will be there, and I couldn't help thinking that might well include his enemies. So, I managed to get an invitation for us both."

He put down his salad fork. "Oh, you did?"

"Right. Since everyone is questioning why he was in the Sierras, I just knew you'd want to go to the party to see all the people Karl knew and hear what they had to say about him. Did I say party? I meant to say memorial service."

He sighed. "Angie, I'm sure all their talk means nothing. It's just gossip."

"And I'm sure the manicotti's warm now." Before long, she came out with a platter of what he saw as very large stuffed macaroni shells. She placed four on his plate, two on hers, added a basket of warm, sliced ciabatta along with butter, oil, and vinegar—his choice for what he wanted on the bread— and then she sat down to eat.

He took one bite and was in heaven.

She let him eat awhile before she asked, "Aren't you curious about what happened? After all, the top restaurant owners and cooks in the city will be there... all in one place... all secretly thankful their prayers to get rid of Wielund's have been answered. You really don't want to miss that, do you?"

Paavo suspected that after the way Angie was feeding him,

he'd agree to almost anything. But he also had to admit she had a point.

If Wielund's autopsy indicated any possible foul play, it wouldn't hurt to hear what people were saying about the deceased. But, he suspected the initial finding of an accident was going to be the correct one.

But then, his talk with Rebecca Mayfield about her unsolved murder of a waitress who had worked at an upscale French restaurant came back to him. What was her name? Right now, he couldn't remember—but he'd find out. His nerves suddenly felt taut—the way they often did at a crime scene when his instincts told him to look further and to take nothing at face value. "You mentioned other restaurant owners should be there. What about the owner of Le Maison Rouge?"

"I would imagine. Since Wielund's was *the* place for everyone who was anybody to be seen, I suspect Karl's memorial will be the same and they'll all show up. I'll point out its owner to you. Why do you ask?"

It was too much of a stretch to imagine that the death of a popular restaurant owner had anything to do with the murder of a waitress some four months earlier. But then, if Angie's friends were right in speculating that Karl Wielund's death wasn't accidental, and if there was a connection with the waitress...

"It's nothing. Just an old case I heard a little about. So, what time should I be here to pick you up?" he asked.

She grinned. "Come by at two. That'll give us plenty of time."

Soon, dinner was over and Paavo said it was time for him to leave.

"Before you go, would you come with me to check on one of my father's tenants? An older woman named Mrs. Calamatti. She's been acting awfully strange lately."

"Alzheimer's?"

"Not like any Alzheimer's I've seen. She seems quite healthy, and walks from Russian Hill down to Polk Gulch to go grocery shopping nearly every day, and she often visits friends. But lately, all she wants to talk about is the economy."

He shrugged. "So do politicians."

"See what I mean?"

They got on the elevator and she pushed the button for the basement. "I thought you wanted to check on Mrs. Calamatti," Paavo said.

"I do."

As they stepped off the elevator, he heard a noise in a corner of the dark garage. He took hold of Angie's arm, ready to pull her out of harm's way, but she stopped him.

"Mrs. Calamatti," she called.

From that same corner came a quavering voice. "Yes? Is that you, Angie? My goodness, you sound so close."

Angie glanced at Paavo then chuckled softly at his puzzled expression as she led him toward voice. "I am. I'm down here, too."

Paavo followed her around the corner of the basement to the area where a dumpster stood at the bottom of the garbage chute. Beside it, Mrs. Calamatti, a thin, white-haired elderly woman wearing a floral housecoat, held her hands out in front of her, gnarled string running from one hand to the other.

"What are you doing?" Angie asked, stepping closer.

"I was thinking about the woman." Mrs. Calamatti tossed aside the string. "It was so sad when she died."

Paavo saw Angie shudder and felt a chill go down his own back. "What woman?" Angie whispered.

"I didn't know her. I guess no one could save her. It was a long time ago. It told me I had to save my money! It's getting so difficult out there. Do you want to help me look for something good, Angie? People throw away things that are still quite useful, you know."

"Not today. Come on. Let's go back to your apartment." Angie put her arm around the woman and gently led her away from the garbage. Paavo followed.

Mrs. Calamatti pointed at the dumpster. "But we could be missing out if we don't look."

"Maybe we'll look tomorrow."

"You're a good girl." Mrs. Calamatti said, then glanced at Paavo, and now aimed her forefinger at him. "Prepare for the coming depression, young man!"

"I'm sure we'll all be fine," Paavo said as he held the doors as Angie led Mrs. Calamatti into the elevator.

It was definitely time for him to head for home.

7

On Sunday afternoon, Angie cast her eyes over a masterful arrangement of canapes and finger foods on the buffet table at Wielund's restaurant. It would have looked much tastier if not for the photograph of Karl Wielund with a black cloth draped over a silver frame.

About fifty people had been invited to the memorial service, and they were eating and drinking with gusto. Their conversation was loud, and often punctuated by laughter. Angie took in the boisterous crowd with amazement. The so-called mourners looked ready to pull out party hats and favors.

What was it about Karl Wielund, Angie wondered, that caused this reaction in so many people? Could it have been his arrogance, always acting as if he were doing you a favor by just acknowledging your existence, gloating over his success, and other people's failures? Seemed she'd just answered her own question.

She stood with Paavo at the edge of the crowd where they could see almost everyone in the room. In the past, Angie had always been in the middle of crowds, taking in everything around her. Since spending time with Paavo, she'd learned that cops liked to stand on the fringe where they could observe and be ready to act if necessary. It reminded her of old cowboy movies where gunslingers always sat with their backs to the wall so no ornery pole-cat could sneak up and get the drop on 'em.

"Here comes Chick Marcuccio," she said.

"Who's he?"

"He's one of my father's closest friends. His daughter, Terry, and I used to be besties until she got married a few years back. I can't stand her husband. Chick's also got a son, Joey."

"Another close friend?"

She grinned. "Hardly. He used to like to knock my ice cream off the cone when we were kids! Chick owns the restaurant, Sorrento."

Paavo's eyebrows rose. So, he did know something about fine dining in the city, Angie thought. Sorrento was the biggest and most expensive of the city's many Italian restaurants. And the best.

Just then, Chick Marcuccio looked in Angie's direction. She waved, and he headed her way.

"Angelina! *Come stai?*" he called out as he approached, his arms open wide. When he reached her, they clasped shoulders and kissed each other on both cheeks.

"I'm doing well," she said with a smile. "And you get more handsome every time I see you." She watched him beam, then added, "I'd like you to meet my friend, Paavo Smith. Paavo, this is a dear family friend, Chick Marcuccio."

Chick was short and heavy-set, with short, wiry, steel gray hair. As he reached out to shake Paavo's hand, the huge diamond in his pinky ring glittered. "Any friend of Angie is a friend of mine," Chick said earnestly. "Let me introduce you to my friend. Janet, get over here!"

The woman he called did his bidding with a pleasant smile. She was tall, slender, and middle-aged, making her a good twenty years younger than Chick. Her suit was gray and sophisticated, her blond hair pulled back in an elegant chignon. Chick introduced her as Janet Knight. She didn't look like Chick's type at all.

As Angie and Paavo shook hands with her, Angie was sure she looked star struck. "I've seen your picture many times, Ms. Knight," she gushed. "Paavo, this is the food editor at *Haute Cuisine* magazine."

Paavo's attempt to express excitement at this news was about as successful as Angie should have expected from a man who's idea of gourmet cooking was adding onion powder to Stove Top Stuffing.

"I've always wanted to do an article for your magazine," Angie said.

Janet smiled. "Really? You should submit one."

"I have," Angie said, her heart sinking as she realized her submittals never even made it past the first-level readers. "Several times."

"Ah. I see." A hint of red showed on Janet's porcelain cheeks.

"Those things happen, I guess," Angie replied, trying, but failing, to hide her dismay that Janet never saw her submittals.

"I'm glad I finally met you," Janet said, addressing Angie. "Chick has spoken to me about you and your family for years."

Years? Angie couldn't hide her shock as she glanced at Chick. She'd never heard he had a long-time lady friend. In fact, the way Chick hung around his ex-wife, Martina, Angie assumed the guy was still carrying a torch for her. "How nice," Angie murmured, struck with a sudden loss for words.

It was now Chick's turn to look uncomfortable. "So what are you up to these days, Angie?"

"I'm working with Henry LaTour on his radio program," she said, hoping he didn't laugh out loud.

"Oh, good. Maybe you can teach him something about cooking."

She raised her eyebrows. "Don't tell me you listen to his show?"

He chuckled. "We all do. When Henry isn't mangling recipes or giving bad advice, he talks a lot about the restaurant scene in the city, what's new, which places are closing, who fired their chef—you name it." Chick looked around. "Speaking of all that, I guess it's time I go and say hello to the competition. Looks like most of them turned out tonight, the snakes."

Angie lowered her voice as she said, "I think everyone's curious about what happened to Karl and what's going to happen to his restaurant."

"All I know is, I'd love to get my hands on his recipes. They've got to be a chef's dream—it's the menu that made Wielund's famous." Chick grimaced. "The way Wielund's was packing in customers, most of the people here probably wished Karl was dead when he was alive. Now, they're all pretending to cry over his death and probably all they want to know is what's going to happen to his restaurant and where's the chef's logbook of his recipes."

"Do you think that's why they're here?" Angie asked.

Chick stared at Angie as if she were crazy. "Of course! These people are all about business and making money, Angie. Never forget that. Well, so long, *cara mia*." He hugged her, then turned to Paavo and shook hands. "Good to meet you."

Chick took Janet Knight's arm and walked into the crowd.

Angie leaned against Paavo's arm. "That was one owner. As for others, over there in the purple dress with the white feathers is Eunice Graves, owner of Europa, an elegant continental cuisine restaurant. She's about as elegant as Roseanne Barr."

Paavo glanced at Angie in surprise. She shrugged. "Over on the far side, the guy in the blue suit with a white carnation--"

"Black hair?"

"Right. That's Peter Fong, owner of the Singapore Palace."

That caught Paavo's attention. "I've actually eaten there and enjoyed it," he said.

"I'll keep that in mind," Angie murmured. "And, the tall woman with the green Chanel suit is Hattie Walker, of Old South. Her place is said to have the best hush puppies and sweet potato pie this side of the Mississippi."

"That sounds delicious," Paavo said.

"Really?" He still managed to surprise her. "Ah, the guy who's now talking to Hattie is Vladimir Polotski. His Russian restaurant is doing about as well as the former Soviet Union. And it'll probably share the same fate."

Paavo shook his head. "All these names are starting to swim together."

"It doesn't surprise me," she said. "But here comes one you'll remember. Mark Dustman, Wielund's sous-chef, is carrying out another tray of canapes. He made everything you see on the table. Looks like he's trying to find a new boss. Anyway, Greg McAndrews, who's now talking to Dustman, owns Arbuckle's Sea Food Restaurant down on the wharf."

Paavo's gaze leaped from one to the other, taking them in.

Angie smiled. "So, what do you think?" But before he could reply, Angie took his arm, her mouth wrinkled with distaste. "If you peek, by the door, you'll see my boss and his wife, Lacy. Late as usual. To hear her, they're the Rachel Ray and Wolfgang Puck of the restaurant set, but word has it she knows even less about cooking than he does."

Paavo glanced where she said. "They're coming this way, Angie."

"Oh no," she whispered, then turned and managed to sound pleased to see them. She quickly introduced them to Paavo.

LaTour gripped Paavo's hand. "Angie talks about you all the

time," he said, pumping Paavo's hand. "I hear you're back at work."

Paavo gave her a quick, surprised glance before he turned back to LaTour. "Yes, I am."

"Back at work?" Lacy cocked her head. Her garish orange hair was piled on top of her head in a curly cluster. "Are you in the restaurant business, too, Mr. Smith? Like my Henry?"

"I know nothing about cooking," Paavo said, giving her a smile. It was small, but Angie could see Lacy was quite taken by how handsome it made him look.

"Oh, it's not difficult." She patted his arm. "Just a little of this and a little of that and stir like crazy."

"Nevertheless, I believe one cook in the family's quite enough," LaTour said suddenly. "You know what they say about 'too many cooks,' right?" His belly shook with his loud laugh. Others turned and stared at him.

Paavo whispered to Angie. "What do they say?"

"That they spoil the broth," she replied.

A waiter carrying a bottle of lightly chilled French Pouilly Fuisse stepped up to them. "May I interest anyone?" They all accepted a glass.

"Speaking of cooks," LaTour said, "has anyone heard what will happen to Wielund's? I suspect it'll sink like a stone. Without Karl, the place is nothing." He looked scarcely able to contain his glee.

"That's why it's so strange he'd go off and leave it when his assistant manager was out of town," Angie said.

LaTour pursed his lips. "He might have thought he'd go up to the Sierras and be back before the big dinner crowd. Maybe that's why he was driving too fast. Speeding on those twisty mountain roads is dangerous even when they aren't icy."

"That's possible," Angie agreed. "But why wouldn't he tell Mark Dustman?"

"Good God," LaTour said. "The man surely could come and go as he pleased without telling his employees."

"But to leave his business that way..." Angie added.

Confused, LaTour looked from Angie to Paavo and back again. "I'm sure I have no idea. Won't you excuse us?" He took Lacy's arm and hustled her away.

"My God, Paavo," Angie said, her eyes merry as she turned to Paavo as soon as the LaTours were out of earshot. "I think he did it. My boss looked guilty!"

Now it was Paavo's turn to look surprised. "Guilty of what?"

"Of whatever happened to Karl. First, LaTour gave silly excuses, and then he walked away instead of continuing the conversation. Don't you watch TV mysteries? That's the formula for the guilty party. And LaTour played it perfectly."

Paavo gave her a side-long glance. "Wish I'd known about that formula. It would have made my job so much easier. But I think LaTour was trying to excuse himself for being happy he doesn't have to compete with Wielund's anymore."

"Well, he could be both, couldn't he?"

───

Mercifully, Paavo thought, the hour was almost up and he could get out of there. Angie was in her element, talking to people, introducing him to them, while he was finding he'd hit overload with all the names of people and restaurants, owners, chefs, and sous-chefs. Even the food, delicious at first, now tasted too rich, too creamy, or too sweet. He draped an arm over her shoulders and leaned in. "I think it's time to go."

"Me, too," she said, moving closer to him, her arm at his waist. "It's actually kind of chilling to realize if Karl was done in, one of the people in this very room could well be a murderer."

"Done in?" he repeated. "You've watched too many old crime shows."

"You know what I mean," she said. "And, if there's any truth to those old shows, my boss would be the guilty one. LaTour styles his hair in a pompadour, and men who do that are always guilty on TV." She suddenly stopped. "Oh! We can't leave yet."

They were near the door when Angie broke away and rushed over to a fellow who, even Paavo had to admit, was striking looking. He had immaculately trimmed gray hair and green eyes in a lightly tanned face.

"Mr. Dupries," Angie cried, stopping him. "I can't believe it's you. We met a few months ago. My name is Angelina Amalfi.""

Dupries glared at the hand on his arm. But then his eyes raised to hers, and his scowl disappeared as Paavo watched his gaze slide from her face downward.

"*Bonjour, mademoiselle,*" he said with a smile. "Please, call me Albert."

Paavo watched the man work his charm. A simple thing like the way he pronounced *Ahl-baerrrr* made his voice come across as smoother than cat's fur, and he had a very French way of moving his lips as he spoke, along with a knowing glint in his eye. Paavo guessed the guy must have studied old Alain Delon movies when he was a kid.

He wondered if Angie would ever remember that they were leaving.

Without breaking her gaze at Dupries, she waggled her fingers for Paavo to move closer. "And, this is Paavo Smith."

Paavo wondered just who this guy was as he extended his hand to Dupries in a greeting.

"Monsieur Dupries is the owner of Le Maison Rouge," Angie said to Paavo, who suddenly grew interested. This was the owner of the restaurant where Rebecca's dead waitress, Sheila Danning, last worked.

"So nice to meet you," Dupries said, shaking Paavo's hand. But then he turned back to Angie and took her hand in both of his. "Amalfi... that sounds familiar. It sounds, in fact, like someone who wrote in some little blog that I charge too much for my chateaubriand." He lifted one knowing, perfectly formed eyebrow.

Angie looked like she wanted to sink through the floor. "I must have eaten there on an off-night."

"I was ready to run a sword through myself when I read your article." His thumb stroked her palm. Paavo noticed she didn't pull her hand away. And then Dupries let it go as he gave a very Gallic shrug. "But I noticed the blog had only three hundred followers, so I let it go."

"I'm so sorry!" Angie gasped. "Maybe I can write a do-over!"

Dupries placed his hands against his heart. "Yes, please, come again to my restaurant. Your next critique will be glowing, I promise."

Angie blanched. "Well... but... I have to be anonymous, you see, or it does no good."

Dupries shook his head as if he were dealing with a child. "Oh, you are too sweet. *Très innocente!* Do you think Bernie is anonymous? Or Nona? *Mais, non.* I wonder, in fact, if Nona will run her review of Wielund's now?" He shrugged. "Why bother? I imagine it will close without Karl and his recipes... unless the new owner gets them. Anyway, take advantage of your power, Miss Amalfi, just as they do. Have a fine meal. With me, in fact. I insist."

She glanced at Paavo, looking unsure of what to do or say. He couldn't offer any help out since he didn't even know who they were talking about.

Dupries cast a glance at Paavo, sighed, then looked again at Angie. "You may even take a friend, if you wish. Call me personally and let me know when I can make a reservation for you both. Our talk has warmed my heart." He bent low and kissed her hand, then gave a curt nod to Paavo and walked away.

Paavo frowned and folded his arms. "His talk warmed my—"

"Stop!" Angie said. "He was just being very French. Good God, that man is sexy!"

"Don't drool on your pretty suit, *ma shay-rie*." Paavo shook his head, trying to forget the way Angie ate up the smooth talk, and to concentrate instead on the man who was once the boss of the murdered Sheila Danning. He thought he might very much enjoy having a serious talk with Mr. Dupries. One on one.

"And who are this Nona and Bernie that he mentioned?"

She took his arm as they slowly, once again, headed toward the doors to leave. "Nona Farraday and C. Bernhardt Eickerman are two of the most widely read restaurant critics in the Bay Area. Nona writes for *Haute Cuisine*, and Bernie for the *Chronicle*. The problem he was giving me is that restaurant reviewers aren't supposed to recognized when in the restaurant. If the restaurant knows who's a reviewer, that could skew the result. So for Dupries to offer to buy the meal I'd be reviewing, was completely wrong. And he implied that's exactly what happens with Nona and Bernie's reviews. That would be unethical."

"*Haute Cuisine*—isn't that the magazine Chick Marcuccio's girlfriend edits?" he asked.

"That's right."

"Doesn't this whole thing seem a little incestuous?"

She shrugged. "Same interests, same friends. Look at the police department. All your friends are cops."

He couldn't help the sudden pang that hit him at the thought of his cop friends, because his best friend, Matt, wasn't around any longer. And every day, he missed him.

"And me," Angie added softly, her hand on his arm and looking up at him as if she'd read his thoughts. Her gesture, her words, touched his heart, and as their eyes met, he nodded.

Just then, Karl Wielund's assistant manager, Eileen Powell, walked to the center of the room. Everyone grew silent. Eileen was attractive in a black suit and white, starched blouse. She gave a polite, nondescript little speech saying what a kind, generous and out-going man Karl Wielund, had been. Everyone knew it was all lies.

Then Mark Dustman got up and slowly stumbled toward Eileen. He'd obviously been drinking.

Dustman was *GQ* model handsome, with sandy brown hair, brown eyes, and a boyish demeanor. But at this moment, his young face was pale and wan, his eyes red and swollen. He looked warily about the room. "I want to tell you all about Karl," the young chef said, his voice hoarse with emotion. "And why he died."

The place began to buzz. Angie glanced at Paavo. He took her hand, and they inched closer as Mark Dustman began to speak.

"I met Karl in Paris at a small cooking academy. He was visiting his friend, the owner, and took me under his wing." He dabbed his eyes with his handkerchief. "I'd lived in San Francisco awhile before saving enough money to go to Paris for training, so I knew this city. Karl told me he had just opened his own restaurant. He said that when I finished my classes, a job would be waiting for me here, at Wielund's.

"I knew Karl would succeed in San Francisco, despite its many fine restaurants. I knew talent when I saw it. And succeed he did."

Dustman looked out over the group. "He succeeded too well, *you* might say. He was clobbering you. All of you. Wielund's was filled up while you went begging for customers. We never had to offer two-for-one or, God forbid, a 'ladies' night' to get customers. We just provided food good enough to cause jealousy in even the kindest soul, and to make your lives a living hell. He was a good, kind and sensitive man, and knowing how so many of you felt about him, hurt and pained him. And that, ladies and gentlemen, is why he died."

Amidst the outraged cries of the group, Eileen grabbed Mark's arm to make him sit, but he shook her off. "I'll keep Wielund's open." He shouted at them. "I'll keep Karl's memory alive. And keep the high quality of food on these tables!"

"Sit down, Dustman!" Chick Marcuccio thundered. "We didn't come here for this."

"Why did you come then?" Dustman leaned toward him, his palms on the table.

The group turned quiet, waiting for Marcuccio's reply. "To pay respects to a dead colleague, of course."

Dustman's eyes narrowed, his voice a rumble. "Night after night I've wondered what made Karl go to that lonely, mountain area in the dead of winter. I can't help but believe it was simply that he wanted to go back to a snowy mountain spot that reminded him of his home in southern Germany. He wanted to get away from this nest of vipers, from you, to find a little peace and quiet. Why on that day? I'll never know. But I'll spend a lifetime wondering about it. And about all of you!"

The room broke into a flurry of reproach, calling for him to sit down, go home, shut up, that he didn't know anything about them, and that a memorial service was no place to talk that way.

Paavo had never imagined this group of elegant restaurateurs could turn so ugly. He'd carefully watched the various mourners all evening as they came by to speak with Angie and to talk among themselves. Dustman was right about one thing —not one of them had appeared truly sorry that Wielund was dead. Yet Dustman's description of Wielund as a caring, sensitive man was completely contrary to what everyone else said about him.

The restaurant owners seemed most furious that Dustman had called their bluff and pointed out their hypocrisy in pretending to mourn. Paavo silently took them in, one by one, committing their words, their expressions to memory. Something was wrong. All those people were supposedly friends, yet there was an undercurrent of dislike and distrust. Wielund had lived in a snowy mountain area in Europe, yet he drove off the side of a major U.S. highway because of what? Ice? Did that make sense? It made Paavo uneasy. He'd worked in homicide many years—long enough to have a sixth sense about it. And his sixth sense had gone into overdrive on this one.

The detective side of him knew it was good he was there, observing this. He could feel in his bones, in every fiber of his being.

"You're looking pleased with yourself," Angie said as she tucked her arm in his. Now, instead of being among the first to leave, they waited until most of the angry people had filed out the door.

He nodded. "Very. Especially since I've learned that next time I go to a restaurant, I'll have to make sure the knife's beside my dinner plate, and not in my back."

8

Monday morning, Paavo carried a cup of coffee from Homicide's vending machine to his desk. He took a sip and his lips wrinkled. After having "Americano" coffees at Angie's, it was hard to even think of what came out of a vending machine as coffee.

He headed back to his desk and sat, then ran his hand through his short, wavy hair.

He'd spent last evening, after taking Angie back to her apartment, thinking about Wielund's memorial service... and about Angie. He'd never seen her so much "in her element" as with those restaurateurs and chefs. It was a world completely different from anything he'd ever experienced. He didn't care for it, and saw it as more proof the two of them really didn't belong together. Unfortunately. But such was life, as he'd learned at a young age.

Back to the service... he couldn't forget the feeling he got in that crowd. There was just one problem with his feeling—it not only wasn't his case, it wasn't anyone's. And, he had no proof it should even be a case.

One way to put this whole situation to rest was to go to the source. He called the Nevada County Sheriff's Department and eventually was connected with a Sergeant Osbourne. "I'm calling about a DOA you had last week, Karl Wielund," Paavo said after explaining who he was. "It looked like an auto accident. The guy went off a cliff. I'd like to know the results of the autopsy."

Osbourne's voice suddenly hardened. "The guy *was* a traffic victim."

"That's what's being said."

"His neck was broken in the fall down five hundred feet of ice-covered rock. That was enough for a death certificate."

Paavo's grip tightened on the phone. "No autopsy?"

Osbourne's long, weary sigh came across the phone wire before he spoke. "Look, we've got more tourists than anything else up here, and they're forever killing themselves on the roads or on the ski slopes. Even if we *wanted* to autopsy every victim, there's no money. Get the picture?"

"Got it," Paavo said. "But I've also got reason to suspect more than an accident happened here."

There was, again, a long silence on the other end. "I see. Let me find out if we still have the body." He put Paavo on hold for a few minutes. "This guy must have been really loved. His body's still in the morgue. No one wants him. Our report says his attorney's contacting relatives back in Germany. So looks like the body will be available awhile. You need an autopsy, Inspector, you'll need the family's okay, and we'll need the money to do it."

"Thanks. I'll get back to you." As Paavo hung up the phone, Yosh walked into the squad room. Bellowing hellos to people in the furthest corners of the floor, he headed toward Paavo's desk.

"Hey, there, partner," Yosh said, pulling a breakfast burrito out of a white bag and placing it on the corner of Paavo's desk. "Looks like you need this more than I do."

"No thanks," Paavo said.

"I got four more in here." Yosh went to his own desk and ripped open the bag, revealing his huge breakfast. "So take it, please. I even have dessert." He held up a package of small, dry, cellophane-wrapped chocolate chip cookies.

They weren't at all tempting. "I'm fine."

"I heard you went to a chef's funeral service yesterday," Yosh said before taking a mouthful of burrito and downing it with Diet Coke. "You know the guys here gossip worse than old women. They also tell me your friend, Angie, used to show up on the society page regularly, and always with a new guy. Sounds like she knows how to turn on the charm."

The last thing Paavo needed was to hear this. "I guess," he muttered.

"She probably makes you feel real important around her, like you're the only guy in the world for her, wouldn't you say?"

She sure does. His mouth felt a little dry. "Could be."

"Yeah. One time in my life I went out with a gal like that. Money, looks, good sex—class all the way." Yosh gave a long sigh. "Then, after a couple months, she stopped returning my calls. I learned she was engaged to a brain surgeon. The least she could have done was picked a guy with an interesting job. Jeez, their pillow talk was probably about stuff that looks like albino earthworms. Served her right, that's what I said. And my Nancy is worth a dozen of her. Nancy's good, down-to-earth."

"Is she?" Paavo really didn't want to hear any more. Yosh's words expressed thoughts Paavo wouldn't let himself dwell on, yet they were always there, dark and malignant, waiting for the opportunity to force their way into the light.

"Damn right," Yosh said. "These other women, they start interfering in your work. Make you see skeletons in every closet, see danger where none is. They make you run around seeing yourself as some knight in shining armor, trying to protect them instead of the people who really need you—the ones you're paid to protect."

A sick feeling hit Paavo's stomach. Had Angie's dark hints about Wielund's death caused him to see trouble where none existed? It was, he realized, all too possible. So, all he could do in answer to Yosh was to nod.

"You're a good guy, Paavo," Yosh said unexpectedly. "I like you."

Paavo glanced at Yosh. Now what?

"I mean, I can see now why all these guys around here try to tell you what you got to do. They like you, too. And they worry about you."

"Sure they do."

"It's a fact. Look, you nearly died; your partner did. That's a lot to deal with, to find a way to get past it and, hopefully, come out whole again. They don't want to see your head turned by someone who just might not be in it for the long term. You know what I mean?" Not missing a beat, Yosh continued. "You're a tough guy. The jerks we arrest, they shake in their boots around you. But, I got to tell you, you're like a babe in the woods around women."

Paavo folded his arms, his body stiff and withdrawn. If this pop-psychoanalysis of Yosh's continued much longer, the guy was going to get a fat lip.

Paavo had experience with women, especially when he was young and in the Army. But once he joined the police department, things began to change. Some women were immediately turned off by a cop. Others were attracted to the job, but even they couldn't handle the crazy hours, the stress, or the dangers for very long. He grew tired of a few good dates, followed by the relationship crashing and burning. It was easier to be left alone.

Yosh looked long at his partner. "You know what, Paav, I think you ought to meet Nancy." Yosh reached over as if to slap him on the back, but then as his gaze caught Paavo's frigid eyes, he withdrew his hand and did nothing more than smile.

"Okay," Yosh continued. "I know I open my big, fat mouth

too much sometimes, and say a lot more than I should, but it's because I care about you, partner. I don't want to see you eating your heart out. None of us do. So, how about Friday night?"

"What about Friday night?"

"It's Hollins' twentieth anniversary with the force. He tried to keep it quiet, but I found out anyway. Everyone's coming by the house. Nancy is cooking. You don't have to *stay*. Don't even have to eat dinner. Just come and give congrats to the Chief. What do you say?"

Paavo respected Lt. Hollins. If it were a gathering for anyone else, he wouldn't hesitate to refuse. But Hollins was different. "All right."

"Terrific! And Rebecca can make it, too. She's a great gal. All the guys think so. Solid, dependable… like my Nancy. And she really likes you, too. So what if she doesn't have lots of money? Money doesn't buy happiness!"

That was one cliché too many. "I already said I'll be there," Paavo muttered, his jaw tight. "You don't have to keep pushing."

Yosh just smiled and gave him a nod. "Nancy will be so glad to meet you."

"Great. But now, I need to talk to Hollins about a case." Paavo hurried away from Yosh. The last thing he ever wanted was a partner who saw himself as Dr. Phil.

Angie opened her kitchen table as large as it could go, then spread a clean sheet over it. Her sister, Bianca, slapped half the mound of pasta dough they'd prepared onto the cloth. She beat it down flat, then Angie took their grandmother's three foot long, wooden rolling pin and started rolling it out.

Bianca was an older version of Angie by fourteen years, her dark brown hair straight instead of wavy, worn in a chin-length blunt cut instead of in feathery layers, and the only color she added was to hide the gray, not blond highlights.

When Angie was young, her mother helped out at her father's shoe stores as well as doing all the ordering, inventory, payroll, and accounting for him—along with raising five daughters and running a household. As a result, Bianca, as the oldest, often found herself being "stuck" with taking care of Angie, the baby. Bianca still often took on the role of mothering her youngest sister.

"Henry LaTour is pompous with nothing to be pompous about," Angie said while pulling and stretching the dough to make it thinner. Then she picked up the rolling pin again. She wished she could stop thinking about her job. That afternoon's show had gone better than previous ones. She was calming down and getting better at quickly finding simple recipes Chef Henri could bloviate over. Still, she didn't like the way he'd snap his fingers for her to find a complex answer quickly, or glare at her if she—and he—misunderstood a caller's question and had to quickly change the answer. "His nose is so high in the air I'm surprised it doesn't get frostbite."

"I don't know why you bother with these radio and TV chefs. I mean, your last boss ended up dead! And you could have been killed, too." Bianca whacked some cloves of garlic with the side of a cleaver, then peeled and minced them. "You know more than 'Chef Ahnree' anyway. You shouldn't be his flunky. When are you going to take charge of your life and stop frittering it away?"

Angie was always amazed that Bianca could both praise and criticize her in a single breath. "I don't think I'm frittering away anything. And I do more than work for LaTour."

Bianca reached for an onion. "Frankly, teaching adult ed classes on San Francisco history seems more a way to keep senior citizens off the streets than for you to build a career."

"I also just sold a magazine article on San Francisco Victorians—homes, not people—and I've got an editor interested in my interview with the retired chef at the St. Francis Hotel where he talks about famous people that once stayed there."

"Well, lah-di-dah. Are those *paying* publications or online vanity blogs? And, work aside, you need to settle down. You aren't getting any younger."

"I'm not ready for a walker, yet, Bianca! You sound like Mamma."

"So? She's right. Is Henry LaTour young?" Bianca asked.

Angie spread more flour on the sheet and with the rolling pin attacked it with renewed vengeance. "No, and he's married."

"Too bad."

"Too bad? Give me a break!" Angie rolled the dough even harder. "That man should be selling snake oil instead of dinners. He's so slick he's lucky he wasn't sucked up along with the last big oil spill. Anyway, I'm seeing someone, kind of."

Bianca didn't answer. It had become clear, before the holidays, when Angie's life was in danger and she spent a lot of time with Paavo, that all four of her sisters and their husbands didn't approve of her sudden interest in the homicide detective. Too dangerous a job, and not enough money in it, summed up their arguments. Her mother, on the other hand, had grown fond of Paavo, and her father hadn't met him yet.

"Has he even asked you out on a date?" Bianca asked.

Angie's lips pursed. "He hasn't had time."

"Of course not." Bianca's tone dripped sarcasm.

"He's been *recuperating!*" Angie insisted.

"I know, I know."

When the dough reached about three feet around, Angie spread a layer of flour over the top, rolled it up, and push it aside. As she did this, Bianca sautéed the garlic and onion in olive oil, then added a pound each of ground beef and veal.

Bianca was opening and closing all the drawers.

"What are you looking for?" Angie asked, taking the remaining dough and flattening it with the rolling pin.

"Don't you have a nice NutriBlade knife? Like on TV? I've got to chop three bunches of spinach."

"Sorry. You're going to have to make do with my professional quality German ones."

"No need to get snippy, Angie!" Bianca clearly was sulking over Angie's not listening to her big-sisterly dating advice.

Deciding the dough had been rolled thin enough, Angie began adding pinches of thyme, marjoram, and rosemary to the meat dish, then took it off the stove and put it in a bowl and added a cup of grated Romano. Shen then dumped the meat filling onto the flattened dough that covered her table top, spread it evenly, and with Bianca's help, carefully unfolded the other piece of rolled dough and placed it on top on top.

"God, this is a lot of work," Angie said, using her arm to push her hair away from her face. "I hope the Knights of Columbus appreciate it."

"They do," Bianca said.

Angie picked up their grandmother's ravioli marking pin—a long roller that had wooden strips that formed squares. Pressing down hard, she firmly and evenly rolled the pin over the dough to seal the dough layers together and enclose the filling. She stepped back to admire her handiwork. The tabletop looked like a computer grid, the raviolis like little puff pillows.

Sitting on opposite sides of the table, Bianca and Angie each picked up a fluted-edged pastry wheel and cut the ravioli apart following the grid lines Angie had made with the marking pin.

"Maybe you'd be better off working in Henry's restaurant instead of on the radio," Bianca offered, carefully separating the ravioli squares she'd cut.

"I'd never do that." Angie wrinkled her mouth. "Henry's restaurant serves mostly burgers, mediocre steaks, pot roasts, and fried chicken. It's good, basic food. A nice place for a family. Kids are happy there—mac and cheese, puffy tater tots, and chicken nuggets. But it's not a place to bring a date, or expect a dinner that'll cause you to sit up and cheer. And, on top of everything, for what they're serving, it's overpriced because its owner has a radio show and that brings in customers. Frankly, LaTour's would have a lot fewer customers if it weren't for *Lunch with Henri* radio listeners who are taken in by all his schmoozing."

"I had no idea," Bianca admitted.

"Anyway, the radio job is better. And maybe, someday, I'll be able to say a word or two on the air."

When they finished, they both wiped the sweat from their brows, washed the flour from their hands and arms, and collapsed in kitchen chairs.

"Now you see why I don't want to work in a restaurant," Angie said. "Cooking for a lot of people is hard work."

"Did you ever think of trying to find yourself a nice dentist to settle down with? Someone like my Peter, for instance," Bianca said, reverting back to her earlier topic, despite Angie not wanting to hear her opinion on the subject. "Or, what about Chick Marcuccio's son, Joey? I was at the house when Chick came over and told papà how happy he was to see you at Karl Wielund's memorial service. They still hope you and Joey will get together. And, Joey's always had eyes for you."

Angie wrinkled her mouth in disgust. "That's because he used to steal my dessert out of my lunch box. He liked it better than his own. I can't stand Joey Marcuccio."

"But Joey makes a lot of money in his financial business," Bianca couldn't help but point out. "I might give him a call just to say hello... from the both of us."

Angie felt as if her hair was on fire. "Bianca, don't you dare!"

9

The Placer County Coroner's Office called Homicide early the next morning. Paavo was already in and took the call. He had managed to get approval from Lt. Hollins to pay for an autopsy by pointing out that Karl Wielund was an important person in the restaurant community in the city—and the restaurant community was important to tourism and therefore important to the mayor. Once he got that done, he worked with the Placer County Coroner's office to contact Wielund's family in Germany—his brother had been named as his executor— and the family okayed an autopsy.

Now, Paavo was about to find out what the results were of all his meddling. He held his breath as the medical examiner told him his finding. The complete write-up would be emailed to the SFPD homicide bureau as soon as it was finished.

The ME identified *atropine* and *scopolamine* as toxic ingredients that had been put into a quiche, eaten by Karl Wielund, and causing his death. As little as seven drops could create a burning sensation, followed by a swelling of the tongue, then paralysis and death in ten to sixty minutes. Consciousness often continued to the end.

Paavo listened to the ME's words with a shudder. It wasn't a pleasant or a quick way to die. The ME also noted that Wielund had been dead for several hours before his car went off the highway in the mountains.

Based on those results, Paavo found it likely Wielund had been poisoned in San Francisco then dumped in the mountains where the heavy snows meant there was a good chance he wouldn't be found until the spring thaws. But, if he were found, everyone would think he'd been in an auto accident and not pursue it any further.

That's exactly what had happened until Angie brought her suspicions to his attention.

Paavo put down the phone then waved at his partner who was getting a cup of coffee. "Just got word that an autopsy on Karl Wielund showed he'd been poisoned."

Yosh's eyebrows rose. "So, when you said the people at Wielund's memorial service seemed to not like the guy, you were right."

"Someone definitely didn't like him."

Yosh's eyes lighted up the more he heard. "Interesting, but is it our case?"

Paavo cocked his head. "His house was in San Francisco. He was dead hours before his car went off a mountainside in the Sierras, and I got Hollins to spring for the cost of his autopsy."

Yosh's lips formed a half-grin. "Unless dead men drive, sounds like it's our case all right."

Paavo called Missing Persons, and within a half hour the report made by Wielund's sous chef, Mark Dustman, was on Paavo's desk. He ran off a copy for Yoshiwara.

Paavo located Wielund's landlord, Hank Greuber, and told him that the police had just learned Karl Wielund was murdered, so the house was a potential crime scene and he didn't want it touched. Greuber complained that he needed to move all Wielund's belongings into storage and rent out the house as soon as possible.

"It'll be released to you as soon as our investigation of it is completed," Paavo said, relieved that the landlord hadn't already cleared it. "Meet us there this afternoon. That'll help move our investigation along."

As Yosh cruised into a parking space in front of Wielund's address, Paavo saw Hank Greuber, a wispy thin man, with a clump of Woody Woodpecker stand-up straight white hair on the very top of his head, waiting beside a big, green Buick in the driveway of the house Karl Wielund had rented. Greuber jiggled his key chain impatiently across his palm.

After quick introductions, Paavo noticed Greuber kept peering at the house and rubbing his arms as if he expected to see Wielund's ghost jump out at them.

"This is just great, Mr. Greuber," Yosh said, patting the landlord on the back as they walked toward the house. "Great of you to join us. Cooperation makes all our lives easier."

Paavo could hardly wait to see Yosh make an arrest. *Hey there, Mr. Murderer, how ya doin'? It's sure great of you to let me read you your rights.*

"I can't believe anyone would murder Karl Wielund," Greuber said to Yosh, his eyes wide and darting nervously. "Good tenant. Clean. Non-smoker. He even brought in his own big, fancy stove and moved mine to the garage. It'll be practically new." He put the key in the lock and opened the front door. They stepped into a small entry, with a door to the garage to one side, and stairs straight ahead. In typical San Francisco fashion, the garage, laundry, and storage facilities were on the ground floor, and a small living area above it.

"Good tenants are hard to find, I hear," Yosh said.

"You better believe it!" Greuber led the way upstairs. "He always paid his rent on time. Quiet. The neighbors never complained. Wait!"

He stopped so suddenly Paavo nearly bumped into him. Paavo whipped out his gun, pulled Greuber back and behind him, then inched forward to see what had alarmed the landlord.

The place looked like someone had tossed it.

"It wasn't like this before," Greuber whispered.

"Before?" Paavo asked.

"I checked the house right after word came of Wielund's death to make sure everything was okay here. It's messy now. As if... as if Wielund came back and threw his papers and other stuff all over the place."

"You'd better wait downstairs in the entry, Mr. Greuber," Paavo said.

With bulging eyes, Greuber looked from Paavo's gun to his face, then backed away.

Paavo went past the kitchen into a small hallway. Off it were two small bedrooms and a bathroom. The possibility that whoever was searching the place was hiding somewhere, was at the top of his mind. He found no one, and holstered his pistol.

"I've never heard of dead men coming back to ransack their house," Yosh said.

"We'll get the crime unit out to dust for prints," Paavo said, the state of the house a mystery.

The front door suddenly slammed shut, making the windows rattle. Paavo glanced quickly at Yosh, then ran downstairs and out the front door.

Greuber was backing out of the driveway. Paavo raced toward him. "Greuber, wait!" he yelled, grabbing the passenger door handle. Greuber sped up, still going backwards, nearly pulling Paavo's arm out of the socket before he let go. His bad shoulder felt as if a hot poker had pierced it. Grimacing, he clutched his arm tight against his chest, doing all he could to stay on his feet as a fierce, throbbing pain made his stomach turn and the sidewalk seemed to sway like a rowboat in a hurricane.

In the far reaches of his mind, he saw Greuber's white face watching him, then Greuber jerked the transmission into drive, gunned the engine and tore down the street.

"Damn!" Paavo said through clenched teeth, both at his shoulder and the uneasy feeling that filled him as he watched the car disappear.

Yosh ran to his side, his face filled with concern. "You all right, partner?"

Paavo slowly eased his hand off his arm. "Sure. It's nothing." He drew in a breath. "Jammed my finger on the door handle."

Something flickered across Yosh's eyes before he turned from Paavo to glance down the now empty street. "Some men just spook easy, I guess."

"I guess," Paavo echoed. But then, the two looked meaningfully at each other, and Paavo stared back at the house, brows locked. "Or, more likely, Greuber saw or remembered something. But what?"

Yosh shook his head. "I'll check out the garage soon as I contact the crime scene unit."

Slowly rotating his shoulder, trying to make it feel somewhat normal again, Paavo went back into the house, and put on rubber gloves to flip through papers, bills for the most part, and a few letters from Germany, as well as opening doors, closets and even cupboards as he passed them. Inside the desk drawer, he saw a small stack of business cards. He flipped through them—restaurants and vendors mostly, but then he stopped at Angie's *Bay Area Cooks* card. Something made him flip it over, and there on the back, in her handwriting, he found her personal cellphone number.

He stared at them a moment. She had said Wielund was a friend. How much of a friend, he wondered. Had they dated?

But she was only twenty-eight, and Wielund was in his fifties. Much too old for her. Wasn't he?

He didn't like the feeling that finding Angie's card gave him. Was it jealousy? Being jealous of a dead man was beyond foolish. There had to be a different explanation for Wielund having such information about Angie. He hoped.

He placed the business cards into an evidence bag, then entered the kitchen to find Yosh.

"I just thought of something," Paavo said. "In the missing person's report Dustman filed, he said he didn't see Karl *or any sign of where he'd gone* when he came to his house looking for him. Nobody asked Dustman how he got into this house to search. Or, the state of the house when Dustman entered it."

"Guess we'll add that to our other questions for him," Yosh said, then headed into the garage.

After a short while Yoshiwara called. "Paavo, you better get down here."

When Paavo entered the garage, he saw Yosh in a corner bending over an open box and holding some photographs in his hand. The box was labeled "golf balls."

"Check these out," he said as he stood and waved the photos in Paavo's direction. "Our victim was into a different kind of golf. Plus, I don't see any clubs around here."

Paavo looked at the photos. Some in color, some in black and white, of women, girls, men, and even animals engaged in activities beyond the imagination of most online pornography site devotees. One woman in particular showed up in again and again in the photos. Paavo shook his head and let the photos drop back into the oversized carton. "The guy was real sick."

"The photos are nothing." Yosh pointed to the remaining contents of the box. It was filled with DVDs. "As soon as I saw the box marked 'Golf Balls,' I knew nobody could have enough for a box this size. That's why I opened it up."

"This stuff isn't commercial," Paavo said, looking at the

DVDs in cases marked with numbers, not names. "Maybe amateur?"

Yosh smirked. "Could be. Looks like Wielund appreciated more than one kind of cheesecake."

Paavo nodded. "The question is, was he a customer, a distributor, or a producer?"

"I know one thing," Yosh added. "Messing around with the people that handle this stuff is a good way to get yourself killed."

Paavo began to look around the garage. "Let's see if there are any more surprises here. I've got a bad feeling about this whole thing."

The memory of Greuber's white face as he sped away from the house came to him once more.

Angie put on her headphones and gave a thumbs-up to LaTour as *The Teddy Bears' Picnic* played to open the show. She vowed she would concentrate on screening the calls as thoroughly as possible; to never again answer any caller's question herself, no matter how quickly and easily she could do so; and to be everything LaTour could ever hope for in an assistant.

Now that she was call-screening and had to talk to callers while the show was on the air, her desk had been moved into the studio next door. A glass window was between the two so she could see LaTour. The two communicated through their computers.

A call was coming in. She sat up straight in her chair and pushed the open-line button. "Welcome to *Lunch with Henri*. This is Angie. How may I help you?"

"Hi, Angie. I'd like to talk to Chef Henri. I love listening to him."

"Great! What's your name and where are you calling from?"

"I'm Dinah from St. Helena."

"Okay, Dinah. What's your question?"

"I'm preparing a small, but very formal, elegant dinner, and I want to cook something really special. But with popular, common, ingredients—nothing over the top, if that makes sense. Any advice?"

Yes, don't ask Chef Henri. But she said, "That's a great question. Chef Henri will surely have a fantastic suggestion for you. He'll be with you in a minute."

She typed out the question so LaTour would know what was coming—just as a good call-screener should do. And then she found a nice recipe for Coq au Vin chicken. It looked elegant, but was chicken—and who didn't like chicken? She transferred it to him.

LaTour read the question and gave her a thumb's up. When the commercial was over, he saw that only one call was waiting for him to answer, he gave his phone number again, and then took the call.

After introducing himself, he made small talk with Dinah and asked her about St. Helena. Her answer took about three seconds. Exasperated, he listened to the question.

"Well," he said, "something elegant but basic for four people.... Ah, I've got it. I would suggest a bacon wrapped pork tenderloin with an apple and wine sauce. You can serve it with fancy mashed potatoes, which you can call Gratin Dauphinois."

What? Angie couldn't believe what she was hearing. She transferred the Coq au Vin recipe to him again.

"That sounds like delicious, and like something my guests would love, Chef Henri," Dinah said. "Thank you so much for taking my call. I'll look for a recipe for that."

LaTour glanced at the empty call-waiting queue. "No need! I know a wonderful recipe for it," he said hurriedly.

Angie was horror-struck. That man didn't know a pork chop from a crown roast. Whatever was he thinking of? She grabbed his cookbook, *Luscious Licks*, and began wildly thumbing through the index.

"That's wonderful!" Dinah said.

"Grab a pencil and paper and I'll give you the recipe, plus it will be posted to our website, w, w, w, dot, L, A, T, O, U, R, S, dot, com. No apostrophe. "

Angie's heart sank as she dropped, quietly, LaTour's cookbook. Nothing even close to the recipe was in it. Whatever was the man thinking?

"You begin by making the stuffing with a green apple, pork sausage, and spices." LaTour said, and then began describing the preparation in so much detail Angie couldn't believe what she was hearing. She stood to look at him and noticed he was reading from a piece of paper. What in the world?

He continued. "Then take a pork tenderloin and cut a one-inch wide pocket through the center of it. Or, better yet, have your butcher cut it!" LaTour laughed.

"Good idea," Dinah said, chuckling with him.

"Put your stuffing in the pork and wrap it with slices of bacon and then grill it until cooked through." Again, LaTour gave a general explanation, and then details for how to do it. "Finally, make your sauce using chopped apples and apple cider, a dry Riesling, chicken stock, sage, and thyme. Put it in a saucepan and simmer until the apple softens, then move it to a blender and puree until it's smooth. After that, boil it until it's cooked down enough to coat a spoon. Slice up your pork tenderloin, plate it, and spoon the sauce around it."

As she listened, Angie's jaw slackened. She couldn't have been more surprised had LaTour turned green and sprouted antennas. Where had he gotten his hands on a recipe like that? What was going on?

When her phone monitor began to blink because another call had come in, it took her a long time to even notice it.

"Thank you for coming by to talk with us. We really appreciate it," Yoshiwara said as he and Paavo led Mark Dustman into Homicide's interview room.

"I'll do anything I can to help. I was surprised to hear from you, I'll admit," Dustman said with a nervous quiver.

The three sat around a metal table. Paavo looked squarely at Dustman. "We've found that Karl Wielund was poisoned."

Dustman's face turned chalky. "Poisoned? You mean someone purposefully..."

"Yes."

"Oh, God!" He pressed a hand to his mouth, his green eyes wide and filled with horror. "I can't believe it."

"You said many people were jealous of his success," Paavo said.

"But not enough to *kill* him!" He gave a shuddering sigh, his voice hoarse. "Are you sure? Poisoned?"

"There was an autopsy."

Dustman looked more closely at Paavo, his eyes narrowing slightly. "I saw you at the memorial service, didn't I?"

"Yes."

"Poison would indicate a chef might have done it. Even me! So... did you already have some suspicion that the death wasn't an accident? "

Paavo studied Dustman, every nuance of expression, every gesture. "Not by me."

Dustman rubbed his forehead. "You were with Angie Amalfi, weren't you? She must have said something... or others did." He lifted his chin. "Well, good! That means it isn't only me who suspected something. I knew someone wanted Karl dead." His eyes darted from Paavo to Yosh. "That must be what I felt. That must be why I felt that there was more to his death than a trip to the mountains that went horribly wrong. Karl was killed by some bastard! Some jealous, rotten, son of a bitch! Damn it to hell!" His eyes filled with tears.

Yosh touched Dustman's arm. "Take it easy, Mr. Dustman. We'll do all we can to find whoever did this."

Dustman squeezed his eyes shut, nodded, then hung his head.

Paavo spoke. "We need to ask a few questions of everyone we talk to in this case."

"Of course," Dustman murmured, trying to compose himself.

"Where were you on Sunday, January 14th?"

"On Sunday? Sleeping in. It's the one day the restaurant is closed. I took it easy all day until seven o'clock when I went to the restaurant to meet Karl, but he didn't show up. I'd tried reaching him by phone, and when I never got an answer, I went to his house. I saw no sign of him or his car. When he was still a no-show on Monday night, I filed a missing person's report."

"Tell me," Paavo asked, "when you checked on Wielund, how did you get in?"

Dustman's head snapped back, his voice growing more shrill with each reply. "I didn't think anyone would care. I just used the spare key in the Hide-A-Key stuck under a potted plant by the front door."

"How did you know it was there?"

"I stayed at Karl's house a few days when I first came to the city. We were close friends...like brothers, or even father and son. He had money, I didn't, so he took me in until I got on my feet and found my own place." His eyes turned red and watery. "Why are you asking me all these questions?"

"Did you ever go back into Wielund's house after that first visit while he was missing?" Paavo asked.

Dustman shook his head. "No. I had no reason to."

"What was the condition of the house when you saw it?"

"The condition? Neat, of course. Karl was fanatical about his house."

Paavo nodded as Yosh asked, "One last question, is Wielund's restaurant still closed?"

Dustman sighed and shook his head. "Yes. Karl's brother in Germany, the estate executor, wants to sell it. Eileen got him to give her enough money to pay the staff two weeks severance, but that's it. I doubt Wielund's will see the light of day again."

10

Paavo left work a bit early that afternoon to visit the young son and widow of his old partner, Matt. He liked to check in on them a couple of times a week. He owed Matt that much, at least. Katie was coping well, all things considered. Also, he took the boy, Micky, to the local playground to let him go on the swing and then play catch for a while. He knew that's what Matt would have done, if he were still here. Afterward, they all went out for pizza.

Later, instead of heading home, he made the mistake of stopping off at Homicide to see if anything had turned up yet from the crime scene unit he and Yosh had called in to Karl Wielund's home. Their report was on his desk. All was so quiet in the office, Paavo sat down to go through the results right then, rather than waiting until morning.

They'd found lots of fingerprints, and were processing them. They also said the DVDs did have porn movies on them, and they'd appeared to be professionally made, not amateur work. They would attempt to find out where they were made. More information, if possible, would be coming to him soon.

Rebecca and Never-Take-A-Chance Bill were the on-call

team that week. Rebecca was at her desk, ready to take any calls that might come in, while Bill Sutter was off doing what he did best, which wasn't much.

It was nearly nine when a call came in to Rebecca from Dispatch. She was strapping on her gun belt when Paavo's phone went off.

He learned there'd been a shooting in the Richmond District and Bill Sutter had a wracking cough and his lungs hurt so much he didn't think he could make it. They'd already contacted Inspector Mayfield were trying to find a back-up for her.

Paavo glanced at Rebecca and signaled her to wait. "I'll take it," Paavo said. He hung up. "Guess who won't be joining you... and who will."

Rebecca just shook her head. "Thanks, Paavo. Let's go."

The crime scene was in a nice part of town, what they called the Inner Richmond, on Clement Street, just a few blocks from the Sorrento Restaurant, which Paavo remembered as belonging to Angie's family friend, Chick Marcuccio.

A driver had apparently lost control of his car and ended up with its front end smashed against a telephone pole. The driver was dead. It was the sort of thing that might happen if the driver had a heart attack or something similar. But the uniformed officers who had been called to the "accident" immediately saw it was more than that.

Paavo and Rebecca arrived, each in their own car, at the same time. The street had been cordoned off.

They walked together to see exactly what was going on. The Medical Examiner, Dr. Evelyn Ramirez, was already there waiting.

"I think you'll find the cause of death clear," Evelyn said as they approached. "How it happened, though, will be your problem."

The two approached the victim's car, a Mercedes sedan.

They could see he was seated, his head thrown back against the car's head rest, and the airbag still wedging him in tight.

The driver's side door was opened. Glass from a shattered window lay on the street. They did their best to side step the glass as they looked inside the car. The driver had a bullet hole in his temple, blood and spatter dotting the sides of his head and clothes.

Paavo heart sank.

"I know this guy," he said to Rebecca. "I just met him at a memorial service for a big restaurant owner, Karl Wielund. He's another owner of a restaurant, Sorrento. It's down the street. I wonder if he was leaving work when this happened."

Rebecca gaped at him. "I've heard of it. Never lucky enough to eat there."

"Me neither," Paavo said, then drew in his breath. "His name—not his actual name, I imagine, but what everyone called him—was Chick Marcuccio."

It was nearly eleven when Paavo left the Hall of Justice late that night to go a couple of blocks for a quick burger since the pizza he'd shared hours ago now had him a bit hungry. He turned up his sports jacket collar as he strode along the sidewalk.

The city glistened as lamplights cast their glow on streets washed clean and slick by the winter rain. Winter in San Francisco was mild. The rain actually warmed up the weather a bit and washed away the fog so that the streets were clear. Having rain but no snow was one of the benefits of life in this town. There weren't many, anymore.

Earlier, by the time Paavo and Rebecca had left the crime scene and went to the Sorrento restaurant, it was closed and the staff had gone for the night. The next day would be spent canvassing the neighbors, hoping someone had seen or heard something, and looking for security cameras.

From Sorrento's, Rebecca had gone to the Marcuccio home to see if anyone was there to talk to, while Paavo returned to Homicide. He told her what he'd learned from Angie about Marcuccio's divorce and affair with the editor of *Haute Cuisine* magazine, Janet Knight.

In Homicide, Paavo learned that Chick, whose real name was Alfonse Emiliano Marcuccio, had been no stranger to the law when he was young and had gotten picked up for shop-lifting a few times. Paavo grimaced. It was scarcely considered a crime any more in the city. But those brushes with the law must have straightened him out, because from age twenty on, he never even got a parking ticket.

Paavo then called Bill Sutter, who didn't cough once while on the phone, and told him what they'd found. Sutter said he'd be in the next morning and would take over and work with Rebecca. Since Paavo had met the deceased as well as many of his colleagues, he felt it would be better if Sutter handled it. Also, he could imagine Calderon's reaction to learn Angie had been close to the victim. There was no reason to bring her—or her relationship with Paavo—into Chick Marcuccio's murder investigation.

He hated that Angie's name might in any way be associated with the victims of these murders. She should live a life free of such ugliness. He could help but think of Angie. She lit up empty corners of his life with her bad jokes and puckish smile, and filled him with her laughter and generosity. He'd been a quiet, normal homicide detective, dealing every day with murder, cruelty, vengeance and seediness, before she'd entered his life. Now, he couldn't think straight. He argued with his friends, talked to himself and... *oomph!*... walked into parking meters in the dead of night.

"Hey, mister," a ragged, scraggly bearded man huddling in a

doorway with an oilcloth over his head and shoulders, held out a pint whiskey bottle toward Paavo. "Looks like you need this more than I do."

The guy was probably right, Paavo thought, and hurried into the diner as if his little dance with the parking meter was part of his usual routine.

But once he entered, he realized what he had been trying to avoid by going there. And knew he was wrong to do that.

The night beacon on Alcatraz that once swept the dark waters of the bay searching for escaping prisoners, now acted more as a warning and reminder against wrong-doings for all San Franciscans as it revolved. Not that they paid much attention. The sharp beam of light flashed in the direction of Angie's rain-dappled windows every nine seconds. She sat in front of the windows addressing invitations for a baby shower for her fourth sister, Francesca. Frannie and Seth had been married three years, and their first child was due in April.

Angie was the only one of the sisters still unmarried, much to her mother's dismay. Angie had never given marriage much thought, enjoying the single life, travel, and pretty much doing as she pleased, until a tall, very single homicide detective entered her life.

But that was then, and this was now. Now, she had the feeling he wanted to avoid seeing her. She had no idea why. Maybe having once been a potential homicide victim wasn't the best start for a long-lasting relationship.

Her phone rang and Paavo's name appeared on the display. "Hello," she said cheerfully. "This is a surprise. What are you doing calling at this hour?"

"Are you still up?" he asked.

Elation at the thought he wanted to see her struck. "Of course. It's not that late."

"Buzz me in. Your doorman has locked up."

"You're here?"

"I am."

She pushed the buzzer to unlock the main door and then waited in the hall until the elevator bonged on her floor and Paavo stepped off. She couldn't help a big smile as he walked down the hall toward her.

"What happened to you?" she said. He looked like a drowned rat.

"Sorry to bother you."

Uh, oh, she thought. The deep, serious sound of his voice told her "Inspector Smith," not Paavo, had come to call. She hurried him into her living room. "It's no bother. Let me take your jacket." It was soaked. His hands felt like ice and she saw his slight wince as he pulled his arm from the sleeve. "What have you been doing getting soaked like this? You must have been working. You've got to take better care of yourself. That shoulder isn't completely healed yet, you know—"

"It's fine."

"But it won't be if you try to do too much, too soon. It'll stiffen up in this cold. And you could catch pneumonia. Then, the department won't have any choice but to wait a very long time for you to solve all its cases. Eleven o'clock at night is too late for you to still be working."

"Angie... " As he turned and faced her, she raced into her bedroom and came back with a bath towel that she tossed over his head and then rubbed to dry his hair.

"Angie..."

She removed the towel and then patted his hair back into place. Okay, she liked having a reason to touch him, his hair, his strong shoulders, despite the way he held himself back from her. "Are you chilly? I've got a wonderful Sherpa lap blanket you can throw over your shoulders, or your legs if your slacks are also wet, which I can see they are around your shoes. How many puddles did you step—"

"ANGIE!"

She froze and looked up at his face, finally taking a moment to see that something—other than the rain—was very, very wrong.

"That's enough!" he murmured.

His expression worried her, and in that moment, she didn't want to hear what he had come to tell her. Was it about the two of them? Or had something happened tonight? Something bad. She placed the towel on a chair. "I was just trying to help."

"I know. I'm sorry. I didn't mean to shout. I shouldn't have, but I stopped by here for a reason."

She nodded, then folded her arms. "I guessed that."

"Right." He ran his fingers through his hair to smooth it back down.

She waited.

"I've got to talk to you about a case."

Her glance went to the gun and shoulder holster he wore. Usually, she could make herself ignore them, but other times, like now, she was forced to remember them and all they meant.

"Okay." Angie didn't like the way he was looking at her, as if he had to tell her something but wasn't sure how. She nodded, walked over to the Hepplewhite and sat. "What's wrong?"

"A man is dead. A friend of yours."

"What?" She drew in her breath.

"Chick Marcuccio."

"No!" She frowned, not wanting to believe his words. "No. It can't be."

"He was shot."

She stood as a cold, ugly feeling, like a block of ice, landed in the pit of her stomach. Chick was like an uncle to her. She'd known him all her life. When she was little, she'd go play at her friend Terry's house, and Chick would often take them to Swenson's for ice cream, or over to the Helen Wills playground for kick-ball. Even after he and his wife divorced, he was always around when Terry or Joey needed him for anything. The thought of him not being there, of being dead....

"No one would shoot Chick!" Even as she spoke, thoughts of not only Chick, but Terry, Joey, even Chick's ex-wife, came into her mind. And her father. Especially her father. He and Chick were the best of friends and had been since they were teenagers. The stories they could tell about the old days. They were both hell on wheels. And now... Tears filled her eyes.

"I'm so sorry, Angie," Paavo whispered, stepping closer to her.

Her father had been doing so well since his by-pass surgery, but how would he handle news like this? What would it do to him? The thought crushed her, and she reached for Paavo, her head against his shoulder as more tears fell.

He gently held her until she stepped back, wiping away her tears. "I'm sorry. You came here with a wet jacket, and now I've gotten your shirt wet as well."

"It's okay," he said softly. "We'll find out who did this to your family's friend. I know how much he meant to you."

She nodded. "I know you will. Now, please. I'll put on some coffee. I want you to tell me everything." She somehow made her way into the kitchen and turned on her espresso machine, trying not to think about what Chick's death would mean to the many people who loved him. In no time, she had a couple of Americanos and a plate of orange-and-walnut biscotti, and brought everything out and placed them on the coffee table. They sat, side-by-side, on the sofa.

Softly, he told her where they'd found Chick and his car.

"So, no witnesses, yet," she said.

"We'll find witnesses or security footage tomorrow, I'm sure," Paavo said. "It's a busy area."

Her lips tightened. "He was like family, Paavo. You know what that means. Find out who did this to him."

He nodded. "One more thing I should tell you," he said. "A while back, I said I didn't see anything criminal about Karl Wielund's death."

He had all her attention now.

"I received the results of an autopsy on him. He was poisoned."

She was shocked. "Poisoned?"

"Someone did it deliberately. He was murdered."

"I don't believe this. Karl and now Chick." She could see the way Paavo studied her that he was making the same connection and may have had the same thought—that this was no coincidence. "Karl was so happy the last time I saw him, and his restaurant was doing so well."

"How long did you know him, exactly?" Paavo asked.

"Eight, nine months, I guess. Chick Marcuccio introduced us. I'd done a review of Karl's restaurant for an online magazine. It was a favorable review, and he wanted to thank me."

"That's all?"

"Well... yes."

He waited. She hoped he was hadn't noticed her hesitation. But then he said, "I found your business card. You'd given him your cellphone number."

"Oh?" Was nothing private with this man? "Well, it meant nothing at the time. It was about restaurant reviews."

"Ah. I see." Silence.

Although who she had or hadn't dated certainly wasn't Paavo's business, she had no reason to keep it from him. "Okay, he did call and ask me out a couple of times."

"A couple of times?" he repeated.

"I didn't go."

"Why not?"

She was getting the feeling this was some sort of interrogation. "I don't know. I guess I didn't much care for him."

He lifted an eyebrow, as if waiting for her to say more. She hesitated, and then blurted, "Something about him struck me wrong. That's all."

"In what way?"

Now, she definitely didn't like his sudden change in attitude. "What is this? Am I a suspect because I gave him my phone number?"

"No. I just want to know."

She wished she could understand what went on in that complicated head of his. "Why? Because he's your case, or is this something personal?"

He didn't answer right away. "I'm trying to understand what kind of man Karl Wielund was, that's all. Strictly business."

It had already been a long, emotional night, and she couldn't stand the Great Stoneface showing up now, when just a few minutes ago Paavo had been here as her friend, her dear friend, and had held her as she cried on his shoulder. "Strictly business, then, I already told you I didn't go out with him."

"You also told me he asked you out *twice*. That means you encouraged him enough to call you back."

"I *what*?" She stood up, disappointed and angry at what sounded like an accusation of some sort.

"Did he say what he wanted? What these dates with you were all about?"

"Dates? I just told you I didn't go out with him!"

"Why are you so mad?" he asked, also standing. "I just want to know why he kept calling you."

She put her hands on my hips. "Maybe because he loved my body!"

He frowned. "That's exactly what worries me."

"*What?*"

He drew in a deep breath and then spoke softly. "Did he

ever, uh, mention anything to you that might have sounded a bit... indiscreet?"

Enough was enough. "Good God, Paavo. The bottom line is he just wasn't my type. He wasn't a guy I was in any way attracted to."

"Why was that?"

She clutched her hair. For a cop, he was completely obtuse about her. "Maybe because he didn't show up late at night with horrible news, and then proceed to interrogate me for no good reason whatsoever!"

"Relax." He leaned back casually on the sofa, his legs crossed at the ankles.

She sat with a huff. "I am relaxed. I mean, if I'd known he was going to get himself killed, I *certainly* would have dated him. Then I could have told you all about him, all his little peccadillos. Is that what you want to hear?"

"Calm down."

"I am calm!"

"Good, that's all I needed to know." He glanced at his watch, then stood and reached for his wet jacket. He threw it over his arm instead of putting it on.

She, too, stood. "What is it you're trying to learn about Karl?" she asked. "Why all the strange questions about him?"

He gave a resigned sigh. "I guess I do owe you some explanation. There may be a connection between Wielund and something illegal. Ugly and illegal. But I can't go into any details, all right?"

She stepped closer. "Illegal? That's interesting."

"I found a few signs that have made me curious about the man, that's all."

She suddenly felt as if she could contribute something. "Tell you what, I'll make a few phone calls. After all, I'm practically in the same business as Karl Wielund, or close to it. We just may be on to something."

"No. Absolutely not. And no more of this 'we' stuff."

It surely hadn't taken him long to burst her bubble. "Why not?"

"It could be dangerous. You don't know who else might be involved."

"I'm not a restaurant owner, just a radio assistant. And I would only talk to people I know well. Some might be jealous, vindictive and even petty, but they're not murderers."

"But someone is, Angie. You shouldn't hang around any of them until we know what happened."

"Don't worry. I'm only talking about a few phone calls."

"Angelina, no!"

When he came out with an "Angelina," it meant he was serious. She smiled. "Inspector Smith, sometimes you are simply too bossy." She then opened the door for him to leave.

11

"I'm glad you called, Angie." Joey Marcuccio's gaze was subdued yet wistful as he looked at Angie from across the table at what would soon become his and his sister's restaurant, Sorrento.

"It's been a long time, Joey," she said. "I'd forgotten how long until I talked to your dad the other night. I really loved him."

"I know. Everyone did. That's why I wanted to talk to you." Joey's brown eyes were big and round. He was skinny as a rail, his curly black hair was already thinning on top, and Angie couldn't stand him when they were kids. As they got older, everyone told her he'd developed a crush on her and he even asked her out a couple of times. She'd always turned him down.

That morning, she called to express her condolences to him and was flabbergasted when he asked her to meet him for lunch to talk. This time she had to accept. It wasn't a date, it was duty.

"Our families are so big now, so spread out. It's not like the old days, Angie," Joey said with a sigh. "Ever since Teresa got married, she's become more serious. The three of us used to have fun together."

"We sure did," she agreed. She'd talked to Terry before calling Joey, but quickly found after expressing condolences, that they had little to say to each other.

"I always had hopes for you and me, you know," he murmured.

She didn't know how to respond.

"Did you know that when we were kids," he continued, "I used to hear my dad and yours planning to make sure we fell in love and got married?" He picked at the *tagliarini* on his plate. As he did, his face took on a worried cast. "I don't think that would ever have worked out."

She saw the change that came over him as he spoke his last words. "Where are you going with all this?" Her voice was soft.

He shrugged. "I need to know, Angie. Does that boyfriend of yours, the cop, have any idea who killed my dad?"

So that was it. She knew how frustratingly close-mouthed the police could be at such times, and how painful it was not to know. She did her best to be honest with him. "Not yet. Not that I've heard, anyway. He doesn't tell me much about his cases."

"What about your boss?"

"LaTour? I can't imagine he knows anything about it."

"What about Wielund's murder? I'll bet he knows about that."

Angie was stunned. "Why would he?"

"Their restaurants are right across the street from each other. Everyone says he's on the verge of going under, that he's having trouble paying suppliers, and he's lost most of his customers since Wielund's opened."

Angie had always thought it was because of his cooking. "That's hard to imagine. They don't cater to the same clientele at all."

"I can tell you another thing," Joey said with a knowing nod.

"You might have always thought I was just another pretty face around here, but I paid attention to my dad and his cooking. I even learned a little about it, although my heart's always been on the accounting side of things. Still, I'll say that was some hell of a recipe Henry gave for German style stuffed pork tenderloin the other day."

"You listen to *Lunch with Henri*?" Angie could scarcely believe it.

"Every chance I get. My dad convinced me to listen. He called it the best comedy around. But Henry often blurts some 'inside baseball' gossip—although I guess it really should be called 'inside kitchen' gossip."

Angie frowned.

"Was the pork recipe yours, by chance?" he asked.

"I wish it was. It surprised me as much as it did most of his listeners, I'm sure."

"That's what I was afraid of." He leaned closer, his voice low. "When Wielund's first opened, I ate that exact same dish *there*. It was fantastic, but Karl stopped serving it because it wasn't as delicious as he thought it should be. The man was a fanatic about his personal recipes, you know."

"It was the same recipe?" she asked.

"Well, at least the same ingredients, same results. I've always checked out the competition for my dad. I do have a good palette, you know. And my nose isn't this big for nothing. So, how is it Henry could spiel off Wielund's recipe that way?"

"Wait a minute," Angie said cautiously. "We don't know for sure it was Wielund's recipe. And he didn't spout it. He read it."

"Ah ha!" Joey nodded. "Well, it sure as hell wasn't Henry's recipe. And if he read it... Whatever did happen to Wielund's recipes, his chef's log?"

"But you don't know that for sure." Joey rubbed his chin.

Angie was stumped. "I don't know. I suspect Eileen Powell and Mark Dustman have them."

"Hmm. They'd go a long way toward helping make a good restaurant a lot better. Maybe even worth killing for."

She could tell where this was going and didn't like it. And she still didn't care for Joey. She glanced at her watch. "I need to get going. It's almost time for the class I'm teaching."

"A class? About what?"

"San Francisco history."

"Oh." He didn't say anything more. That was the typical reaction to her class, she was sorry to admit. At least the seven people in it enjoyed it.

"Thank you for the lunch, and I'll be sure to keep you posted if I hear anything."

Joey helped her with her jacket. "Give my best to your family," he said, and then kissed her cheek.

As she hurried from the restaurant, she fought the urge to wipe her cheek where his too wet lips had touched.

12

"I give up," Yosh said, tossing Karl Wielund's porn photos back into Paavo's little-used briefcase. "Everyone denied ever seeing any of them, and we have no way to prove otherwise."

Paavo remained silent as he drove them back to Homicide. His mind kept retracing the pitiful lack of evidence and clues they had so far. Dirty pictures, a poisoned restaurateur, a shot restaurateur, and, on top of that, Greuber's wife had called to say the landlord hadn't come home after going off to meet the detectives at Wielund's house.

Also, Wielund's car had been hoisted from the cliff where it had rolled and was delivered to San Francisco's crime scene unit. They found it hadn't been tampered with, and was lousy with fingerprints, as was his house. For a loner, this guy had a lot of people in his life.

Paavo and Yosh had interviewed Eileen Powell and, as Dustman said, she had been in Paris at the time Wielund was killed, talking to restaurant owners and chefs. She had the receipts to prove it. She claimed she was there to find the latest in decor, menus, and wines so that Wielund's would remain at the top of its game, which meant to be as much like a Parisian dining experience as possible, even though its menu featured "continental" over strictly French food. She, like Dustman, had no idea who would want to kill Wielund.

Waiters, waitresses and kitchen help at Wielund's corroborated Dustman's story about him trying to track down Karl, handling Karl's work as well as his own, and contacting the police.

Neighbors had seen nothing strange about Wielund. Relatives in Germany were interviewed with the help of translators and they, too, expressed shock at Wielund's death. He'd given no indication of any problems to any of them. Shop owners up and down Polk Street were questioned about anyone or anything near the restaurant that seemed odd to them. Another big zero.

For that reason, Paavo and Yosh decided to focus on the pornographic photos and films. They were the only thing sketchy about Wielund's life. They decided to see what reaction they might get from other culinary figures about them, despite knowing they might just be wasting a lot of time.

As they reached their desks and sat, Yosh began to chuckle.

Paavo frowned. "What's funny?"

"I was just remembering the expressions on the faces of Wielund's staff along with the other restaurant owners when you whipped out those porn pictures and asked if they knew any of those men or women, or ever saw Wielund with any of them."

Paavo shook his head and grinned. "I never before heard the sound of jaws dropping."

"Or saw eyes popping out of heads," Yosh said with a chortle as more laughter bubbled up in him. "Vladimir Polotski looked like he didn't want to give the pictures back. Mark Dustman didn't want to touch them, and Dupries gave them a sneering glance. I suppose that was very French of him."

Paavo nodded.

Yosh laughed harder. "I almost lost it when Henry LaTour stopped to put his reading glasses on to see better—'as a public service,' he'd said. Considering the pictures, maybe he meant to say 'a pubic service'?"

"Ohhhh," Paavo groaned, then despite himself, he, too, laughed.

Neither one of them felt much like laughing, though, when a phone call came in a few hours later.

At the crime scene, the patrolman who called in the report was leaning against his black and white, his complexion the same color as Hank Greuber's green Buick. The car had been parked along the tree-lined drive through Lincoln Park, near the Palace of the Legion of Honor. Although tourists visited the beautiful museum by day, at night it stood secluded and empty. Not until the patrolman noticed the car had been parked there for over twenty-four hours, did he slow down to investigate.

An oddly shaped white object sticking against the windshield had intrigued him enough to get out of his car. Only as he got closer did he see it was hair, human hair. The rest of the man's body was sprawled across the front seat, the back of his head gone. Hairy scalp, blood, and brains had somehow managed to stick to the windshield, creating the grotesque white flag that alerted the officer to trouble.

"So now we know why no one saw Greuber after he left Wielund's house," Yosh said.

"Damn!" Paavo wanted to shake the old man awake again. He wondered if Greuber saw something, or if someone had been hiding in or near Wielund's house when they arrived. That might have been why Greuber got spooked and ran outside. Or, possibly, an intruder grabbed him to make a fast get away. He might have been in the back seat of Greuber's car... inches away from Paavo as he tried to stop Greuber. "This never should have happened."

"You nearly lost your arm trying to stop him."

"But he lost his life."

After seeing Joey and teaching her history class the day before, Angie had gone to her parents' house in Hillsborough. She wanted to be sure her father was doing all right after the horrible news about his friend.

Salvatore Amalfi liked to act tough, but around his family, especially his daughters, his soft side often came through. He brought out the port, along with walnuts and fresh fruit as they sat, along with her mother, Serafina, and he reminisced about the good old days when he and Chick were young.

He especially liked recounting the old story of how, before Christopher Columbus became a *persona non grata*, the Italian community in San Francisco would get together for their own celebration of the arrival of *Cristoforo Colombo,* as he was known in Italy. They would gather at Aquatic Park, a small beach, so that Columbus could ride in on a rowboat and "discover" America.

One year, Chick played Columbus and Angie's father was an improbable Indian there to guide him to the shore. Why a native American was guiding him, no one knew, but also, no one cared.

The two of them, in costume, sat in a tiny gray rowboat on the far side of a pier, out of sight of the beach, drinking whiskey, supposedly to stay warm, while they waited for enough Italians to gather. By the time that happened, Chick and Sal were unsure if it was 1492, 1942, or any other date. Since there was no wind, and no sails, Sal was supposed to row them to shore while Chick stood, nobly viewing land. But Sal couldn't get the boat to go anywhere but in circles. He yelled at Chick to stop making the boat "lopsided," but when Chick shifted, his heroic pose dissolved into a flurry of arm-waving and pleas to Heaven as he pitched head first into the water. The crowd hooted.

The laughter increased when Sal tried to pull him back into the boat, and instead, join his friend in the water. Dripping wet, drunk, and seasick, they crawled to the beach. "Columbus" had to be held up to receive blessings from another friend playing "*Il Papa*,"—the Pope—while his "Indian" companion began to loudly sleep it off.

Angie was about seven years old before she realized Columbus didn't land in San Francisco when he discovered America.

All in all, it had been a good evening, and she was glad she'd spent it with her family. It might make the upcoming funeral a little easier to bear.

Then, in the morning, Angie had to break the speed limit to get to KYME radio in time for the show.

She made it to her desk at exactly twelve noon—just in time to see LaTour glaring at her for being almost late.

As the theme music ended, LaTour began his spiel. "Welcome to *Lunch with Henri*. It's so nice of you to join me today at our cozy little table for two. Our waiter is lighting the candles on our white linen tablecloth. He's turning over our crystal glasses to pour a Beaujolais—a bright red color, fresh, with the unexpected scent of blackcurrants, a young wine, yet with nothing thin about it..."

Angie stopped listening. LaTour would continue talking for a while, setting the scene for his listeners. This was something new he decided to try, thinking it'd make his female callers feel more "intimately attached" to him despite Angie telling him he was just wasting time. After that, he would give a monologue about cooking, often throwing in some restaurant news, and then he would read a couple of commercials before going to the phones. It was time for Angie to start screening the calls.

She looked at the telephone monitor. A call was waiting. She pushed the connect button. "*Lunch with Henri* radio show. This is Angie. Can I help you?"

A loud whistle suddenly blasted over the phone line and wouldn't stop. Angie broke the connection before it broke her eardrum.

A minute later, the phone light indicated that another caller was waiting. "*Lunch with Henri* radio show. Can I help you?"

Again, a loud whistle made the connection unbearable. What was going on here? Angie took off her headphones and tapped them, hoping that whatever was out-of-whack could be jiggled back into place. She played with the receiver's buttons for a while, waiting for another call to come in.

Eventually, one did, but again, Angie couldn't hear anything but a whistle.

A commercial was playing now, which meant it was almost time for LaTour to begin to take calls from listeners. She ran to his studio. "My earphones aren't working," she whispered. "You need to take the calls!"

He looked blankly at her. "What?" he mouthed.

She pointed at the earphones. "They aren't working!"

He nodded. "Okay. Where are the calls?"

She responded. "There aren't any."

"That's all I need. A talk show with no callers!" LaTour just then became aware that the music had stopped. He cleared his throat.

Unsure what to do, Angie stayed in the booth with him.

"And now," LaTour said, "it's time to go to our phones, so that you, our callers, can ask me anything your hearts' desire about cooking." He glanced at the blank phone monitor, then at Angie with an ever-deepening frown. "We seem to be having a bit of trouble with our phone lines, so I know it makes it diffi-cult for you to call in. My, my, my, whatever shall we do, since you know I *live* for our lunchtime together... when I can share

my knowledge about cooking with you, my dear listeners."
Angie's cringe grew ever deeper as his voice droned on. She'd
never been around so much B.S. outside of a cow pasture. "Let
me give you the numbers to call once more," LaTour said, "then
we'll take a little station break, and when we get back..." The
incoming call light began to flash. Angie waved frantically at
Henry, then pointed to the monitor. He nodded.

"Good news, ladies and gentlemen! Our phone system is
ready to be tested again. Let's see if it works." He hit the on-air
button. "Welcome to *Lunch with Henri.*"

"Hello, Chef Henri."

Angie glanced up from the monitor. She'd been debating
whether to try to take the next call, if and when one came in,
when her attention was caught by Henry's caller's strange voice.
It was oddly muffled, and Angie couldn't tell if the caller was a
man or a woman.

"I didn't catch your name," Henry said.

"Pat."

"Well, Pat, what can I do for you?"

"I'm concerned about the restaurateur killer in your city."

Henry's eye caught Angie's. "Thank you. I'm sure the police
will capture whoever is behind them right away."

"I'm glad you think so, because... *you're next.*"

Henry jumped up and slapped the phone's disconnect
button. "And now," he said, his voice quivering, "a word from
our sponsor."

Paavo was in the KYME by 1:30 that afternoon, a half-hour after
the show ended.

LaTour had been much more of a trooper than Angie ever
would have given him credit for being. The commercial break
had given him time to compose himself and he came back on

the air all laughs, saying it was a friend just pulling a fast one on him, then went on to say he regretted the tastelessness of the joke and sent his apologies to the families and friends of those who'd been lost. He did it all in less than thirty seconds, then continued his show as usual.

Angie, however, was less fortunate. She was a basket case. The threat brought back memories of the horrible murders that had happened around her while she worked on the staff of a television cooking show. Why, she wondered, had she gotten involved with any kind of cooking show and their "celebrity" hosts? Once was bad enough, but twice? Never again!

With her ailing headphones mysteriously working once more, it was all she could do to concentrate on the callers' questions.

When Paavo and Yoshiwara arrived, Angie and LaTour explained had happened, but there was really nothing they could do. The station never bothered to tape LaTour's show. But it didn't matter since they both were sure the caller had used some sort of voice-changing device.

Paavo and Yosh would contact the phone company to see if they could determine where the call had come from. As they got ready to leave, Angie stopped them. "I just thought of something."

"Yes?" Yosh asked.

"The caller used the word restaurateur instead of saying 'restaurant owner.' Not many people know or use that word and often think there should be an N in it—saying something like 'restauranteur' instead of the real word. I think that means our caller is someone connected to all this. It might not be the prank call we'd like to think it is."

"Oh, no!" LaTour all but fainted at her words.

13

That evening, Paavo dropped by Angie's apartment.

"You didn't have to come by," Angie said as she opened the door. "I'm sure you're quite busy with all that's going on."

"I know." His arms started to reach for her as if from their own volition. He managed to stop them and drop them back to his sides. "But I just wanted to see how you're doing after this afternoon's scare. And... if you thought of anything else that might help with this investigation."

She smiled as she ushered him in. Of course, he wouldn't admit to wanting to see her. But at times, like just a moment ago when he almost hugged her, he would let the wall he'd put up around himself slip just enough that she knew he wanted to be with her. Someday, she believed, he'd admit it, as well.

She led him to the sofa and then sat beside him. "I'm better, I guess. After you and Yosh left, LaTour ranted and raved at everyone, saying he should get a medal for being there since his life was now at stake. He wants to know who'll protect him if someone attacks the studio. This situation, after what happened at the TV station, is more than I can handle. I swear, I'm giving serious thought to quitting."

"Are you sure?"

"If LaTour was a nicer guy, that might make a difference. But right now, one—well, maybe more than one—little mistake and he carries on as if I'd just murdered Betty Crocker."

"You can't have done anything that terrible."

Her jaw tightened. "I didn't! I just mistakenly blurted out the answer to a caller's question as I was screening a call… once or twice." Then she stood. "Can I get you a beer? Coffee? Anything?"

"I'm off duty so a beer sounds good."

She hurried into the kitchen, continuing to talk as she found a beer, bottle opener, and glass for him. "It's this call-screener roll. Sometimes it's hard for me *not* to answer questions. I mean, I've *always* answered questions. Even when I was in kindergarten and the teacher would ask the class a question, and most kids would sit on their hands, guess who always raised hers?"

"Angelina?"

She returned to the living room and placed everything in front of him. "You're darn right. My teachers *expected* it of me. They praised me for it. So did my parents. Everyone would count on me to say *something*. Well, no more. I'll be mute. A regular Marcel Marceau. A Muppet without Jim Henson. Milli without Vanilli."

"Who?"

She breathed a weary sigh, then sat beside him. "It doesn't matter. I'm quitting tomorrow."

"I'm sure Henry will get over it. He might even apologize to you and the others."

"I doubt it."

"Give him another chance, Angie."

"Give *him* another chance?"

"He needs you, remember?"

"He does?"

"Why else would he have hired you?"

She perked up. "That's right, isn't it? To think, I'd forgotten. You're absolutely correct! How could I forget? Paavo, you're so wonderful."

He didn't quite know what to say. *Wonderful* wasn't an adjective he'd often heard applied to himself. Maybe never before, in fact.

"There's something else I almost forgot," she called as she dashed into her bedroom. "I was so upset after I left the studio today that I went shopping. Did I ever tell you I love to shop? Anyway, I found something for you."

"For me?"

She came back carrying a large Neiman Marcus box and handed it to him. "I didn't go shopping *for* you, but when I saw this, I couldn't pass it up."

He stared at the box in his hands. "It's sure big."

"Open it, silly."

"It's not my birthday, or anything. And Christmas just passed."

"And all I got you for Christmas was a card and a fancy basket of nuts and chocolates. I mean, I should have known you aren't much into snacks."

He remembered the snacks basket. It was huge.

With more than a little trepidation, he took the lid off the box. Inside was a double-breasted camelhair overcoat. His heart sank and he could only think one thing...it looked god-awful expensive. Still, he couldn't stop himself from touching the material. It felt like velvet.

"Try it on."

He swallowed. "I can't accept this."

"Of course you can! This way, if you're working and it's rainy out, you'll stay warm. It'd take quite a drenching for water to soak through this baby. Let's see how it looks on you. You can take it back and they'll tailor it, of course, but I described to the salesman how you wide your shoulders are, and how long your arms are, and he thought this size would be perfect, so...."

As she talked, he put the coat on over his sports jacket. She smoothed his collar, then ran her hands over the shoulders, then downward, against his broad chest. "Perfect," she said, adding a sigh over how handsome he looked. "Come see." She took his hand and led him to the full mirrors on the sliding closet doors in her bedroom.

He stared at the perfect fit of the coat. He'd never worn anything like it before.

"You look dressed for the Top of the Mark on a winter's eve. Wow! I *knew* that coat was you, I just knew it."

He raised his arms, holding them right out in front of him. So often when he did that, the sleeves of his jacket would nearly bare his elbows. This coat scarcely showed the cuff of his shirt. He loved it. Quickly, he went back into the living room, took it off, and handed it back to her. "I appreciate it, but it's too much."

"Too much what?"

"Money."

"Money? It's a gift. What do you mean?"

"I mean, hell, anyone sees a cop with a coat like that, they'll figure I'm on the take for sure." He slid his hands in his trouser pockets, not giving in to the temptation to touch the soft material once more.

"That excuse is so lame, Inspector. When the fog and biting breeze come in off the ocean, even a cop can get cold. Take the coat. Please." She held it toward him.

He shook his head, unable to find the words to explain that as much as one part of him was warmed and touched by her present, another part was troubled. He rarely received any presents at all. And for sure, no one had ever given him a present this expensive. Not ever.

"Okay," she murmured as she placed the coat near him on the sofa, and then sat beside him again. She met his eyes, the pale blue eyes she'd come to love as she softly said, "Did you know that I was beside myself when I got home today? I didn't know what to do. I felt like such a failure... again."

"None of this is your fault," he said.

"Still, I felt bad. But to have you stop by here to see me... I can't begin to tell you how much that means to me."

He looked pleased, but a bit puzzled. "It's good to hear you say that. But it's nothing for me to come by... to check on how you're doing after the scare you had."

"You're wrong, Inspector." She touched his arm, her gaze intense. "That *coat* is nothing. How one person makes another feel inside, that's what's important. That's everything, Paavo."

She was right, he thought. She was being generous and warm and caring... and he was the one being petty. He glanced again at the coat, then nodded. "I guess I can wear it if I ever take you to one of those operas you're always talking about."

Her face lit up. "You'd go with me to the opera?" She threw her arms around his neck, holding him close. "That's wonderful. In fact, I've got a friend who's offered me a couple of tickets to *Götterdämmerung*."

"To what?" He was smiling as he lifted his head to look at her. He was close, too close, she realized. She loved his smile. And she loved the touch of his hands against her waist.

She drew back, realizing what she'd done, holding him that way. In the past, she'd pretty much only put her arms around him when she was scared, not happy. This was something new. She smoothed her hair and tried to ignore the pounding of her heart, how much she had liked holding him that way... how much she had liked how close he had been to her.

"It's by Wagner," she explained. "The twilight of the Gods.

Four and a half hours. Valhalla's destroyed and Brunhilde rides a horse into her lover's... who's also her nephew's... funeral pyre. There's so much loss, it's wonderfully *emotional!*" She got up then, worried that her hug might have crossed the boundary he'd built between them, she hurried into her den. When that line was crossed, she wanted him to be the one to do it. She knew she was pushy and impatient, just as she knew he was cautious. She needed to wait. "I'll go check the opera schedule."

Paavo picked up his new coat, not quite sure how they went from a heart-to-heart to the twilight of the Gods. The time on the big wall clock in her dining area showed he'd been here a lot longer than the quick stop he'd intended to make. But he waited patiently for her to return, and then he'd be on his way.

The opera. He couldn't help but grin as he thought of what Calderon would say about that.

14

The next afternoon, Angie sat in her living room and read online newspaper headlines from the greater Bay Area. Reporters were having a field day with the culinary killings, using headlines like "Menu for Murder," "Dinners of Death," or the less lurid, more chilling, "City's Restaurant Owners Fear For Lives in Wake of Latest Murder." A portrait was painted of a crazed killer going around terrorizing restaurateurs.

She saw Paavo on the local news on TV that evening saying he was sure the murders were not random, that there was a definite reason the two restaurant owners were killed, that the men had known each other, and there was no reason whatsoever for other restaurant owners to be frightened. He appeared reassuring and calm and even smiled pleasantly at the reporters. But she also saw that he could scarcely contain his anger when a reporter stuck a microphone in his face and asked if the public should stay away from restaurants until this killer was caught. The answer he gave was smooth and skillful. Probably only people who knew him really well could see that he thought the reporter's intelligence was somewhere around that of a slug.

It was probably a hard time for everyone in the restaurant business, she thought, as she then considered someone else Chick had loved, and who had loved him. Someone who probably didn't have anyone to grieve with. She called the manager at Sorrento and explained who she was and what she needed to know.

Janet Knight lived in a gated condominium apartment south of the city on Highway 1, facing the Pacific Ocean. Angie couldn't help but reflect on the irony of how secure Janet's home was, and that the man she loved was gunned down on the street just driving home from his restaurant. No matter how much you planned, life was full of surprises. Mostly bad ones.

God, I've been around Paavo too long, she thought. Because that really wasn't how she felt. As she walked toward the condo, her eye caught the Pacific in the moonlight. She stopped and looked out at the water a moment, and despite the death and dreariness around her, she felt a slight easing of her low spirits. She breathed deeply, knowing it wouldn't be easy to face Janet.

Mercifully, facing Janet wasn't as bad as she had feared. Janet seemed to be a beacon of strength in a world gone topsy-turvy. Or, maybe she was still in shock, but she took Angie's condolences and gift of homemade biscotti with grace and invited her to have some coffee.

"Thank you for coming by, Angie. No one else has."

Angie nodded. Being so close to Chick's ex-wife, she'd felt a little guilty herself for coming here.

"The thing that hurts the most," Janet said, "is that the last time we were together we fought over something silly."

"If it was silly, I'm sure Chick didn't take it too seriously."

"He always took his restaurant seriously. Strangely, our fight was about Karl Wielund, and an article we were doing on him in *Haute Cuisine* magazine. I'd sent Nona Farraday, my food critic, to Karl over several days to interview him. It was going to be a big spread. Then, when he was killed, Nona quickly put together an article on Albert Dupries instead." Janet sighed.

"What was wrong with that?" Angie asked.

Janet gave a half-smile. "Nothing, except Chick thought the article should have been about him."

"Ah," Angie understood the implications of professional trouble that would have caused Janet. "I see."

"He wanted to know why I'd published such trash in my magazine."

"Did he mean the article was trash, or Dupries?"

"He might have meant both. He despised Dupries. But he also said the article Nona wrote on Wielund was far superior. It went into what a fanatic the man was about his recipes as well as how his customers were treated. He thought it was realistic and should have been used as a tribute to a great restaurateur —even if Karl Wielund wasn't especially popular. But since I didn't do that, Chick thought that I should have at least written about Sorrento."

Angie put her hand lightly on Janet's. "In time, Chick would have realized why you couldn't do an article on him, I'm sure. It's not worth upsetting yourself over. Chick was completely devoted to you."

"Was he?" Janet asked.

"I'm sure." Angie was also sure that in Chick's old-world, Roman Catholic Italian heart, he still thought of his "ex" as his wife, even though their love had died and they couldn't live in harmony together. But that didn't mean he loved Janet any less.

Angie hoped her visit had been a help to Janet because it had left her feeling upset and lonely. There was only one place in this entire city that would help her to feel better.

Her only question was, dare she go there?

15

That evening, Paavo went to Yosh's house to celebrate Chief Hollins' twenty years with the SFPD. All inspectors were invited, along with spouses or "significant others." Paavo realized what a solitary group they were when he walked in. Only Hollins, Calderon, and Yosh were married.

He'd met Mrs. Dottie Hollins before—a nice matronly woman who spent most of her time working with charitable organizations.

Nancy Yoshiwara was every bit as warm and friendly as Yosh had claimed she was. Their three teenage children, two girls and a boy, made a brief appearance and then fled.

Although Calderon was married, his wife didn't like going to anything involving his job. Rebecca and Bo Benson, like Paavo, were unmarried with no current SO, and Bill Sutter had married and divorced more times than he would admit to.

Paavo wondered if Nancy wouldn't take a look at Yosh's new colleagues and insist he return to Seattle. He also couldn't help but wonder what Angie would think if he had brought her to this party. Would she fit in at all, or would she feel as out of place as he had among her "restaurateur" crowd?

As they ate hors d'oeuvres, cake, cookies, nuts, and chips, and drank beer, whiskey, and even rum and coke, everyone loosened up and soon were having a good time of it until Rebecca and Bill Sutter's phones rang. They were the on-call team that night.

"A gang shooting," Rebecca said. "Glad I didn't drink. I was afraid something like this might happen."

Bill Sutter on the other hand, had downed nearly a six-pack all by himself. Everyone knew he had a bit of a problem with drink, but he stood up, swaying slightly, and said he could handle the call, anyway.

"I don't think so," Yosh said, taking his car keys from him. "We'll get an Uber to take you home, and I'll go with Rebecca. By the way, Rebecca, if you want to go home and change, I'll cover for you, too."

Rebecca was actually wearing a dress and high heels, meaning she towered over everyone but Paavo, Benson, and Yosh. And she'd left her hair down and flowing around her shoulders. "I can do my job dressed this way," she said firmly.

"And Yosh," Paavo said, "it's your party. You need to stay and play host. I've got this."

"You sure?" Yosh said. "I can—"

"Thank you, Paavo," Nancy Yoshiwara said to him. "I can use Yosh's help here with this crew! I'm so glad we finally met."

Soon, Paavo and Rebecca were out the door, and heading for the area out on Third Street, near Hunters Point, where the shooting took place.

Flashing red and white lights filled the street as they reached the scene. Paramedics were already there.

"My God," Rebecca whispered as she caught up to Paavo and walked with him to the bodies. "They're just kids."

The two who were lying on the street looked fifteen, sixteen at most. One boy had been killed outright, and the other was being worked on by the paramedics.

The third boy, also a gunshot victim, was sitting up against the tire of an old Chevy. His teeth chattered as his hand clutched his side while too much blood oozed between his fingers and onto the street. "This kid needs help, too," Paavo called.

"We'll be there asap," one paramedic answered. "But this one's sinking fast."

Paavo and Rebecca could see the beginnings of shock on the face of the boy they were with, and knew he had to be kept warm if he were to have any chance of making it. Rebecca knelt on the ground and took his hand, telling him to hang in there. His eyes were wide and scared but he listened carefully to her words.

Paavo grabbed a blanket from the ambulance and gave it to Rebecca. It was ridiculously thin. He ran to his car and pulled out his as-yet-unworn camelhair overcoat. What the hell, he thought, he probably wouldn't have felt right wearing it, anyway. He laid it over the boy. It was thick and warm, and he tucked it between the boy's shoulders and the tire so that it wouldn't slide off him.

"Hang on, kid," he said, and lightly touched the boy's shoulder. The boy gave a slight nod, his fear easing a bit as gratitude softened his features.

"I'm okay here," Rebecca said to Paavo. "You can deal with the crowd."

Paavo nodded even as he hoped Rebecca realized, the way he did, how bad the boy's condition was. He headed over to the small group watching the drama. "All right, folks, we're going to talk about what you saw and heard."

A couple of people started backing away.

Paavo pointed at them. "I mean, everyone. You can give your names, contact info, and anything you saw to the officers around you now, and make this as fast and painless as possible, or we can bring all of you down to the station where we'll have really long talks."

The people backing up froze in their tracks. Quickly taking in the authority and icy glare of the broad-shouldered detective, along with the uniformed officers giving him back-up, they meekly followed orders.

Rebecca joined him as the paramedics took over care of the boy. The two then began talking to the bystanders themselves to find out if any of them knew who did this.

The detectives were lucky. They were given the name of the alleged assailant, along with the make, model and license of his car, from four witnesses, but it still took a couple of hours before he and Rebecca could leave the scene.

Just as they were getting ready to leave, a call came in that the boy whose hand Rebecca had been holding had also died. She looked stunned as they walked to their cars.

When they reached Paavo's Mustang, she saw his overcoat lying on its hood where it had been tossed after the paramedics took the boy to the hospital. She held it up and looked at the blood stains, grease and dirt on it. "This must have been beautiful," she murmured. Her voice shook, and he could see her begin to tremble as the intensity of the crime scene investigation passed and the cold, harsh aftermath set in.

He nodded. "It was."

"Maybe a good dry cleaner..."

"It doesn't matter."

"No." She shook her head, then lowered her gaze as she could no longer hold back the silent tears she had fought ever since hearing of the young, frightened boy's death.

His chest tightened. He remembered how bad it could hurt, how some cases, especially when kids were involved, just got under your skin, and no matter how much you told yourself this was a job you had to do, you reacted like a civilian, not a cop. And even when you tried to be tough, the ugliness and cruelty that men could inflict on each other, would crush you. "You okay?" Paavo lightly held her arm.

She shook her head. "I just need a moment. I'm sorry."

"No need to be," he murmured. She sounded so forlorn, he placed his hand on her back to walk her to the car.

But after a couple of steps, she stopped and bowed her head. "They were so young. It's such a waste, so hard to accept. Maybe... maybe I'm not cut out for Homicide."

He couldn't help but put an arm around her shoulders and give them a quick squeeze. Normally, he'd never do anything like that to another officer, but no other cops were around, and she was new in Homicide and hurting. "You did just fine, Rebecca. No one ever gets used to seeing something like this. Some of us have learned, over time, to stop the tears from showing. That's all."

You're the lucky one, he wanted to add. *You can still cry. The rest of us just feel the anger and pain... and emptiness.*

She wiped her tears and nodded. "Thank you for saying that." Then she gave him the briefest, lightest of hugs before she got into her car.

He got into his old Mustang and put his new coat, all bunched up now, on the passenger seat. He placed his hand on it.

It's just a coat, he told himself, as he remembered how happy Angie had been to give it to him. He knew she wouldn't care that he'd used it the way he had—that she would have wanted him to, in fact. But he cared. Not about the coat, but because he'd taken something lovely from her, and destroyed it.

He saw so much destruction that night—three young men, still boys, really—dead now. For what?

But that was his life. He glanced at the coat again. Good things didn't belong in it. Not a good coat. Not a good woman.

His jaw firm, fighting the ache that filled his heart, he drove back to the Hall of Justice to begin the lengthy reports he would have to complete.

16

It was two-thirty in the morning before Paavo turned his car onto the street where he lived. Angie's white Ferrari was parked in front of his house. He could scarcely believe it. Was she all right?

He pulled in behind it, ran to the window, and then saw her curled up asleep. He stood there and watched her a moment, taking in just how very pretty she was, and realizing he probably had a ridiculously sappy look on his face.

He couldn't help it, though. It felt too good seeing her here for him to not pause a moment and enjoy simply looking at her.

He sighed as his more responsible self annoyingly tapped him on the shoulder. It was cold out here, and she was twisted like a pretzel on the seat, probably every muscle aching for relief. He had to get her on her way. He drew himself back and looked around, glad he lived on a quiet street where no one had bothered her lying there alone at this time of night.

"Angie?" He knocked on the window. Across her lap lay a thick book called *Design for the Rebuilding of San Francisco After the Great Earthquake and Fire of 1906.* No wonder she'd fallen asleep.

She awoke with a start, then sleep-dazed eyes met his and she smiled. He felt a tug to realize that even half-asleep her reaction to him was so warm. As she unlocked the door, he opened it from the outside and gave her his hand. "What are you doing here?" he asked.

Slowly, she let him pull her to her feet. "Trying to make my class interesting."

That made no sense, and he didn't care. In the dim street light, she looked sleepy, warm, and inviting, a sanctuary from the bleakness he'd just left behind. She blinked a few times and then stretched her arms with a big yawn that made him want to reach out for her. He ruthlessly clamped down the urge.

"I was waiting to see you," she replied.

"Do you know the time?"

"No." She yawned again. "I guess I fell asleep."

"It's nearly three a.m. Don't you think you should go home?"

"Okay." She then looked down at herself, then at the car. It took a moment before she seemed to realized she was standing outside the car, with the door open.

The befuddled look on her sleep-softened face broke Paavo's control. He reached into the car for her handbag, shut and locked the car door, then put his arm around her waist and led her toward his house.

"What's wrong?" she murmured.

"You're sleep-walking. One cup of coffee, and then you'll be on your way."

"Okay," she whispered as she snuggled closer and shut her eyes, letting him direct her steps.

Paavo lived in a brown-shingled cottage tucked away in the northwest corner of the city, far from crowds, and not far from the Pacific Ocean. It was so old it had no garage and was mere inches away from similar cottages on either side of it.

He opened the front door and Angie left his side to step into the small living room with its overstuffed, mismatched sofa and chairs. She'd been there before, when he was saving her from people who wanted her dead.

Paavo's big, pugnacious tomcat, Hercules, bounded off the patchwork cushion he loved to sleep on, and padded across the red and blue hook rug straight to Paavo, where he began rubbing against Paavo's leg and meowing loudly.

"Hello, Herk," Paavo said, then looked at Angie as he shut the front door. "This cat thinks my sole function in life is to open a can of food for him as soon as I walk in the door."

"While you do that," she said, rubbing her eyes, "I'll put on some coffee."

"Are you awake enough?" he asked.

"I think so." She staggered toward the kitchen like a drunken sailor.

Grinning foolishly, he followed her, with Hercules running between his feet.

The kitchen was almost as old as the house, but so big Angie felt a twinge of envy every time she saw it. It had high shelves, not one of which slid out or rotated like those in a modern kitchen which meant things could get buried and lost forever. Judge Crater, Jimmy Hoffa, and Amelia Earhardt could all have been stuffed away back there. The refrigerator had only one door, and the old gas stove needed a match to light a burner... just like Angie's parents' kitchen when she was growing up and before her father's business started to make money.

Going to Paavo's house for Angie was like going home again, in more ways than one. She liked the feel of the homey surroundings, the easy life-style where comfort and function mattered more than looks and price, where a big, affectionate cat slept on cushions and trimmed his claws on throw rugs or the sides of chairs and no one cared. She liked... Paavo.

She'd given him a bag of gourmet Italian roast coffee when she'd learned that he had nothing but Taster's Choice in the house. It lay in the tiny freezer, the seal unbroken. She rubbed her eyes, still yawning. In a cupboard under the counter she found a nearly new-looking Melitta coffee pot, but there were no filters anywhere. Taster's Choice it was.

Paavo put a bowl of 9-Lives on the floor for Hercules. As soon as the coffee water boiled, she made them each a cup, and they took them into the living room. As they sat side-by-side on the sofa, Angie folded her arms against the cold. They had both left their jackets on.

"I'll put the heater on." Paavo headed toward the wall heater.

"A fire would be nicer," Angie suggested. She loved his big stone fireplace, the one architectural amenity in the house.

He looked at her a long moment. "It's a little late," he said finally.

She dropped her gaze to the hooked rug on the floor, studying its colors, and then nodded. "You're right." He'd said what she feared he might. All she had wanted to do was to spend some time with him. After her visit with Janet Knight, she saw what loneliness looked like. It made her want to be with the one person more than any other... Paavo.

So, she showed up here.

She had expected his party for Chief Hollins' anniversary wouldn't last much past ten o'clock. Who knew homicide inspectors were such party animals he wouldn't get home until nearly three in the morning?

And now, he wanted to boot her out, anyway. She almost laughed, but it wasn't funny.

He turned on the heater and sat beside her. They both reached for their coffee and took sips, then both put their cups back on the coffee table.

Looking at him, it was all she could do to stop her hand from reaching out to touch his face, the high, angular cheekbones, the way-past-five-o'clock shadow on his cheeks, chin and upper lip, the big, baby blue eyes that made her heart thrum just to look at.

She should go home, now. But it hurt to leave him. Could this be what withdrawal was like? Maybe she was addicted to Paavo? "It's after three," she murmured. "Some people might call it late, but for others, it's very early."

He took her hands in his and it seemed a hundred emotions played on his face before he confessed, "I just don't know what to say."

She drew back her hands and folded them. "My goodness, all this angst just because you can't decide if it's too early or too late to build a fire in the fireplace? Next time, I'll just bring a Presto-log."

He grinned.

"All right, home with you." He stood, pulling her to her feet, then put his arm around her to walk her to the door.

She stopped walking and faced him. "Why do you smell like perfume?"

"Yeah, I'm sure. I use it all the time." He pulled the front door open.

Eying his jacket, she saw a long blond hair on the shoulder. She lifted it off, feeling as if a ten-ton weight had landed on her shoulders. No wonder he didn't get home until so late.

"What's that?" he asked.

"Lint." Her tone was brusque, and she held her head high. "You don't need to walk me to my car. Goodnight."

She pulled her coat tight around her as she marched from the house.

17

Paavo was back at his desk Monday morning. He'd had no word from Angie since finding her at his house Friday night… or more correctly, the very early hours of Saturday morning.

He'd gotten so used to her calling or texting he found this silence upsetting. He knew something bothered her when she left his house, but for the life of him, he had no idea what it was.

She couldn't have expected to stay, could she? They'd never even kissed. Not that the thought hadn't crossed his mind somewhere between one and a thousand times since they'd first met.

He did his best to stop thinking about Angie and to concentrate instead on the murders of Karl Wielund and his landlord, Hank Greuber. He also kept tabs on Rebecca and Bill Sutter's investigation into Chick Marcuccio's murder. All the inspectors believed the three murders—Marcuccio's, Wielund's, and Greuber's—were connected and now all of homicide was working on them.

He also had told Rebecca about meeting Albert Dupries, the boss of her murder victim, Sheila Danning. They had looked into Dupries a bit, together, but had found no connection between him and Danning, or even between Danning and Karl Wielund, beyond Danning being a waitress and both men owning restaurants.

This investigation was growing broader and stranger at every juncture. The press kept up its clamor about the dangers of being a restaurant owner in the city, making it sound as if getting gunned down or poisoned was as common as getting stiffed with a bad credit card.

The only sure lead Paavo and Yosh had was that the gun that killed Wielund's landlord, Hank Greuber, had also been used to kill Chick Marcuccio. But that caused the detectives an even bigger problem. How was Greuber connected to any of this?

Or, did he just happen to be in the wrong place—Wielund's house—at the wrong time?

Every aspect Paavo and Yosh pursued came up empty. They had found no known associations with criminals, no known enemies, no police records, no family troubles, no financial troubles, and no bizarre habits, hobbies or associations beyond Wielund's interest in pornography.

The mayor and police chief were briefed daily on what was happening. The city's leaders didn't want anything to scare the public from going to expensive restaurants, which were one of the city's main attractions.

Paavo had requested all the accounting books from both Wielund's and Sorrento restaurants. Often, when all else failed, following the money trail would lead to a development in an otherwise baffling case. Money had been called the root of all evil, and in Paavo's mind, that held doubly true for homicide cases. He got Sorrento's books right away and was going over them closely. Karl Wielund had used a German bank, and the SFPD had to go through hoops to get them to release their records. Finally, they came in.

They weren't set up quite the same as American records, and required extra time to figure out, let alone different languages and acronyms. Yosh wasn't very good working with numbers, but he was better than Paavo at pounding the pavement and getting people to talk to him. He was out doing a lot of that while Paavo worked the Sorrento accounts and tried to make sense of Wielund's German bank records.

"Need help, Paavo?" Rebecca asked.

He glanced up. Ever since the dinner at Yosh's and their investigation of the gang murders, Rebecca had been friendlier than ever, and she'd always been pretty friendly. They got along well, he had to admit. Yosh, Calderon and the others constantly reminded him of how stalwart Rebecca was. She was a woman he could understand, and who understood him. She wasn't the type to jump first and ask questions later, nor was she impulsive, whimsical or zany. She certainly wouldn't show up at his house, uninvited, late and night and then, for no good reason, leave in a huff. She was cautious, logical, and serious. A paragon. In short, she was much like him.

"I'll muddle through," he said.

"I've studied some accounting."

Accounting, too? Was there anything practical this woman hadn't dabbled in? "I didn't know that."

"It was too dull, so I dropped it."

"Let's see how much you remember."

He handed her Wielund's German bank records and was starting to take a look at them with her when his phone rang. "Smith, here."

"A Miss Farraday to see you, Inspector."

"I'll be right there."

Rebecca picked up a set of books. "Let me take these. I'll get back to you."

"Thanks." But before he even got up from his chair, the door to the squad room opened and Nona Farraday sauntered through it. She wore a plum-colored suit with a short skirt and a v-necked cream silk blouse that showed off her sleek, tall figure to perfection. Her long, blond hair glistened and swung freely as she walked. Every eye in the place turned her way.

She spotted Paavo immediately.

He stood. "Miss Farraday, this is a surprise."

She gave him her hand. "Call me Nona, Inspector Smith. I know we haven't been introduced, but I know you're working Karl Wielund's murder investigation."

"Yes, and I know you're a writer for *Haute Cuisine* magazine. Won't you have a seat?"

She looked pleased that he knew her and took the offered chair by the side of his desk. She flicked her mane of hair off her shoulders, then crossed her long legs, letting her skirt ride up high. "I have some interesting information for you."

"Oh?"

"Tell you what," she leaned forward, her elbow on her thigh. "It must be near your quitting time. Why don't we go to dinner and I'll tell you all about it?"

From the corner of his eye, Paavo saw Rebecca staring hard at him. Benson gave him a thumb's up. Calderon rose from his desk, and on the pretense of searching for something, moved closer to Paavo, eying Nona the whole time. "You can tell me about it now," Paavo said.

"But this is a long story... and I have a restaurant to review. Arbuckle's, on Fisherman's Wharf. It'll be my treat."

Greg McAndrews, owner of Arbuckle's, was one of the restaurateurs at both Wielund's and Chick's memorial services. Might be worth going. He glanced up to see that Calderon's frown had grown deeper as his gaze jumped between Paavo and Nona.

That decided it for Paavo. He was going. It'd give Calderon more to fret about and might, hopefully, put Angie out of his mind for a while.

"Sounds good." He picked up his jacket and led her past gaping looks as they walked out of the squad room.

Arbuckle's Sea Food Restaurant was large and catered to the upscale tourist trade. After Greg McAndrews greeted Nona lavishly, they were given a secluded table with a view of the Bay, and instantly, two waiters hovered nearby to fill their every whim. Paavo saw what it meant to be a well-known restaurant critic in this town. All of Angie's worries about a critic needing to be "incognito" when reviewing a restaurant obviously didn't concern Nona at all.

She perused the menu. "I've been told the food here is elegant. I'll order for both of us, if you don't mind, and that way I can taste two of each item."

Paavo shut his menu and leaned back in the chair. "Fine."

"For appetizers," Nona began, causing the waiter to spring to attention, "for me, scallop crudo, for my guest, the seafood gratin."

"Ah, excellent choices, Miss Farraday," the waiter declared.

"The salads don't look especially interesting. What do you recommend?"

"The smoked mussels. Definitely. Served on a bed of arugula with warm goat cheese and roasted red peppers. It is uncompromising."

"And for my guest?"

"I suggest grilled scallops wrapped in cucumber, with caviar and saffron sauce."

Nona smiled, clearly liking the waiter's suggestions. "And for the main entrée you suggest...?"

"Striped bass filet, sautéed and served with citrus sauce and braised fennel for your guest, and perhaps our world famous house cioppino for you?"

She shut her menu. "Excellent. I trust you'll bring the proper wine with each course?"

"*Naturellement.* May I recommend our desserts, Miss Farraday? The perfect ending to a perfect meal."

"Dessert! How could I forget?" She opened the menu again and then glanced at Paavo, a sly smile toying at her lips. "I think the passion fruit bavarois sounds very promising. After all that food, we'll share it. Don't you agree, Paavo?"

He wasn't used to feeling like something on a menu. "Right," he replied.

In no time, the waiter had served wine and brought their seafood gratin, which Paavo discovered was minced squid and tiny brown shrimp swimming in a thin, milky soup. He took a few bites and slid his bowl to Nona. Not a favorite.

In no time, the waiter, who was watching them closely, returned to take away the appetizers and put the "salads" on the table.

Paavo liked the grilled scallops, but not the caviar or sauce on them. Soon, he gave that dish to Nona as well. "What was it you came to the office to tell me about?"

She patted her lips with the napkin, then leaned close to him. "Have you heard what Mark Dustman is up to?"

"No."

"I'm sure you know that he and Eileen Powell didn't get to keep Wielund's open. The lawyers for Karl's brothers back in Germany shut it down immediately, even though Wielund's was on the verge of being the best restaurant in the city."

"And so what is Dustman doing?"

"He's taken a job with LaTour's!"

"You're joking." Paavo couldn't hide his surprise, especially imagining Angie's reaction to a respected cook like Dustman going to work for Henry LaTour.

At that point, the waiter showed up yet again, to remove their scarcely eaten "salads" and to bring their entrees. Paavo took a bite of his bass filet and finally found something he really liked. It was delicious. There was only one problem. The piece he'd gotten was so tiny, he'd finish it in two bites if he wasn't careful. And he had to leave some for Nona. Her bowl of cioppino should have been called a cup. He thought she was ordering too much food, and now he knew he was going to have to get himself a pizza on the way home.

Once the waiter left, Paavo quickly returned to their conversation. "Why in the world is Dustman going to work at Henry LaTour's restaurant?"

Nona laughed. "*Bravo*, Inspector! I see you've learned enough about our little restaurant world to be shocked, yet amused. Mark Dustman fancies himself to be a gourmand, with designs to become a top chef in the city. Working at LaTour's will destroy his reputation! LaTour's needs a short-order cook, not a gourmet chef. Isn't it ludicrous?"

"Why is he doing it?"

"I guess he needs the money. These days, even in San Francisco, there aren't many openings for a creative chef. Maybe he hopes turning LaTour's around will help his reputation in the long run... if such a thing is possible."

Paavo shook his head. "You seem to know Dustman pretty well."

"Not really. But I knew Karl Wielund *very* well."

"You did?"

"I spent several days with him practically 'round the clock, a week before he died. I was doing a special article for *Haute Cuisine*. After he died, though, they didn't want to publish it."

"You still have the article, then?"

"It's at my apartment. I can give it to you tonight. After our passion fruit."

Angie was having dinner with Lacy LaTour at a small eatery on Fisherman's Wharf, known for its Crab Louie salad. Lacy had invited her there to talk more about *Lunch with Henri* and how to make it better.

"This radio show is very important for the success of our restaurant," Lacy said. "You don't know how tough the restaurant scene is in this city. And now, the news about the murders is scaring people from showing up at all! Aside from that, every time you turn around, there's a new place that's hogging all the attention from the media. The cost of paid advertising in San Francisco papers is through the roof, and of course, TV and radio are completely out of our reach. So all we can do is hope for word-of-mouth and free advertising, which is what our lunchtime radio show is all about."

"I recognize that," Angie said. "But I don't know what more I can do. My job description is rather limited."

"I have an idea, and that's what I wanted to talk to you about," Lacy said as she worked on removing crab meat from a claw.

Angie waited, bracing herself.

"Right now, the cookbooks and recipes you find for Henry to use on the show are, frankly, rather dull. I mean, they're good recipes, but they don't make anyone sit up and take notice."

"That's because most of the time, I give him answers to questions, not whole recipes."

"That's what I'd like changed," Lacy said with a smile as she finished one piece of crab and reached for another.

"I don't understand."

"I think... oh, no! Will you look at that!" Lacy sounded disgusted as she pointed out the window they sat by. "Nona Farraday is coming out of Arbuckle's. Don't tell me she's doing an article on it! What's so special about a fish restaurant on

Fisherman's Wharf? Like, *duh!* What else do you expect down here?"

Angie turned to look at Nona, not surprised that the woman had caught Lacy's ire. Truth be told, Nona Farraday was one of Angie's least favorite people, too. But when she turned her head, she nearly fell out of her chair. Not because of Nona, but because of the man with her. Paavo!

"Look, Angie," Lacy said. "Isn't that the fellow I saw you with at Wielund's funeral?"

It took a moment for Angie to find her voice. "Yes," she squawked. "Yes, it is."

Lacy faced her, lifting an eyebrow. "I thought you two were an item. You seemed close."

"No. Not at all." Now, Angie's voice was way too high. She swallowed hard. "We're just acquaintances. He's actually the detective working on Karl's murder investigation. He wanted to check out the people at the memorial service."

"Hmm," Lacy frowned. "It looks like he also wants to check out Nona Farraday!"

"Enough of them," Angie said, trying to sound dismissive, and not wanting to look at the two of them walking down the street together, and especially not at the possessive way Nona hung onto his arm. She was so close to him, Angie was surprised they didn't trip over each other's feet!

Would serve them right, too.

"What I'd like, Angie... *Angie?* Yes, what I'd like you to do, is to give Henry a simple answer to whatever is being asked. Who knows? Maybe you can ask Siri to give an explanation and then send it to him once you're sure it's correct. But then, I want you to follow up with a great recipe. An interesting recipe. One that will cause listeners to salivate so much we may put the entire Bay Area in danger of flooding!"

Angie stared speechless at Lacy a long moment. The

thought of LaTour reading long, complicated recipes on the radio was enough to make her cringe.

"Let me think of a good way to do that," she said, unable to sit there another moment and pretend her life hadn't just turned upside down. "Right now, it's getting late. I need to get going. Thank you so much for the dinner. It's been... memorable."

18

Salvatore Amalfi didn't like him. Paavo knew that the minute Angie began to introduce him to her father.

At the moment, Angie didn't seem to much like him either. And he still didn't know why she was so irritated with him. But since he'd promised to accompany her to Chick Marcuccio's funeral buffet, catered and held at Chick Marcuccio's Sorrento Restaurant, he had shown up at her apartment, on time, as promised, to attend this event with her.

She actually appeared surprised to see him. The car ride to Sorrento could have taken place in the Arctic, it was so cold.

But here, now, Paavo studied Sal Amalfi. The man stood eye-to-eye with Paavo, hawk-nosed, olive-skinned, broad-shouldered, and with a keen, assessing way of looking at people... a sharpness now mixed with sadness over the funeral of his old friend.

Their handshake held cautious appraisal.

"So you're the one my wife and daughter talk about all the time." Sal's words were softly accented, his manner one of elegant sophistication, yet the ravages of his heart condition showed in the gauntness of his cheeks and in the touch of frailness this obviously once-powerful man now bore.

"I hope what they say is good," Paavo replied.

"It is."

"I've heard a lot about you, too, Mr. Amalfi. All of it good."

Sal eyed him slowly. Angie's head bobbed from one to the other, not knowing what was going on.

"You want a drink?" Sal asked.

Paavo shrugged. "Sure."

Paavo noticed Angie's cautious smile. She seemed to breathe easier at Sal's invitation, as if she thought everything would be all right since they were all going to have a drink together. Paavo doubted that was the case.

"Angelina, go talk to one of your sisters or your friends," Sal said, dismissing her. "We'll be right back."

Her smile disappeared as she looked from one to the other. "You want me to…? Oh? Okay. I guess."

Sal led Paavo across the restaurant to the bar.

Chick's restaurant was packed with the friends and relatives who'd attended the funeral, as well as the restaurateurs Paavo had seen at Wielund's. In contrast to the falseness of the guests at Karl Wielund's service, the people here looked genuinely saddened by their loss. All around, he heard snatches of conversations of people speaking in glowing terms about Chick, telling each other stories of adventures and schemes, usually humorous, that he'd been involved in. The more Paavo heard, the more he realized what a fine man had been killed.

Over the group, too, was the pall that murder brings. It was a feeling Paavo knew well. Where Wielund's death had been thought, at first, to have been an accident, Chick's was known to have been cold-blooded murder. And where the restaurant owners had been able to distance themselves from Karl—a new-comer to the city, his body found in a remote area of the Sierras—Chick was a friend to all these people, someone who came here as a young man, married, raised a family, began a business and then was gunned down in the neighborhood he loved. His death gave them all cause to be nervous. Why had he been killed? And, who was next?

"What'll you have to drink?" Sal asked.

"Just some tonic, with a lime twist," Paavo said to the bartender.

"Jack Daniels on ice," Sal said, then looked back at Paavo. "I was wondering when I'd meet you."

"Same here."

Sal took a sip of his whiskey. "Angelina sounds serious about you."

Paavo slid his hands in his pockets. He was too old to be given a once-over by "the father of the bride" and made to feel wanting—especially since he'd never even gone on a date with Angie. Besides, he wasn't convinced that anyone, ever, would be his bride. He was too much of a loner. All he had to do was to look at Angie, who was constantly getting exasperated with him for reasons he often didn't even understand, to realize he wasn't marriage material. "That's an overstatement, I'd say. We're friends. That's all. Angie's a fine woman," he said. "Good-hearted."

"She is. And ever since I was able to provide for her, I always gave her the best of everything."

Paavo nodded. "I've noticed."

Sal's dark brown eyes were stern. "Angelina is special to me. She's my youngest. She knows history, music, art, and she can write about anything she wants. I sent her to the Sorbonne... in Paris... for one year. Did you know that?"

"She's mentioned it."

"You get my drift, then."

Paavo got it, but he wasn't about to let the man off that easy. "No. Not at all."

Sal's expression said he knew exactly what Paavo was doing. "So, you want to hear the words."

Paavo took a deep breath. It'd been a long time since he'd been told he wasn't good enough for something... or someone. He guessed that was a benefit of becoming a cop—people watched what they said to him. He kept telling himself this was Angie's father, that the man was only doing it because he loved her, and that Angie all but worshipped the ground Sal walked on.

Sal sipped his drink, then stared at the ice. "I don't want her to be hurt. That's all this is about."

"Neither do I." Paavo fixed his gaze firmly on Sal. "Look, Mr. Amalfi, as I said, there's nothing going on between Angie and me. We've become good friends over what happened when her life was in danger, and we spent a lot of time together. But it was always on the up-and-up, a cop protecting a potential victim, all right? And now, with these killings of her friends, she's naturally nervous. She knows the people involved, she hears things, and then she calls me. That's all."

Sal shook his head. "That's what you say—maybe what you believe. But I have eyes. I see how she looks at you... and you at her."

Was it really that obvious? Paavo had to wonder. His lips tightened. "It means nothing."

Sal smacked his drink onto a coaster, hard. "I'm not a fool. You, both of you, need to stop this, now, before it's too late! I don't want to see my daughter hurt—and not you, either! You don't have the money for her taste. You don't have the time to spend with her. And as long as she's with you she's going to live every minute you're away wondering if she's going to get a phone call or a knock on the door and have someone tell her that you're dead."

Paavo's stomach twisted. "These days, that can happen just

walking down the street... or heading for home in your car after closing up your restaurant for the night."

Sal shook his head. "No. It's not the same. You know it, and so do I. Don't take this personal, because it isn't. I think you're probably a good fellow. My Serafina, she says so all the time. And I've asked around about you. Commissioner Barcelli is a friend. All I hear is praise. But none of it matters. *I don't want you for Angelina.*"

Paavo did his best not to let his irritation show. His voice tight, he said, "That's for Angie to say, not you."

"Maybe it's for *you* to say." Sal's dark eyes bored into him. "I love her too much to watch her throw her life away with someone like you. You're a smart cop. You know I speak the truth. If you have any feelings for her at all, you know I'm right. Angelina's strong, she's young. She'll get over it."

Hearing Sal express his own thoughts, his own doubts, made Paavo feel as if he'd been given a body blow. Paavo's expression was rigid, his voice low and firm. "Whatever happens between Angie and me is up to us, not you, to decide."

"As her father, I have a say in what's right or not right for her. And I will speak. Do we understand each other?"

"Perfectly."

Sal walked away.

Paavo stood alone, then ordered a scotch on the rocks. Sal Amalfi's words gnawed at him. Other words, too, like those of Calderon and Benson. Even Yosh, good-natured Yosh, looked askance at the possibilities of a lasting relationship between him and Angie.

And, frankly, so did he.

Paavo took a taste of his drink. He had tried to explain to Angie's father there wasn't really anything between them, but apparently, he hadn't been very convincing.

For good reason.

He wanted there to be something between them. And he

knew she did. Why not just go for it? All the way. See what happens? How bad could it be?

But then he thought of the coat she'd given him. That damned coat. He'd taken it, beautiful and pristine, and rich—so rich—and didn't have it a full day before he'd managed to soil it, all but destroy it, because of his life, his job, his world.

What if he did the same thing to her?

He drew in his breath, wondering if Angie knew how strongly her father felt? He suspected not. He suspected that Sal, just like Paavo, did all he could to protect her from what was harsh and cruel in the world. He knew she adored her father. If things ever were to progress to the point where she had to make a choice between the two of them, what would she do? And what would *he* do, knowing that asking her to make such a choice would tear her apart, and that he couldn't bear to hurt her?

He looked at Angie standing in the middle of a crowd of old friends and relatives, including Chick Marcuccio's kids, Angie's friend Terry and her brother Joey. The closeness of the group, their many years of friendship, could be felt across the room as they gave comfort to one another. Plus, their wealth and position hung about them like a Swiss bank account. She fit right in, and he, always the outsider, didn't fit in at all. Why had he ever expected otherwise?

He took another sip of his drink.

A sultry voice behind him said, "Haven't I met you somewhere before?"

He looked over his shoulder at Nona Farraday. She gave him a big smile. He took in her enormous green eyes, a perfect, heart-shaped face and flowing, shoulder-length blond hair. She was the kind of tall, willowy, blonde, female he'd always thought of as "his type" until petite, brunette Angie confused his esthetics along with everything else. He wondered if Nona could help him forget about Angie.

"Shouldn't that be my line?" he asked, forcing a smile.

Her lips curved up in a wicked grin, suggestive of all kinds of promise. "What brings you here this afternoon, Paavo?"

"Let's say I'm a friend of the family." The thought of how much of 'friends' he and Sal were brought a grimace to his lips. His gaze drifted over Nona again. The cost of the dress she wore easily ran into four figures. She screamed money. Like Angie. "What about you?" he asked, trying to muster interest.

She gave a toss off the head. "I thought I'd do a story on memorial service fare. Which restaurant is the best place to have a dearly departed meal? They've had so much experience lately, it seems."

Snooty and cynical. How charming. "Right." He looked over his shoulder for Angie, wondering where she'd disappeared to.

"We should get together again soon," Nona said, placing an elbow on the bar and leaning against him, shoulder to shoulder. "I have another couple of restaurants I want to try out. Do you like Japanese?"

He stared at his glass, watching the ice slowly circle. "Given all the funeral meals I've been to lately, I've decided I don't like any food. In fact, I may never eat again."

She laughed, low and wicked. "That's an illness, you know. I have a remedy for it, too. I'll give you a call in a day or two, but right now, Mark Dustman's headed this way. I promised him I'd see him after the service ended. He's extremely anxious to find a way to keep Wielund's, you know, and is willing to do just about anything to get it. But he has no money, the poor dear. Never has. He owed his soul to Karl Wielund." She placed her forefinger on Paavo's shoulder. "See you later."

He watched her walk away as he finished his drink.

"Careful! I don't think I've seen a neck swivel that far around since the last time I watched *The Exorcist*."

He recognized the voice and quickly turned. "Angie! What are you talking about?"

"Oh, nothing. Just wanted to let you know I'm ready to leave."

"Angelina! Paavo!" The shrill tones of Angie's mother, Serafina Teresa Maria Giuseppina Amalfi, cut through the murmur of voices around them. Her black dress had long, wide sleeves, and a black hat sat squarely on top of her five-foot-one, one hundred fifty pound frame. "I'm sorry, I couldn't talk to you earlier! This funeral, it's so, so sad," Serafina cried as she swooped toward them.

"I know, Mamma," Angie began, ready to offer her mother comfort, but Serafina went straight to Paavo, put her hands on the back of his neck, pulled his head down and gave him a kiss on each cheek.

She continued to keep her hands on his shoulders as she spoke. "Paavo, *caro*, how nice of you to come here, to share our family's grief. He was such a good friend. Shot down...so young. *Terribile*."

"We're trying hard to find whoever did it, Serafina," he said, his hands gentle on her waist. He unashamedly loved this woman. She'd been good to him during the time Angie was in danger, making him feel a part of her family, of her life, and she even came to visit him and Aulis while he was recuperating. He would never forget her kindness. Plus, she was the sort who could take over a room and still manage not to irritate anyone, who could be bossy and nosey, yet do it all with an honest, bigheartedness that put others at ease.

"I know, *caro mio*." Serafina grabbed his hand and Angie's giving them both a squeeze. "I've been so busy... so many people I haven't seen in years and years, all came here to pay respects. It's a shame we have to wait for a funeral to see each other. But Chick was a good man."

"I can see he was well liked," Paavo said.

"And how are you, Paavo? Angelina told me you've gone back to work. How do you feel?"

"I'm fine."

Serafina stepped back, studying his face left then right, peering closely at him, then turned to her daughter. "He looks a bit pale, Angelina, and too thin. Don't you give him enough to eat? He needs big dinners with liver, some nice blood sausage, to make him strong."

"I don't make him dinner, Mamma. I mean, it's not like we're dating!"

"Hmph, and you won't be, you treat him like that! *Mangia*, Paavo, and get Angie to cook for you. Don't let her be so lazy."

"We were just leaving, Mamma," Angie interrupted. Her arms were folded and Paavo could see she was steamed.

Serafina gripped his elbow, stopping him from leaving just yet, her dark brown eyes, so much like Angie's, seeming to read clear through to his soul. "You met Salvatore?" she asked softly.

He nodded.

She patted his arm. "He worries too much. But he means well. You do what you have to."

Her unexpected words, the trust she showed in him with her daughter, touched and meant more to him than all the medals and commendations he'd ever received. Do what you have to, she'd said. Her simple words, combined with the logic of Sal's, made clear to him what path he must take. "I will," he whispered, then bent over and kissed her cheek. "It'll be all right. *Ciao*, Serafina."

"*Ciao, caro*," Serafina said.

As Angie stood with her mouth hanging open looking at the two of them, he took her arm and led her from the restaurant.

Angie knew that something was wrong as Paavo rode with her in the elevator up to her apartment. She was tired of being irritated at him over Nona Farraday, despite the fact that if he'd watched Nona walk away from him at the memorial service any more intensely, his eyeballs would have been seared onto her backside. But aside from that, he didn't actually look sorry to watch her go. And he'd paid zero attention to her the rest of the afternoon, which wasn't the way a man in love would act.

She was wrong, and glad of it. Now, she wanted to make amends. She invited him to join her for coffee and to talk about the people at the memorial service.

"I think, instead of coming in, I'll just say goodnight here," Paavo said when she opened the door to her apartment.

"No time for some coffee to settle the stomach after all that rich food?" she asked. "Or to talk about any possible motives—"

"It's later than I thought..."

Again, the brush-off. Was she wrong about his feelings for Nona? Was there someone else? Or some other reason? She spun toward him, ready to ask, then stopped as she saw his closed expression, the reserve he wore like a barrier reef. "I suppose you have to get to work really early tomorrow. Lots of crimes to investigate."

"True."

No, she wanted to scream, it's more than that. Disappointment and confusion filled her. "Heaven forbid you come inside my apartment, then. What if you lost yourself over my wiles? You might not get a good night's sleep."

He looked at her as if he could scarcely believe what she was saying, or why. "You know that's not it."

"No? What is it, then?" She drew in a deep breath. "Tell me. Was it something my father said about me?"

He lowered his gaze. Sal's words had replayed in his mind all evening. He put his hand on the doorframe. "This isn't the time. We just got back from a funeral."

Her blood turned to ice. "Seems to me, that makes it perfect."

He sucked in his breath. "All right, then. I think this... this closeness that seems to be developing between us... is a mistake. You need to see other people. So do I."

His words hurt her heart. "Is there someone else?" she whispered.

Big blue eyes captured hers, his voice soft. "No. Not for me. Not yet, anyway."

"Not *yet*?" She shook her head. "Well, that says a lot about how you feel about me, doesn't it?"

He ran his fingers through his hair. "I didn't mean anything by it. It's just that we aren't right for each other. Hell, you know it as well as I do, Angie. We've both always known it."

"I do?" *I do. Bad choice of words there, Amalfi.* She turned her back on him and swung her apartment door open wide. Everything between them seemed to be upside down, and wrong.

"Angie, let's give ourselves a little time... a little space. Okay?"

She bit her bottom lip to stop its trembling. "You really mean it, don't you?"

His gaze held hers. "Yes. I mean it."

She wished he didn't look so heart-stoppingly handsome in his dark grey suit and pale blue shirt—a blue that perfectly matched his eyes—as he stood there saying goodbye to her.

She wished she didn't remember so well the softness that came into those beautiful eyes when he gazed at her with affection and warmth, instead of with the bleak, cold look they wore now.

She wished she didn't understand how much he cared about people and making things right in the world, or how well he took care of those few people he allowed close to him such as Aulis Kokkonen and Matt Kowalski's son and widow.

And most of all, she wished she didn't know how it felt when he was near, or how much she liked it when he held her close.

If all that meant nothing to her, it would be easy to say goodbye to him now. But she was never one to insist that a man stay with her. Quite the opposite, in fact. "If that's how you feel, then fine," she said, forcing her voice to sound strong. "So, goodnight, Inspector Smith. You needn't bother to call me again."

She stepped inside her apartment. He turned and walked toward the elevator. She hurled herself against her door, slamming it shut. Almost immediately, she regretted her action and pressed her palms and forehead against the door. She hadn't meant to say that to him!

She stood at the door a moment, waiting for him to come to his senses, but instead, she heard the elevator doors open, then close. *He can't have gone!* She opened the front door a crack.

The hallway was empty.

She couldn't believe it. She stood there a long, long while, watching the elevator doors, willing them to open so he would come back to her. But they didn't. She shut her eyes, shut out the tears that threatened, and went back inside.

After getting ready for bed, while washing off her make-up, Angie gave herself a good talking to. *If he's got the bad taste to walk out on me, so be it!*

But tough words didn't help.

Yet, despite what Angie saw, in her heart she believed Paavo was no more interested in Nona Farraday than *she* was. He was no gigolo, not even a mere playboy, and he *did* have feelings for her. Strong feelings. A couple of times, he'd even allowed her to see them. If she didn't believe that to her very core, she would have run from him and never stopped. And deep down, something—call it intuition, a sixth sense, whatever—told her he was worth the effort it took to try to get him to truly trust her.

But what, now, had caused this terrible chasm between them?

Could something have happened that made him think this case might be dangerous for her? That could be it. Perhaps he wanted to protect her from those dangers, knowing how much she cared about Chick and wanted to find his killer.

She twisted her hands. Please, let that be true, she thought. *He cares, I know he does. He can't change that fast. Not Paavo.*

As she walked through the apartment turning off lights, on the floor beside the sofa she noticed his briefcase, an old-fashioned one, with handles on the top, and a wide bottom. He told her he'd needed it for his job that morning, but then, rather than going back to Homicide, he'd gone straight to her house to go with her to the funeral.

For that reason, he'd brought it to her apartment because his car's door locks were easy to bypass and nothing left in a car on city streets was safe anymore. Not even people.

But now, he'd forgotten it.

Maybe on purpose, or so she hoped. Even if subconsciously on purpose, she would take it.

He would come back to get it, and then, maybe they'd talk. Or not.

19

ngie bustled about the next morning making a healthy quiche filled with cheese, eggs, and lots of vegetables, as well as straightening out the living room in preparation for Mrs. Calamatti joining her for breakfast. But once again her gaze went Paavo's briefcase.

Why would a homicide detective be carrying around such a thing? A notebook, rubber gloves, and evidence bags were all he usually had on him, along with his Sig Sauer handgun, of course. But then, maybe it wasn't even connected with his job.

Curious, she walked over and picked it up off the floor by the sofa where he'd left it and placed it onto one of the wing-back chairs near the windows. It didn't seem right to leave it lying on the floor. As she looked at it, she couldn't help but wonder if its contents had anything to do with Chick's murder. That should be Paavo's main case, as far as she was concerned.

She really shouldn't peek. But what if the briefcase contained something that had to do with Chick's murder? Or Karl's? Might it give her, an "insider," a clue to the murderer that an outsider like Paavo wouldn't be aware of?

Surely, he would have told her anything interesting he'd

learned about Chick's murder, considering that she knew all these people.

Who was she kidding? He was the most close-mouthed person she knew, much to her frustration. So maybe, she *should* look. In fact, wouldn't it be her civic duty to look inside Paavo's briefcase to help him out? Of course it would.

She tried the clasp that held it shut. It wasn't locked, so clearly that meant nothing truly secret was inside. She pulled the briefcase open and saw a tablet, a folder with some papers, a large manila envelope, and two DVDs.

She picked up the DVDs with interest. They were in clear plastic cases with no names, but only serial numbers: 911,974 and 911,221.

What could they mean? 9-1-1 on both DVDs. Was it some sort of emergency hot-line number? And why would Paavo have them? She was tempted to put them in her DVD player...

An immediate sense of guilt struck her, and she carefully placed the DVDs back, as if they were infused with the fires of Hell. She felt like she was a kid again, in class, and Sister Mary Joseph had just caught her peeking at the answers on her neighbor's test paper. She knew it wasn't right for her to go through the briefcase. But as she was about to shut it, she noticed a handwritten note stuck on the outside of the envelope. She didn't actually remove the envelope, but just slid it upward enough to read the note.

P—

These'll take your mind off your little Italian friend!

Ha, ha!

Yosh

She reread it. What in the world did it mean? Little Italian friend? Was Yosh talking about her? What was this all about?

The temptation to look in the envelope was all but overwhelming. But she forced herself to slide it back in place, shut the briefcase, and refasten the clasp. She respected Paavo's privacy and the confidentiality of his case... sort of... as she slowly backed away from the severe amount of temptation sitting on her wingback chair.

She hurried into the kitchen to put the biscuits in the oven to go with the quiche. She had asked Mrs. Calamatti to breakfast to see how the woman was doing and to get a sense whether her neighbor should continue to live alone.

Promptly at ten on the dot, Mrs. Calamatti arrived. "I'm so glad you could make it," Angie said. To her surprise, her downstairs neighbor was wearing a jacket and carrying a large handbag. She hoped Mrs. Calamatti realized they weren't going out to eat. "How are you feeling today?"

"Just fine. I'm happy to be here." Mrs. Calamatti removed the jacket, draped it over the arm of the chair Angie had directed her to, and placed her handbag on the floor beside it.

The two then sat in the living room a while and had a nice chat about health and the weather until the kitchen buzzer told Angie breakfast was ready. She excused herself to go into the kitchen to remove the quiche and biscuits from the oven.

When she returned to the dining area carrying a tray with their plates, she saw that Mrs. Calamatti was standing near the wingback chairs, handbag on her arm as if she was ready to leave. "Brunch is ready," she called.

Mrs. Calamatti spun around and then smiled. "So it is. I was just enjoying the view from up here. It's so much nicer than being on the third floor!"

Angie took a moment to enjoy the view as well. No matter what else was going on in the world or in her life, San Francisco Bay was a beautiful thing to behold.

Paavo did his best to check in on the man he referred to as his father about once a week. Aulis Kokkonen was up in years, and lately, Paavo could see that he was growing frail. It pained Paavo to see the change in the man who was once so strong. Born in Finland, Aulis had worked his way to the U.S. as a young man, eventually reaching San Francisco where he found a job working for a carpenter.

Paavo always felt Aulis could have done a lot better for himself in this country except for the fact that Paavo's mother had dropped him and his older sister off at Aulis' apartment one day and never came back for them. Paavo was four, his sister Jessica, nine. Aulis had raised them from that day on. He always said he never regretted, not even for a single moment, having them in his life.

On this day, however, Paavo didn't go to Aulis only to check on the old man. He needed to talk to someone about the subject most weighing on his mind... Angie.

"I don't know what to do, Papa," Paavo said as he looked at the small, white-haired man seated across the wooden table from him. "Angie's father objects to the two of us being together. When he explains why, it's as if I'm listening to all the reasons I tell myself to stay away from her. Yet, at every chance I get, I run right back to her side."

"I got to know her when she came here while you were recuperating," Aulis said. "I understand why you feel as you do about her. She's a little off-putting at first, but then she grows on you. Yes, that she definitely does."

"I don't understand her," Paavo added. "If I treated just about any other woman the way I do her, walking out on her, telling her to leave me alone, it wouldn't be tolerated. But Angie forgives me. I don't get it."

"She accepts who you are. As you must who she is. Why not give her, and yourself, a chance at happiness?"

Paavo rubbed the back of his neck. "I'm not sure I dare to. Everything has come easily for her, the way paved by her father. But this, between us, if it were to go anywhere, will only get harder as time goes by—as she learns more about the ugliness I deal with every day. I know that, but I don't think she does. It makes me doubt she'll feel the same way in a year. Hell, in a month. Breaking it off with her now is probably the best thing I can do for her as well as for me."

Aulis' turquoise eyes studied the proud man the ragged little boy had become. He, more than anyone, understood where Paavo's reserve came from, and why he feared so much to open his heart. He still clearly remembered how, years ago, four-year-old Paavo had sat by Aulis' apartment door day after day, his jacket in his hand, insisting that his mother would come back to get him. His sister, Jessica, never waited for their mother's return. She was only age nine, but already much too wise about the harsh side of the world. She never expected anything from it.

Then, one day, Paavo stopped talking about his mother, stopped asking about her. That day, Aulis realized, Paavo had decided not to put his faith in anyone anymore. It took years for Aulis to get Paavo to even trust him. The only person Paavo had unquestioningly, immediately, loved and trusted was his older sister. And then she died.

Aulis put his hand on Paavo's shoulder. "There are no guarantees, son. But sometimes you have to put your heart at risk. Only you can decide if she's worth it."

Paavo shook his head. "That's not the point."

"What is, then? You worry, I think, that you'll just be together a short while. That what you have now won't continue for eternity. But tell me, do you wish Jessica had never lived at all? Because if she hadn't, you wouldn't have had to lose her, either."

"Of course I don't feel that way." Paavo ran his fingers through his hair. After Jessie's death, it had taken nearly ten years for the nightmares to stop, the visions of Jessie as she'd been at age nineteen, laughing and beautiful, going on a date with a strange man, a man he'd never seen before—a man with small, gray, penetrating eyes and a large, black, beetle-like mole on the side of his face, a man whose hand lingered a little too long on Paavo's hair as he stroked and ruffled it when they met.

Then he remembered his uneasiness when Jessie didn't return that night, his search for her, and finally, finding her dead from an overdose of heroin. "She died and, much as I wish I could have done something to stop it, there was nothing. This is different. This time, *I've got control.* But I'm not sure what I should do with it."

"There's only one way to find out. Either you decide to trust Angie—trust her with your heart—or you don't."

"How do I decide such a thing?"

"You are so practical, Paavo," Aulis said, his mouth forming a slight scowl. "Sometimes too practical. You try to figure out everything logically. But at times that doesn't work. This is one of those times. You'll have to find a way to listen to your heart, not your mind. There are no guarantees that happiness will follow. But if you follow your heart, at least you'll know you tried your best. There really isn't anything more a person can do than that."

Paavo's gaze dropped to the now cold cup of coffee before him on the table, and after a long moment, he asked, "What if my heart is silent?"

Aulis studied him, again seeing the troubled boy, not the man, before him. "I'd say it's a bit scared right now. Give it time."

A loud rap sounded on the door. Angie knew that knock. She had been waiting for it ever since she'd returned home from the radio studio where, fortunately, nothing dangerous or surreal had happened during the show, and not a single death threat was made. Hearing Paavo's knock, her heart bounded, but then she forced back the feeling.

He was there to pick up his briefcase. That's all. The fact still remained that last night, he had told her they were finished. She had no reason to think he'd changed his mind.

But what if he had? What if he regretted his words and behavior? What if he wanted to apologize?

He knocked again, and she ran to the door, then skidded to a halt. She didn't want to make things *too* easy for him. Not after the hell she'd gone through last night after his goodbye.

"Who is it?" she called sweetly.

"It's me."

With folded arms, she leaned against the door. "Who?"

She could all but hear his teeth gnashing. "Paavo."

"Back so soon? I thought you didn't want to see me."

Silence. Good, she thought. He was steamed. "Angie, open the door."

"But then you'd see me."

"I left my briefcase," he said finally.

"I don't think I quite heard you."

"I need my briefcase! Just give it to me, and I'll be on my way."

Stan's voice, from the apartment across the hall, called out, "Angie, open the damned door! I'm trying to take a nap!"

She yanked open the door. Paavo stood in front of her and a sleepy-looking Stan stood in his doorway. She gave Stan her attention. "You should be at work."

"I'm sick today."

"*Again?*" She glared at Stan who quickly backed into his apartment and shut the door. She then faced Paavo, her nose in the air. "All right, come in."

He walked in and picked up the briefcase. "The clasp is open." He faced her, his expression accusing. "Did you go through it?"

She swallowed hard. She had opened it, but she was sure she snapped the clasp shut again. "Was it locked?"

"I didn't think I needed to lock it." His eyes showed disappointment. "Guess I was wrong."

"I didn't go through it, Paavo. I... I may have looked to make sure it wasn't empty."

His lips tightened as he opened the briefcase.

"I had a manila folder." His voice was cold. "Where is it?"

She knew what he was talking about. Knew it had been in there. She stepped to his side and looked inside the case. It was gone. "I didn't take it!"

"But you saw it."

Her voice tiny, she confessed, "I... I may have noticed a strange note on it."

His shoulders sagged. "It's not what you think, Angie. Yosh was just joking."

"He was making a joke about me?" she asked, now confused.

"Photos were in the envelope—photos we found in Karl Wielund's house. Now, what did you do with them?"

"What kind of photos?" she asked.

He looked as if he were grinding his teeth. "The kind that, in some cases, could be illegal to own or distribute."

She felt shocked by his words, but then, her eyes grew round as a thought struck. "Oh, dear! I think I know what might have happened to them. Mrs. Calamatti came to breakfast today, and she wandered around the living and dining area as I was dishing out our quiche."

"You think she took—"

"We'll go get them!" Her breath came fast. "I'll phone and make sure she's home." She made the call, but it went to voice mail.

"She's not there?" Paavo asked, increasingly annoyed.

Angie swallowed hard. "I've got an idea."

She went to the over to her garbage chute and stuck her head in it. "Mrs. Calamatti! Hello!"

No answer.

"Mrs. Calamatti, are you down there?" she called again, much louder this time.

"I hear you, Angie," the thin, reedy voice cried out. "Where are you?"

"God damn it!" A deep male voice echoed up from the chute. *"Can't you broads use the phone like everybody else!"*

"We've got to talk," Angie called. "Can I meet you at your apartment right now?"

"Well, I think so. Give me a minute and be there."

"I said—" the man bellowed.

"Go stuff it!" Angie yelled, and shut her garbage chute door.

2 0

Mrs. Calamatti looked startled to see both Angie and Paavo waiting at her front door as she got off the elevator. "Angelina. Is anything wrong?"

"No, not at all. We just need to ask you about something."

"Okay." The woman looked nervous, and Angie knew she had to calm her down to get anywhere.

"Let me handle this," she whispered to Paavo as they entered the apartment. It was like stepping back in time. The two of them sat on an avocado-color sofa with white antimacassars over each arm. Mrs. Calamatti dashed into the kitchen and came out with a small platter of some hard, circular Italian cookies with white icing and set them on the coffee table.

"Can I get you some coffee or tea?" she asked.

"No, thank you," Angie said. "This will only take a minute. We were wondering if you happened to find any pictures yesterday."

Mrs. Calamatti forced an innocent look on her face. It was as Angie had come to suspect during their breakfast—the woman was only as ditzy as she wanted to be. "Pictures?"

"Photographs, actually. They were in a manila envelope."

Mrs. Calamatti's face flushed red. "I did see something like that."

Angie all but cried out with relief. Keeping her voice calm, she said, "And did you pick them up by any chance?"

"Me? Pick them up?"

"Yes." *Come on, Mrs. C., confess that you took them, and please, please don't say you threw them away.*

"The only pictures I saw couldn't possibly have been yours, Angie."

"Actually," Paavo said, "they're connected to my case. It's important I get them back."

Mrs. Calamatti's mouth dropped open. "Oh, I see." She then scooted back in her chair and seemed to think a moment. "Well, that makes sense, then. Yes, it does." She shook her head. "My sister's boy takes pictures like those, too. It breaks her heart. He used to be such a good boy. An altar boy, even. And now..." She gave a "What can you do?" type shrug.

"Yes, I'm sure," Paavo said forcefully. "But, *do you have the photos*?"

Mrs. Calamatti grimaced at his tone and turned to Angie. "Those pictures are no good, Angie! Just like my sister's boy. She thought he was a fashion photographer. Hah! Some fashion. *Un*-fashion, they should call it—"

"Paavo needs the pictures back, Mrs. Calamatti." Angie spoke softly and smiled sweetly.

Mrs. Calamatti gave him a fisheye. "I know why men need pictures like that!"

Paavo looked ready to writhe on the floor.

"Please," Angie coaxed. "Where are they?"

"Oh, all right."

Angie and Paavo watched as she got up and pulled the pictures from a bottom drawer in her bedroom. She clutched the envelope tight as she walked back into the living room. "I didn't want them out where anyone could see them. I didn't want anyone to think I like things like this. I'm surprised you looked at them, Angie. What would your mother say if she knew?"

Angie nearly dropped to her knees in thanks. "Actually, I never saw them."

"Oh?" Mrs. Calamatti raised her eyebrows. "Well, maybe you should see the kind of filth your friend here works with. It might make you think twice about who you hang out with!" So saying, she turned the envelope upside down and let the photos fall onto the coffee table.

Angie's eyebrows rose even higher than Mrs. Calamatti's penciled-in ones.

"I'm not surprised to see that girl in them." Mrs. Calamatti said, pointing to one of the more lurid X-rated photos. "The way she was acting."

"That girl?" Paavo stared at her. "Do you know that woman?"

Mrs. Calamatti scowled at him, as if he were personally responsible for the smutty photos now spread over her coffee table. "Not exactly. But I watched her nearly get herself killed and then try to knock me over!"

"Oh, no!" Angie said, but Paavo put his hand on her arm to stop her from speaking.

"What do you mean?" he asked.

Again, Mrs. Calamatti's eyes bored into him, then she faced Angie as she said, "I was doing my grocery shopping on Polk Street. As you know, I like their stores. I was pulling my little two-wheel cart—it makes it so much easier than to carry bags up all the hills to this apartment. Anyway, that girl ran right out to traffic. It was a mercy she didn't get killed! Cars managed to stop on time, but instead of slowing down, she came right across the street toward me, as if she scarcely saw where she was going. She ran into my cart, stumbled and nearly fell over it. I wrenched my arm holding it tight. I was lucky she didn't knock me down!"

"That sounds terrible," Angie said. "You're lucky you didn't get badly hurt."

"I know." Mrs. Calamatti grimaced at the memory. "I tell you, after all that, I wasn't surprised at what I found out about her."

Paavo glanced at Angie, his brow furrowed, then turned back to Mrs. Calamatti. "What did you find out?"

"The very next day, I saw her picture in the paper. She was found dead out in Golden Gate Park. They said she'd been strangled."

Paavo blinked a couple of times. Rebecca's case! He picked up the picture of the heavily made-up face of the woman in the photo and studied it. He looked at Mrs. Calamatti. "You're talking about Sheila Danning, aren't you?"

"Hmm... that name does sound familiar. But it was a few months ago. I'm not good with names, but I've always been very good with faces."

Paavo dug in his briefcase and pulled out a photo of a young, pretty, very innocent-looking woman. "Is this her?"

Mrs. Calamatti took the photo, then slowly got up and walked over to her reading glasses on a corner table, and put them on. "I think it's her. Could you bring me one of the smutty picture of her, young man? The light here is better."

Paavo did as told and placed the two photos side-by-side. As he did, Angie thought of something Mrs. Calamatti had said earlier, and took out her phone and snapped as many of the other photos that might have been Sheila Danning as she could before Paavo turned around.

"Yep, same girl," Mrs. Calamatti said. "She sure aged fast, didn't she?"

As they joined Angie again, Paavo said to Mrs. Calamatti.

"Let me get this right. You're saying you saw Sheila Danning the day before her body was found?"

"I guess I did. Is it important?"

Instead of answering, he asked, "Do you remember where, on Polk Street, this happened?"

"Of course. It was on the block with those two fancy restaurants. There's no good shopping on that street—a waste of real estate, if you ask me. But I'm sure Angie knows the restaurants. She's a gourmet cook, you know. Anyway, the woman was going from Wielund's to LaTour's. I was walking past LaTour's, on the shady side of the street, so that's why I remember."

Paavo glanced at Angie. "Sheila Danning was dead about twenty-four hours before her body was discovered. That means she was most likely killed a short while after Mrs. C. saw her."

Angie's gaze swiveled from Paavo, to Mrs. Calamatti, to the photos, and back. It sounded as if this could be big, although she had no idea who Sheila Danning was or why Paavo cared about her case.

Paavo gathered up the photos and put them into the envelope. "Mrs. Calamatti, you may have been more help than you'll ever know."

Finally, the old woman smiled at him. "Good. Then, maybe you police can start to do something I consider important, like helping the people in this city prepare for the depression. It's coming, you know!"

Angie rode down the elevator and out to his car with Paavo. "I'm not positive," she began cautiously, "but as I was concentrated on Sheila Dannings' face, she seemed familiar. When Mrs. C. mentioned Wielund's, I can't help but think I might have seen her with Karl."

"Since these pornographic photos of her, among others,

belonged to Wielund, I wouldn't be surprised. Do you remember where or when you saw them together?"

Angie was momentarily shocked to hear the photos were Wielund's. She thought hard about Paavo's question. "One night, when I went clubbing with some friends, Wielund was there with a woman who looked way too young for him. I think it might have been her, but I wouldn't swear to it."

"Unbelievable." Paavo shook his head. "It wasn't my case, but from the files I saw, everyone had her pegged as a sweet kid from Tacoma, young, innocent, and working as a waitress at Le Maison Rouge when she was killed. But little else."

"Since she worked there, I'm sure she kept those 'photography' sessions a secret," Angie said.

"That would make sense," Paavo agreed, then leaned against his car facing Angie. "And then there were four: Wielund, Marcuccio, Greuber—"

"Who?"

"Karl Wielund's landlord."

Angie's eyebrows rose. "Was he a cook, too?"

Paavo stopped and stared at her a moment, then continued. "No. And now, we add another non-cook, Sheila Danning. She's no cook, but is connected to Wielund. Maybe we've been looking at this wrong. Maybe the connection isn't restaurants, but is pornography."

"Chick Marcuccio had nothing to do with porn," Angie indignantly stated.

"We don't know that for sure. Just like we don't know how much Sheila Danning had to do with restaurants."

"What are you saying?"

"I'm saying it's a mess. We've got clues galore, but all they do is confuse everything. Anyway, I'm heading back to Homicide with this new info. Thanks, Angie. What I thought was a disaster, is actually a big help."

She shrugged. "I guess that's what I'm here for."

21

R ebecca walked into the homicide bureau late the next afternoon. "When's the funeral?"

Paavo and Yosh looked up at her. "Whose funeral?" Yosh asked.

"I don't know. I figured someone must have died, the way you two look."

"Gallows humor has no place in homicide, Inspector." Paavo barely glanced at her as he spoke, then went back to the report he was writing. "But you are just the person I want to see."

"If you're looking for news on the Marcuccio killing," she said, "all we have is a dark sedan, license plates removed, driving toward Marcuccio's car as he slowly drove down Clement Street. The sedan stopped as Marcuccio passed it. Two shots were fired, one missed, the other hit its mark. I'm guessing his foot was on the gas as he was hit and that's why his car smashed into a lamppost. And, then, our mystery driver sped away. No clear view whatsoever of the driver. It's beyond frustrating."

"What's the make of the get-away car?" Paavo asked.

"Old Toyota Camry, black or dark gray. They're a dime a dozen in this city. We'll try to find a match, but with the plates gone, it looks like a planned execution."

"It does," Yosh agreed as Rebecca continued toward her desk.

"Wait, Rebecca," Paavo called. "I have something you need to see."

"Oh?" She stepped closer.

Paavo picked up the envelope lying on the edge of his desk, then hesitated. Despite himself, he found it hard to hand a woman, homicide detective or not, a pile of pornographic still photos.

"What's your problem, Smith?" She grabbed the bag from him and took the photos out. "Oh, yuck!" She eyed the photos. "These are wild. Where did you get—?"

Paavo and Yosh glanced at each other.

"Oh, my God," Rebecca murmured. "This can't be Sheila Danning! It's hard to tell with all that make-up on her eyes and mouth, but still..."

"I believe it's her," Paavo said, and proceeded to tell her the story he'd already told Yosh, about Mrs. Calamatti.

Rebecca hurried to her desk and pulled a file out of the bottom drawer. "I should have turned this over to Central Filing by now, but I just couldn't let it go." She ruffled through the pages, then placed an 8x11 graduation photo on Paavo's desk.

With two large photos, it was easy to see that the shape of the face, nose and ears were basically the same in both photos. But the eyes that sparkled in the graduation photo had grown dull quickly for one so young.

"Her parents sent that picture down to us," Rebecca added, "saying she hadn't changed much. Boy, were they wrong."

"Why did she come to San Francisco?" Paavo asked.

"No special reason. Her parents said she wanted to find a job here."

"Looks like she did that, all right." Yosh's voice was tinged with weariness, with the dismay of seeing, once again, the pointless loss of youth.

"I never could find out what she did before getting the job at Le Maison Rouge," Rebecca said. "All I know is no one gave any hint that she would have considered posing for pictures like these, let alone done it. The investigation turned up nothing more than her being a nice, wholesome girl who worked as a waitress and happened to be in the wrong place at the wrong time."

"Forgetting to add that she happened to pose for porn photos," Yosh said.

"And who may have dated Karl Wielund, who's now also dead," Paavo added, "and who kept these photos of her in his garage."

"She also worked for Albert Dupries, another restaurant owner," Rebecca added.

"I think it's time we visited Mr. Dupries again," Paavo said.

Yosh reached for his jacket, but so did Rebecca. "It's my case, remember?" she said.

Paavo and Yosh exchanged glances, then Yosh went to his desk and sat. "I don't mind holding down the fort."

Rebecca smiled at Paavo. "Are you ready?"

"I guess." He gave Yosh a quick wave as he followed Rebecca out the door.

Paavo drove Rebecca to Le Maison Rouge. He was surprised to find a parking spot in front of the restaurant—and equally surprised that a valet didn't come running to move his old Mustang out of sight.

The maître d' gave him and Rebecca an ingratiating smile as they entered. "A table for two?"

"We won't be eating," Rebecca said, pulling her badge from her jacket pocket. "Inspector Mayfield, with me is Inspector Smith. We'd like to speak to Albert Dupries."

The maître d's expression changed to one similar to a man who had just heard them announce themselves as Health Inspectors. His eyebrows lifted archly. "I shall see if Monsieur Dupries is available."

In no time, Paavo and Rebecca were shuttled toward the back of the restaurant to a small office. Dupries sat behind a desk, but stood as they entered. Paavo noticed his face paled a bit as he gazed at Rebecca.

"Inspector Smith, what a surprise," the restaurateur said, holding out his hand, then smiled and looked at Rebecca. "I've spoken to you before, I believe, Inspector Mayfield."

"Yes, about Sheila Danning. That's why I'm back."

"Of course! Pardon, Mademoiselle. It is inexcusable for me to have forgotten someone who is so lovely."

Rebecca stared at him as if he'd just crawled out from under a rock.

"But you cannot believe I have more information for you after all these months," he said with a rueful smile.

"We believe you can be quite a help, Mr. Dupries," Paavo said.

"Well, umm," he waved his arms helplessly, then gestured toward the straight-backed wooden chairs. "Shall we sit down?"

The three sat as Paavo opened his briefcase and took out the pictures. "There's someone I'd like you to tell us about," he said.

"Yes?"

"This person." Paavo placed the graduation picture on the table.

"But of course. This is Sheila Danning."

"And," Paavo continued, "this one."

Dupries glanced at the naked woman in the photo and jerked back in his chair. "I don't understand."

"Don't you?" Rebecca asked.

Dupries looked closer. "*Mon Dieu!* This is Sheila Danning, too?"

"Isn't it?" Rebecca asked.

"Well... I suppose."

"Are you saying you didn't know she made such photos?" Rebecca asked.

"I had no idea."

Paavo jumped in. "Did she still look like the girl in the graduation photo?"

Dupries glanced up at him, then his eyes saddened and he shook his head. "No. She was not so innocent. Especially after her *amour* with Karl Wielund. But then, I didn't pay much attention." He drew in a deep breath. "She was a waitress. He met her here one evening. Sparks flew between them. I don't get involved in such things."

"How long did she work here?"

Dupries shrugged. "A long time. Nine months, a year? I don't remember. Then she died."

"You had no recollection of anything at all about this woman several months ago, Mr. Dupries," Rebecca's voice was cold. "I'm curious about why you remember this now?"

Dupries pushed out his lips in thought. "It must be because of my conversation with a mutual friend of Inspector Smith. Angelina Amalfi. She came here for lunch today after her radio show. She was with Joey Marcuccio, the son of my friend, Chick, may God rest his soul. We had a most enjoyable time. She said that Karl Wielund was seeing one of my waitresses. That was when I remembered about Karl's interest in Mademoiselle Danning. So strange, isn't it, that both met tragic ends?"

Blood rushed to Paavo's head. Hadn't he just told Angie to

keep out of his case? And he thought she couldn't stand Joey Marcuccio! "So, Angie told you about the waitress and Wielund?"

"I hadn't paid much attention before. Sheila Danning was a waitress, nothing more."

Paavo's throat began to tighten, his breath grew harsh. "Had you, by chance, thought of this before talking with Miss Amalfi?"

He shrugged. "I doubt it. I'm not one to pay attention to gossip."

"Was any of your current staff friends with Sheila Danning?"

"I don't know. We can ask them."

Paavo and Rebecca learned nothing of note until they reached Tiffany Carson. She had been on maternity leave during the time of Sheila's death and was never contacted when she returned to work.

And Tiffany had a lot to say. "Sheila's main interest was to make it big in movies. She jabbered about wanting to move to Hollywood all the time. But while here, she seemed willing to do anything to get a big break, and I do mean *anything*."

"Is that so?" Rebecca said, sounding interested.

"I didn't like her attitude, frankly," Tiffany admitted. "But she didn't seem to have many friends. Early on, I kind of felt sorry for her and invited her to a party. Well, never again."

"Why was that?" Rebecca asked.

"I don't like to talk badly about the dead, but I'll make an exception here. We went to the party, as I said. We weren't there ten minutes when a good-looking fellow who claimed to be writing a movie screenplay, asked her to dance. Now, I know this fellow. He's been working on the same screenplay for six years, and doesn't have a chance in hell of selling it. Of course, Sheila didn't know that. From what I could see, they didn't even finish the dance, but went into the bathroom—together. Well, that didn't leave anything to my imagination. I was born at night, but not *last* night! If Sheila had asked me I'd have warned her to stay away from that jerk. Did she? No! So, I never invited her to anything else. Never felt sorry for her again, either."

Paavo took the name of the ersatz screenwriter, Jared Albright.

He and Rebecca then went to pay him a visit.

Albright lived in a small apartment on Twin Peaks. He remembered Sheila Danning and wasn't surprised she'd been murdered. "She lived on the edge," he said. "I dated her a couple of times, but before the third date, she said she expected to be paid. I thought she did what she did because she liked me. She laughed and said she didn't think anyone living in this town could still be so naïve. I never saw her again. Then, I learned she was dead."

"Any ideas about who did it?" Paavo asked.

Jared shook his head. "Maybe she asked the wrong guy for money."

2 2

Earlier, that same afternoon, on the way home from her boring lunch with Joey at Le Maison Rouge, Angie got an idea for a completely unique way to help move Paavo's case along before anyone else got killed. Instead of going to her own apartment, she knocked on Mrs. Calamatti's door.

"Mrs. Calamatti, would it be easy for you to contact your sister's son, the one who has a connection to studios that take those pictures like the ones we saw yesterday?"

"You mean my nephew, the zucchini brain? Sure. He's not married, so my sister makes sure she knows where he is. Even though he's a jerk, she still has to be sure he eats right."

"Could you ask him to come over tonight, or for us to go to see him? I have a very important issue to talk to him about?"

"Ooooh, sounds exciting!" Mrs. Calamatti said gleefully. "And it's not like Scotty is ever busy. Let me call him right now. I'll ask him to come by for dinner tonight. He always likes food. Then, after he eats and is in a good mood, I'll call you to join us."

She placed the call and soon told Angie he'd be there at six o'clock.

"Fantastic," Angie said. "And how about I cook the dinner for you? Does he like Italian food?"

"Lasagna is a big favorite of his."

Angie had some frozen in her freezer. "You got it!" The two high-fived.

As planned, before Mrs. Calamatti's nephew arrived, Angie brought down a platter of lasagna, a green salad, and for dessert she made *zabaglione,* a custard spiked with Marsala, and topped with sliced strawberries. She added a bottle of cabernet sauvignon.

Less than thirty minutes later, Mrs. Calamatti called. "Scotty all but licked his plate. And loved the wine. Come on down before he falls asleep!"

Angie no sooner arrived than she discovered that Scotty thought his aunt had set this dinner up as a blind date for the two of them.

"I'm suuure happy to meet you, Angie," he said with a smile. He was short, stocky, and wore an old tee-shirt and sweat pants, which made him look even pudgier than he was. His hair was thinning and stood straight up on top—more due to lack of being combed than style. "Auntie Grace told me you cooked that meal. I wish you'd enjoyed it with us. I think it was the finest Italian I've ever eaten. Come on and sit here by me. Auntie Grace, do you have any of that wine left?"

"No thanks," Angie said quickly, joining Scotty on the sofa but not too close. "Actually, I wanted to talk to you about something important." She then went into a song-and-dance, buttering Scotty up about his vast experience as a photographer, and slipped in the fact that she understood some of his photographs were very exotic "boudoir photos" of beautiful people. He looked more and more confused as she continued talking.

But then she whipped out her cellphone and asked if he would look at some photos she had. Like a shot, he slid across the sofa, landing hip-to-hip next to her, one arm behind her back. "Suuure, Angie. I'll look at anything you want to show me."

She showed him the photos she'd taken of the porn pictures Paavo had. "I'd like to know if you have any idea who might have taken these photographs."

Scotty's jaw nearly hit the floor as he looked at the photos Angie showed him.

"I... uh, I... didn't see you as the type interested in—"

"I'm not. I just want to know who does this work. It's rather special, wouldn't you say?"

He swallowed hard, then took the phone from her. "Suuure is." He swallowed hard again, and Angie had to wonder if this idea of hers hadn't been a big waste of time and a good bottle of cabernet sauvignon.

"Actually," he said. "When you look at the background— that sort of weird, swirly purple and pink pattern on the walls, there's only one place where I've seen that. It's in Berkeley, though, not the city."

"That's okay. Berkeley's just across the bay."

He found the address on his own phone and sent it to her. "I can take you there, if you want."

Angie hesitated. It wasn't a place she wanted to go, and definitely not a person she wanted to go with.

"It sounds fine to me," Mrs. Calamatti said. "Let's do it, Angie. It's a bucket list item if ever I heard one!"

"Where shall I drop you?" Paavo asked as he and Rebecca got into his Mustang after their visit to Le Maison Rouge.

As she gazed at him, he could see the curiosity but also the hesitancy in her eyes. "How about dinner?"

He had to admit he was hungry, having skipped lunch. "I guess we could go back into the restaurant for dinner."

"And blown our paychecks for the week?" she said with a rueful smile. "Anyway, I'm more of a Jumbo Jack kind of girl."

"As you wish, Inspector," he said, happy to avoid the possibility of another pricey but skimpy dinner like the one he'd had with Nona Farraday.

They ate their oversized, juicy cheeseburgers and fries in the car, washing them down with large, black coffees-to-go. When done, he drove her back to the Hall of Justice parking lot.

As she reached for the door handle to get out of his Mustang, she said, "I don't live too far from here. Would you like to come over? You can follow me and we'd be there in ten minutes." Then she quickly added, "It's not very late."

Her offer shouldn't have surprised him—the other inspectors were constantly telling him she had a bit of a crush on him. A part of him said he should take her up on the offer, that he needed to see other women, needed to forget about Ms. Society Belle and all she might have meant to him.

Rebecca was a nice person. Quite attractive. A good detective. And he liked her, as a colleague. That was why he couldn't be anything less than straight with her.

"No, thanks."

She looked at him a long moment, as if waiting for an explanation. He knew better than to make excuses, and she didn't need to hear the blunt truth. "Okay," she said. "Maybe next time?"

"Probably not, Inspector."

Her face flamed. "You make yourself clear." She caught his gaze, then sheepishly smiled. "I guess I should say thanks for that."

He looked uncomfortably at the fog-misted night lights lining the street, then murmured, "Not at all."

She got out of his car. "Well," she said, her voice heavy, "see you at work tomorrow."

"Goodnight, Rebecca. Good job with Dupries," he added, then felt like an ass for doing it. She didn't want to hear, right now, about being a good cop. He knew the feeling.

He waited a moment before leaving to make sure she got safely into her car for her drive home.

23

It had been bad enough when Angie received calls from so-called friends telling her about Paavo's being seen at an Arbuckle's restaurant with Nona Farraday. But the next morning, she received several text messages telling her Paavo was seen the evening before at Le Maison Rouge with a mysterious blonde woman, one none of them knew.

With friends like these..., Angie thought.

Had Paavo become so intrigued with the whole fine dining scene he now was taking *all* his dates to such places? One visit to a good restaurant with Nona Farraday, and he'd dumped Angie like a fallen soufflé?

What, she wondered, what was going on with him? Had he really meant it when he said they should give each other a little time, a little space? Had he already been thinking about other women he wanted to be with?

Sharp stabs of jealousy struck deep. She had no idea what to do.

It hurt. She'd never really been in love before, but she guessed she must be now. That could be the only explanation she could feeling so miserable because of some man.

She hated the feeling.

But what if he wasn't actually "dating," and simply taking dates to restaurants to help him find out more about the people who might be involved in the deaths, just as she'd done when she went to lunch with Joey Marcuccio?

All of this only confirmed the actions she'd already set in motion. She would help him. She knew these people much better than he did. She could handle it.

Clutching that thought made Angie feel somewhat better as she got ready to go to the KYME studio.

Lunch with Henri was mercifully uneventful that afternoon, and as soon as it ended, Angie hurried back to her apartment house. Mrs. Calamatti and Scotty were outside waiting as she pulled up to the front door in her white Ferrari Portofino.

If Scotty wore false teeth, they would have been on the ground as he looked at the car. "If we take my car," Angie said to Scotty, "the back seat is a little small, and I'd hate your aunt to be uncomfortable back there."

"I'll take the back," he said as he reached out to touch a fender. "Woo-hoo! I don't mind at all. Did I hear right, Angie, that you're single and have no current special boyfriend?"

"Get in," she said with a grin, and then helped Mrs. Calamatti into the low front passenger seat.

Angie's Ferrari would have broken the speed limit crossing the Bay Bridge then heading north on 880 to Berkeley, except that there was too much traffic.

Finally, they reached the town and Angie drove down Telegraph Avenue until she spotted a parking garage on a side street. It was worth the big tip to the attendant to be sure he'd keep a watchful eye on her Ferrari.

Scotty then led them down Telegraph to a brick building on

Dwight Way, surprisingly close to the University of California Berkeley campus.

Telegraph Avenue was a 1970s nostalgia lover's dream. It was modern and filled with college students but it still had the ambiance that reminded people of a time and place when the Grateful Dead were still young, Janis Joplin still hung around with Bobbie Magee, and the University's Free Speech Movement was considered the start of a revolution.

"Spare change, lady?" A teenage girl stopped her, but the girl's chubby-faced, healthy looks told Angie she was in no danger of starvation.

"*Hari Krishna, hari Krishna...*" Angie glanced at the group of chanting, men in their saffron robes and Birkenstock sandals as she passed them. They seemed pretty old, but their shaved heads hid any gray or bald patches. Maybe that was the secret of their popularity?

As Angie hurried past them, a cacophony of sounds from students and street people struck from every direction, along with the pervasive smell of marijuana.

"Free abortions, NOW!"

"Got any change?"

"Save the Berkeley Five! Give donations!"

"*Falafel!* The taco from Morocco. Get your *falafel!*"

"Sexism sucks!"

"*... hari rama, rama, rama...*"

"*Gimme some change!*"

Finally, Scotty stopped at a two-storied building with a brick façade, storefronts facing the street, and a glass door on one side. He opened the door and led them up a steep flight of steps.

At the top was a sort of reception area, stark, in need of paint, and windowless, with a middle-aged man sitting behind a high counter. He looked up and stared at the strange three-some through black-framed eyeglasses thick as coke bottles. He had a mustache and beard, and his black hair was practically gone on top, but long and bushy on the sides. He had it tucked behind his ears, making it look like he had a whiskbroom stuck to the back of his head.

Angie had expected some kind of photography studio, but this looked like a factory office.

"What's up?" Whiskbroom Head asked.

"I'm a photographer," Scotty said. "Just want to look around, see if we might arrange some kind of deal, you know?"

Whiskbroom Head smirked. "If those two represent your products, no need for me to call the boss. It's a no."

Scotty rubbed an ear. "Uh, no. They're my sponsors."

Whiskbroom Head looked confused, then he grimaced and without another word, went through the door directly behind him. In a short while, he returned and faced Scotty. "They're making some videos right now, so the boss said okay for you to go back there, but not the women."

Angie's eyebrows rose at the sexist comment. She was surprised when Scotty glanced her way. She watched his Adam's apple bob like it was on a trampoline. He then said, "Yeah, makes sense," and went with Whiskbroom Head through that same door, shutting it behind them.

Angie wasn't happy. How was she supposed to find out anything here? She decided to take a peek past the door. She needed to see the place.

***

For days, whenever time permitted, Paavo and Rebecca worked together on the accounting books from the Wielund's and Sorrento restaurants.

"Look at this, Rebecca," Paavo said. "I may have finally found something. It's a monthly deposit into one of Wielund's personal accounts in Germany. I'm not sure where the money comes from. It's a lot, and changes only slightly each month."

Rebecca scooted her chair closer to study the figures Paavo had before him. "It isn't coming from the restaurant," Paavo continued, "that's for sure."

"So what's going on? Money laundering?" Rebecca suggested.

They turned their heads back to the books and found that, for the past three months, roughly ten thousand U.S. dollars would show up in Wielund's personal account—the amounts varied slightly only because of changes in the exchange rate from dollars to euros. Then, a week later, the money would be withdrawn from his personal account and his business would have an upsurge in receipts. Without that ten-thousand dollar infusion, the restaurant would most likely have been in financial trouble.

"When you look at all he's buying for the restaurant," Rebecca said, "it's pretty clear where the money is going. He might not be laundering it at all. It might be that to run a top-notch restaurant, to make it big in this town, it simply takes this much time and this much money."

"Could be," he said, rubbing his chin. "Let's see if we can find the source of his funds."

"Even easier, let's get someone from the Financial Crimes Unit to help us track the foreign transactions. That's what stumping us."

Paavo nodded. "Good idea."

24

Angie gave Scotty and Whiskbroom Head a minute for a head start and then opened the door they had gone through.

When she did, she came face-to-face with a flashy-looking fellow who seemed as stunned to see her as she was to see him.

He studied her with confusion, and then a sly look spread over his face as he stepped into the reception area, pulling the door shut behind him. Angie couldn't help but back up to Mrs. Calamatti as he approached her. Something about him shouted "Danger."

He was of medium height, trim but muscular, and somewhere in his forties. His short, bleached blond hair was combed forward, Napoleon style, and framed a darkly tanned face. With his scarcely buttoned denim blue shirt, turquoise and silver Navajo rings, necklace, and bracelets, he looked like someone who should be on the beach in Los Angeles, not a studio in Berkeley. But then, Berkeley attracted all types.

It was his eyes, she realized. They were gray, but expressionless—flat, as if he had no soul. She felt chilled as she tore her gaze from them.

For a moment, she thought he had some kind of bug on the side of his face. But as he continued closer, she saw it was a large, black mole.

"What do you want here?" he demanded when he stopped moving toward her.

She stopped backing up. "Do you take pictures here?" she asked, her voice small.

He frowned. "Could say that." He had a small goatee between his bottom lip and his chin. She wondered if the goatee was to attract attention away from the mole. It didn't work.

"I was thinking of having some photos taken of me for my boyfriend," she said.

He laughed. "Yeah, and pigs fly."

"I was!"

"You want a tour of the studio, I take it?"

Angie hesitated to go anywhere with this guy, but this was her chance. "Yes, I would."

"Okay, but Grandma has to stay here. You go sit down, Granny," he said. "We'll be right back."

"I don't know," Mrs. Calamatti said, looking worried. "Angie?"

"It's okay. I won't be long," Angie said, hoping she was right. She didn't like the way this guy, whoever he was, was looking at her, but before she was able to say anything, he gripped her arm and led her through the door that had been kept so carefully shut.

Angie found herself in a large, warehouse-like movie studio, alive with activity. Making such movies, she suddenly realized, really was big business.

Mole Man led her by a series of cubicles with six-foot high partitions. Each cubicle appeared to be a movie set. Beds and precious little else were in the them, all arranged for the cameramen to do their work as quickly and efficiently as circumstances allowed. The cubicles were set up so that once a scene had climaxed, so to speak, the camera could swivel around to another cubicle's rising drama.

A woman wearing a short yellow robe stood with a thin, pock-marked man, in her hand a sheaf of papers. "Oh, oh, oh," she said. Her voice was a flat and nasal. She turned to the cameraman. "Do you think I expressed enough emotion? I don't know how I'm ever going to remember all these lines."

Angie nearly backed into a partition.

Off to the right, a group of people were standing around a brightly lit cubicle.

"They're filming," Mole Man whispered in her ear.

"Filming?"

"Want to see?"

She swallowed, then murmured, "Why not?" He led her through the group to a set illuminating a bed with sheets yellowed with dirt and age. On the bed, two G-string wearing women knelt. Seated between them was a man, fully dressed in a tuxedo and top hat, with a dopey look on his face. The scene, as best as Angie could tell, was that the women were trying to seduce the man, and one woman had to take off his clothes, while the other was supposed to slip ropes on his hands and feet without him knowing it.

"Action!" the director shouted.

Angie held her breath as the man's shirt came off and the ropes went around his hands. He lay flat on the bed, but then he had to scoot himself closer to the head of it for the ropes on his wrists to reach the bedposts. Angie figured verisimilitude was the last thing on anyone's mind.

One woman unzipped his trousers.

Angie's eyes nearly popped out of her head. Men in these movies didn't wear G-strings.

"*Cut!*" the director yelled.

Angie jumped, her attention now on the chubby, greasy-haired director.

"Dammit," he yelled. "I want the Statue of Liberty, not The Blob, for cryin' out loud!"

The man on the bed yanked the ropes loose, then lifted himself up onto his elbows. "Hell, all these hours, being poked and prodded and shoved around! I'm tired!" He jutted out his lower lip. "I'd like to see you do better."

The greasy-haired man turned purple. "Where's someone who can do something with Don Juan, here? Right now!"

Angie scooted away from the cubicle. She didn't know what anyone was going to do about Don Juan's problem, and she didn't want to know.

Mole Man took one look at her face and laughed out loud. She knew she looked shocked, but she couldn't help it.

He led her back to the reception area where Scotty and Whiskbroom Head were now waiting.

Whiskbroom Head turned about twenty shades paler than he had been as he looked at Angie and her "tour guide."

"Oh, my, Mr. Klaw, I didn't mean for these people to disturb you. I'm so sorry!" Whiskbroom Head looked ready to pass out.

"No problem." Klaw didn't look at his employee, instead he kept his gaze fixed on Angie. "Tell you what, sweetheart, you want to make photos, that can be arranged. You ask for me, Axel Klaw. I own this joint."

She swallowed hard, then put one hand on her hip and tried to look tough. "Sure thing, Axel. I'll be back."

"I look forward to it," he said, then gave her a toothy grin.

Scotty then hurried Angie and his aunt out of the studio.

25

Paavo and Rebecca turned over Wielund's German accounts to a specialist in Financial Crimes. While they were waiting for her findings, they had to work through the weekend as more and more pressure was being put on Homicide to find the killer.

Paavo didn't mind. Weekends were the worst time for him. Sitting at home on a Saturday night and thinking how, if he was smart, he'd be with Angie instead of his cat, were hard to take. Now, he was busy and that left less time to dwell on all he was missing.

With the connection found between Sheila Danning and the restaurant owners, Paavo took another look at Danning's murder investigation.

He began with discussions with Never-Take-A-Chance Bill Sutter and quickly realized Never-Take-A-Chance had done a piss-poor job. Now, Paavo and Rebecca needed to start over.

According to Sutter, if witnesses and friends could be believed, Sheila Danning had been such a loner she must have strangled herself.

Paavo wondered if her death might have somehow been the catalyst for everything else that had happened. But if so, why?

He looked over Danning's birth records, then contacted the authorities in Tacoma to ask if they could find out anything about her life there that might connect her to the murders taking place here now.

The police in her home town had, fortunately, done a thorough job investigating her background at the time of her death, talking to family, school friends, employers, and old boyfriends. The picture that emerged was of an ambitious girl with above-average looks and below-average brain-power, who wanted to make her mark in the world if it killed her, which it had.

Her life had become a blank after she moved to San Francisco. When her body was found she'd been easy to identify only because she'd applied for a passport so her fingerprints were on file. But although the police had a name, birthdate, and her hometown, and even her current job and address, they had been unable to find anyone who would want to kill her. It was finally decided that she had simply been in the wrong place—a pretty young woman walking alone in a large, woody sector of Golden Gate Park—and there she was strangled. There was no evidence of a sexual attack.

Interestingly, the crime scene unit didn't believe that was where she'd been killed. They didn't find any signs of the kind of struggle that most likely had taken place before she was strangled to death. But no other spot was found that met CSU's "criteria," so it was dropped.

Now, Mrs. Calamatti put the young woman near two big restaurants around the time she very likely had been killed.

Paavo and Rebecca went to the building that had housed Sheila Danning's small studio apartment and interviewed her neighbors. No one knew her well enough to say more than "hello," but they all had noticed that she seemed to be away more than home.

The detectives also talked to the apartment owner, who said Danning was often late with her rent, but would come through eventually. She seemed to be struggling, but the landlady knew no details. In short, they learned no more than Bill Sutter had.

They were about to leave when the landlady called them back. "I just remembered," she said, "a few times I saw a fancy-looking big blue car pull up in front of the house and wait there with the engine running. Sheila would run out to the car, and off they'd go."

Paavo glanced at Rebecca. "Wieland had a blue Audi."

"Henry," Angie said after their lunchtime show ended on Monday, and they were in the studio putting things away until the next day.

"Yes?"

"I've been thinking about how very much you know about food and its preparation." What she didn't say was that all the restaurant owners were abuzz with the news that Henry LaTour had managed to get Mark Dustman to be his chef at LaTour's Restaurant.

LaTour glanced smugly at her. "Oh, really? That's very complimentary of you, Angie. Yes, I do have quite a store of knowledge. But then, look at how white my hair is. Had to learn something in all those years. Ha, ha!"

"I can't help but wonder if having a restaurant isn't the key to learning so much."

He looked surprised. "You want to buy a restaurant?"

She smiled and shook her head. "Maybe someday. But, for now, I wouldn't mind working in one." Especially one with a fine chef like Mark Dustman, she thought, but didn't dare say. After all, Dustman had worked with Wielund. Perhaps from inside the kitchen she could learn some reason for these deaths.

"Restaurant work is grueling," LaTour said. "I don't know that you'd be up for it."

"I could do it!" she insisted. "What would you say to taking me on as your apprentice? I wouldn't expect you to pay me, of course. I'd do it for the learning experience—to work beside you and anyone else who might be a chef at LaTour's. I'd love to go to your restaurant's kitchen from time to time and soak in the knowledge there. I'll chop, clean vegetables, even wash dishes if it'd help."

Henry puffed up like a ball of yeasty dough. "That's very flattering, Angie, but I can't imagine you'd enjoy it."

"I certainly would. And all the best chefs in Europe have apprentices."

His eyebrows rose with interest. "They do?"

"Of course! It's a sign the chef has 'made it big.' As you have. So, can we try a couple of days a week? If it doesn't work out, well, then, that'll end it. So you'll get free labor at no cost. Is it a deal?"

He gloated. "How could I turn down such an offer! "

She smiled and quickly turned around so he wouldn't see her face. Despite her visit to the porn studio and all the hubbub surrounding Sheila Danning's photos, Angie was sure the restaurants were behind the murders of Karl Wielund and Chick Marcuccio. And she was going to find out why.

Paavo was typing up the useless interview he'd had on Sunday with Eunice Graves, owner of Europa restaurant, when Yosh came into the squad room. He tossed his notebook onto his desk.

"She's done it again," Yosh said.

Paavo looked up. "Who?"

Yosh took a deep breath. "Your Italian tornado."

Paavo's eyebrows rose. "Angie?"

Paavo had never seen Yosh scowl at him before. It wasn't a pretty sight. "Don't play innocent, Paavo. You *know* that every time we turn up to talk to a restaurant owner about Karl Wielund, she's already been there asking her questions. I was at Perestroika trying to get some information out of Vladimir Polotski, and he all but answered the questions before I even asked them."

Paavo tried to shrug it off. "She knows these people. It's just small talk."

"Small talk with someone who's dating the detective working on Wielund's and Marcuccio's murders!"

"We aren't dating. How many times do I have to say that? I told you I'm not seeing her anymore."

"You can say it all you want, but these people don't know that. They remember what they say to her and have to be sure they tell me the same thing. They all talk to each other, Paavo, you know that. Ask one a question, and fifteen of them chime in with the answer... and it's always the same answer. God damn. If I didn't know better, I'd think this was like *Murder on the Orient Express* where they're *all* guilty."

"I know the feeling."

"Paav, you've got to do something." From time to time, like now, Yosh's jolly façade would slip. His face would grow serious, his dark eyes grim, and Paavo could almost see the wheels turning in his logical mind. And now, Paavo knew, Yosh was right.

"I can't very well stop her from talking to her friends, Yosh."

"Don't you hear what your partner is telling you, man?" Calderon said as he stepped nearer. "You got to do something about her. You can't let your personal life mess up a murder investigation."

"My personal life isn't messing up a damn thing."

"No? That's not what I just heard Yosh say."

Paavo looked at his partner. He could see Yosh's hesitation. While Yosh didn't want to get involved in the constant bickering between Paavo and Calderon, at the same time, it seemed, he couldn't dispute Calderon's words. He shrugged, looked at the floor, then turned back to his desk, sat and began going through some papers.

"You got to face it, man," Calderon said. He pulled out the chair by Paavo's desk and straddled it backwards, his hands clutching the top chair rail.

Paavo just stared at him, the muscles in his jaws tight.

"Look, man, hanging out with a cop is just a lark for her. She can have anything money can buy, but one thing it can't buy is excitement. She's just some bimbo who finds murder exciting. She wants to be in the middle of it—gives her a thrill, you know? Maybe more than you do."

"Get the hell away from me, Calderon." Paavo's voice was icy.

Calderon stood and slammed the chair back against Paavo's desk. "Just remember when you get dumped after she learns the filth and ugliness this job's really about, remember we told you that you were being played for a sucker. *This* is the only family you got. The only one that matters. And don't ever forget it."

"She's not like that."

"They all are! I'm just warning you, nothing more."

Paavo slowly rose to his feet, eyeball to eyeball with Calderon. If possible, his voice had grown even colder. "Who made you my savior?"

Yosh quickly stepped between the two. He put his hand on Calderon's shoulder and turned the man as he spoke. "Thanks, Luis. It's five o'clock. Time for all of us to get out of here. It's been a long day. A long week."

Calderon shook his head as he walked away toward the door. When he reached it, he turned and looked at a still-seething Paavo. "You know, man, *pavo* means turkey in Spanish. You're really livin' up to your name." With that, he stomped out the door.

Paavo stared after him, brows knitted.

"The problem's with his wife," Yosh said softly.

Paavo spun around to stare at his partner. "Carlota?"

Yosh nodded. "She told him she's had it. Wants a divorce. Same old story."

Yosh didn't have to say any more. With a sinking heart, Paavo knew. All cops knew. Too many nights Calderon's wife had to stay alone when she needed him with her, too many promises that things would change that never did. Too much danger. Too much worry. Too much loneliness. "She walked?"

Yosh nodded. "Took the kids and went to her mother's somewhere around San Diego."

Paavo remembered the pained expression on Calderon's face. He'd thought it was anger. Now he knew it went a lot deeper. Something in him twisted for another man's pain, for his own emptiness. "Hell."

If Carlota Calderon couldn't handle this life, Angie didn't stand a chance.

"All right," he said quietly. "I've got Angie out of my private life. Now she has to be out of my public one as well."

Yosh looked surprised but gladdened by this sudden change. "That's what I was saying."

"Do whatever you can to let the restaurant owners know that Angie no longer has any connection to any of us. Word will spread and you won't have to worry about her interference anymore."

Yosh gave him a long look. "You sure about this, partner? I mean, she'll hear as well."

"Maybe this way she'll believe it. So yes, I want it done."

"Okay, it will be. Listen, Paav, why don't you go home on time for once? Take it easy. It's five o'clock. Quitting time."

Paavo glanced at the pile of lab reports he had to read and notes he had to write up. "What the hell? Why not?" He grabbed his jacket and shrugged it on as he headed out the door.

Earlier that day, Paavo had gotten a text message from Angie saying that she had what he wanted and he should call her as soon as he was a free.

She had what he wanted in more ways than one. But he'd broken things off with her, to a degree, and now, one text from her and he was ready to go running back?

Damned right.

But he also convinced himself that by seeing her, he could explain that she needed to stop talking to her friends about his cases. He would even let her know how upset the other detectives were by her interference. And then he'd end it by repeating, firmly, that he simply couldn't see her any more.

He no longer had a choice in the matter.

But as always, as he approached her apartment door, anticipation made his heart thump a little harder. This time, he tried hard to squelch the feeling. This time, he reminded himself of the words her father had spoken, and that the man had been right. Paavo would hear what she had texted him about and then leave. He knocked.

She opened the door. "Hello! Thank you for coming by."

The smile he'd missed seeing lit her face, but he also saw the caution in her eyes. He felt his own wariness, despite the emotions that roiled through him, so he said nothing, but marched sternly into the room.

The living room was dark except for the blue glow from her television. Watching T.V. wasn't like her—she much preferred to read and listen to music. Moans and heavy breathing caused him to walk over to the T.V. He couldn't believe what he saw.

"What's this? The *Playboy* channel?" he asked.

She switched on some lamps. "No. I bought three movies. Research." She pointed to the DVDs on the coffee table.

He turned his back to the television set and picked up the disks. "*Behind the Green Door, Deep Throat,* and *Debbie Does Dallas.* Are you kidding me?"

"I heard these are the 'classics,' the ones to watch. I was curious after what I'd learned about Sheila Danning, so I bought them—cash sale. I didn't want to leave a trail back to me." She grinned. "They don't have much of a story line, but hey, if my radio career doesn't work out..."

He shut his eyes and took a deep breath. He knew her well enough to know she wasn't looking at these movies out of curiosity, and he was steadying himself for what the truth behind this just might be.

He shut off the T.V. "All right, Angie. Tell me all about it."

"You'll never guess what I found out!" She looked beyond ready to tell him. "But first, how about a beer? Or, if you have to go back to work, maybe coffee? And I've got nuts, and chips, and—"

"A beer sounds good."

Since he enjoyed Guinness a lot, that was what she brought him, pouring it slowly into a glass so the head was creamy, just the way he liked it.

She then sat on the sofa, primly folded her hands in her lap, and with an angelic smile announced, "The Sheila Danning photos are from a studio on Dwight and Telegraph in Berkeley."

He thought there was little Angie could do that might still surprise him, but he was wrong. In a strained voice he asked, "How could you possibly know that?"

She looked well pleased with herself as she explained. "Scotty, Mrs. C's nephew, brought us with him to the studio. Of course, I wanted to make sure it was the right spot before I told you. And Scotty said he was sure that one of the, uh, rooms they used for Sheila's photos had the same purple-and-pink background as in the photos you had."

"He *what?*"

"And I even," she announced, "watched them shoot a movie."

He was floored. "You aren't talking about a pornographic movie, right?"

She couldn't stop a small grin. "I am."

"Good God!"

She laughed at his shock. "I agree! It was kind of fascinating, although more than a little weird."

He grimaced. "Look nobody waltzes into a porno studio and gets them to give you a guided tour. What's the real story?"

Her eyebrows rose indignantly. "That is the real story. I simply told them I wanted some photos taken of me."

His heart plummeted to his stomach. She wasn't joking. He stood. Every ounce of his self-control was gone, vanished. As she sat there looking up at him, all he could think of was the horrible risk she'd taken, and all he could feel was fury. "Don't you know those people can be dangerous?" he bellowed. "Especially if they realize you're just being nosy about them?"

She leaned back against the sofa. "I know it. But what they're doing isn't illegal in California."

"But the people in that business are no saints," he shouted, "in case you haven't heard!"

"I know that!" she yelled back. "And I'll admit, I was even a little scared at first. But I knew I could get out of there. I had Mrs. Calamatti and her nephew with me!"

"Oh, yeah. Great!" He paced, trying to calm himself. It didn't work. He stopped in front of her bending low. "So you took the chance of meeting with dangerous people making videos that are illegitimate in *most* of this country, and you learned that one of the rooms used *might* have once had a *backdrop* that looked like the one in the Danning photo?"

"Well, yes, but Scotty was sure—"

"*Who cares what he thought! What if you couldn't get away? What if they tried to force you to...to...*" He couldn't say any of the horrible things that flashed into his mind, things he'd heard had happened to women in such places, women with no idea what they were getting into. He ran his fingers through his hair. She just didn't know how quickly things could turn ugly, or how bad it could get.

"Nothing happened," she said. The enthusiasm she'd had when she told him about finding the studio vanished from her face.

It tore at him, but he couldn't stop himself from raging at her. "I can't believe you'd be so foolish! What in the hell did you think you were doing?"

She folded her arms. He could see the red spots of anger forming on her cheeks. "I was trying to help you. And Chick! He was my friend. If those photos had anything to do with why Karl was killed, and if Karl's death had anything to do with Chick's murder, then it's my business as well as yours!"

He pointed his finger at her. "You have got to stay away from all this. Whoever's behind it is very likely responsible for at least three murders—Wielund, Chick, and Wielund's landlord. And possibly four, if he also killed Sheila Danning. It's too dangerous for you to go snooping around."

She jumped to her feet, her nose near his, or as near as

possible with a ten-inch difference in height between them. "I'd stay away from all this *if*, Mr. Inspector, you and your force would be able to catch Chick's killer. I don't see that happening, though, do I?"

"I'm warning you, Angie. Keep out of it." He drew in his breath. "I don't want you getting any more involved in Chick's *or* Wielund's murders."

"Involved? But I didn't—"

"I don't want you asking the restaurant owners, or Wielund's employees, or Mark Dustman, or Eileen Powell, or anyone else, anything about Karl Wielund. The same goes for Chick's friends and employees."

"What do you mean? Those people were my friends."

"*And I don't trust a single one of them.* And if, by chance, you stumbled across the one who's guilty, do you realize the danger you could be in?"

"Nonsense!"

"When you talk about the case, they think your words are coming from me, or from some other inside information you might have."

She folded her arms. "So what?"

"When we question them, they answer with whatever they've already told you."

"*Already?* So, that's it! You're mad because I've been ahead of you. I've gotten there first. Well, I guess I must apologize for being so prompt at *your* job!" She turned her back on him.

"Just keep away."

"Don't worry. I will. Especially if you're there!"

He walked toward the door, but as his hand touched the doorknob, he couldn't help but glance once more at Angie, still with her back to him, one foot tapping angrily. He felt as if his heart had dropped like an ugly, black stone to somewhere near the floor. His gaze slowly drifted up her high, high heels, her shapely legs, nicely rounded derriere, and tiny waist before he forced his eyes away from her. But then he took in her apartment—richly beautiful, yet with warmth and comfort... just like Angie.

Hers was a world so different from the one he knew he wouldn't have believed it real had he not seen it for himself.

She glanced over her shoulder at him, her expression quizzical as if wondering why he hadn't left yet. As his gaze met hers, he steeled himself against her pull. Somehow, he found the humility to say, "Thank you for finding all this out, and for letting me know. Now, please, leave the rest of the investigation up to me."

And then he walked out the door.

Paavo got word from Nona Farraday that Mark Dustman had started his new job at Henry LaTour's restaurant. She didn't know if it meant anything to his case, but she let him know in case it mattered. Paavo thanked her, and he and Yosh decided it was time for another interview with Dustman.

They found him in LaTour's kitchen.

"Things should change for the better at LaTour's soon," Dustman said.

"Why do you say that?" Paavo asked.

"Because I'm preparing the food here now."

"I thought you'd wanted to keep Wielund's open?" Paavo asked.

"I did. But Karl's family wouldn't cooperate, the fools. I'll have the last laugh, though, because without me the place is worthless. They'll get nothing from its sale."

"From everything I've heard, working at LaTour's is a step down from Wielund's. Why take a lesser position?"

"I wanted a job where I could run things my way. Here, I can. Henry LaTour knows he's a lousy cook. He'll let me be in charge."

A female voice rang out from the doorway. "Isn't that a little harsh, Mark?"

Paavo felt his blood in his temples begin to pound. He knew that voice. Angie. He slowly turned.

She was wearing a jaunty white pants suit with a nautical look. The double-breasted gold buttons and braiding on the waist-length jacket caused him to notice that she filled out the jacket in a way sailors never did. Her short hair was a tumble of curls today, falling onto her forehead and framing her face, making her lashes seem longer than usual, her eyes wider and more shiny.

She ignored him, though, and kept her attention on Dustman as he crossed the room toward her. "What a surprise! I didn't think you meant it when you said you'd come by this afternoon to help."

"Of course I meant it." She gave him a hug. Paavo's teeth ground watching them, and a volcanic swelling in his chest told him this wasn't something he could put up with for long. Luckily, they broke it off, and Dustman turned to face the inspectors, his arm still around Angie's shoulders.

Paavo had the strong desire to take Dustman's hand, which held Angie's shoulder a little to snugly, a little too possessively, and make sure LaTour's new chef couldn't use it to even pick up a soup spoon for several days.

"I'm being quizzed here by two of San Francisco's finest," Dustman explained to Angie. "But, of course, you already know them."

"I do," Angie said. "How have you been, Inspector Smith?" She raised her brows ever so superciliously as she gazed at him.

"Better than ever," he replied, keeping his voice as calm and steady as possible given the provocation.

Yosh's head swiveled from Angie to Paavo, then he moved closer to the refrigerators, as if he feared being too close to the line of fire.

"Gentlemen, I must tell you, this is the best restaurant critic in the country," Dustman said to the detectives. "She was the first one to give Wielund's a wonderful review. I still have it on the wall in my living room, Angie."

"You're so sweet, Mark. That's a quality I appreciate in a man."

Paavo's teeth clenched.

"I'd say we're done here," Yosh announced, with a hand on Paavo's shoulder. "If we think of anything more, Mr. Dustman, we'll give you a call."

"Very good," Dustman said.

Yosh started toward the door, nudging Paavo ahead of him.

"If you need to ask me anything about Karl or Chick," Angie called, "I'll probably be here for many, *many* hours."

Paavo's step faltered. His jaw tightened as he glanced over his shoulder to see Mark beaming down at her like the fox who just had a chicken walk into his den.

"Paav," Yosh called in a hushed voice.

Paavo nodded and led the way out of the restaurant.

Once Paavo and Yosh had gone, Angie stepped away from Dustman to look at the menu and decide for herself what she could help with. Anything but julienning more carrots.

Dustman looked confused. "You were acting pretty friendly, Angie. It couldn't have had anything to do with the cop who was glaring at us, would it?"

"Don't be silly," she said, sharpening a knife.

"Yeah, right," Dustman said and then hurried from the kitchen to deal with the supplier about the poor quality of the supposedly fresh vegetables. With him gone, Angie finally found a chance to do what she'd taken the intern job for. She wanted to look at both LaTour's and Dustman's notebooks and recipe collections. LaTour reading off that fancy pork tender-loin recipe still bothered her. Where had he gotten it?

As much as she hated what these murders were doing to her relationship with Paavo, she couldn't just sit back and do nothing after her friends had been murdered.

Mark Dustman's chef's log of recipes sat open on his work-table. Angie sat down and began going through it.

She turned a page, and suddenly the handwriting changed. The way the numbers 1, 7 and 9 were written now looked German. She'd spent time in Germany and knew some of their handwritten letters and numbers differed from the way they were written in the US. She realized this had to have been Karl's chef's log.

The notebook might not have been Dustman's to take, but she could understand why he did so. It would have been a shame for a bunch of lawyers to get it. They would either over-rate the value and lock it up, or underrate it and throw the log book away. Either way, Karl's recipes would have been be lost.

She read through several recipes and knew why any chef would want this log book. Quickly scanning the pages for the pork tenderloin recipe, she was frankly stunned when it wasn't there. She then started looking over the recipes more carefully, but stopped when she reached one for fresh cream truffles. At the bottom of the page was a number: 911,394.

For some reason, it seemed familiar. And then she remem-bered... 9-1-1. The DVDs Paavo had in his briefcase had numbers on them that also began with the emergency call number.

She wasn't sure if the numbers, other than that, were at all similar. Numbers weren't exactly what she'd been focused on at the time.

Why would Karl write the number down on this recipe? She copied it. Maybe someone should take a look at it?

She could tell Paavo about it, and he could tell the Berkeley

P.D. But what good would that do?

On the other hand, she probably could get back inside the porno studio without much trouble. She went once, and no one bothered her, despite Paavo ranting and raving at her about her visit there. The place was filled with people—women as well as men. How dangerous could it be, really? And it wasn't illegal in this state.

But then, Sheila Danning was dead.

"What do you think you're doing!"

Angie jumped a mile as Mark Dustman's voice boomed out at her. She'd been so lost in thought she hadn't even heard him come back in. "Nothing." She shut the notebook and stood.

Dustman's jaw twitched. "So. you found my little secret."

"I don't suppose you told his family about it," she said.

"I was more like family than any of them! Besides, none of them cook."

"So, it doesn't matter then."

He put his hands on his hips and took the notebook from her. "Look, I need these recipes to turn this restaurant around. It was part of the deal I made with LaTour when he took me on. He wanted to see Karl's recipes, and wants me to put some of them on LaTour's menu."

"Why?"

"These gems will give me—and Henry—a chance to make something of ourselves. Something big. Okay?" Passion blazed in his eyes.

It wasn't her business to get into this. Particularly since she could sympathize with his ardor. To a chef, recipes were works of art, and Karl was a great artist. An artist whose work might have been lost if it weren't for Mark. She knew what he'd done was wrong, but she also meant it when she said, "I'm glad you'll keep Karl's work alive."

He shut his eyes a moment as if in thanks, then turned around to sort out the vegetables he'd just bought.

Angie stood outside the plain glass door in Berkeley with the number she'd found in Wielund's notebook clasped in her hand. She looked at it one more time, memorizing it, then put it in her jacket pocket. Surely, she needn't worry about going inside again. There wasn't anything frightening about the place. Not really. It was a legitimate business establishment... a type she'd never dealt with before... but legitimate nonetheless. There was nothing for her to be frightened about.

Why then was her stomach jumping maniacally?

She opened the door and went up the stairs to the reception area. Whiskbroom Head sat at the front counter just as the last time she was there. She shivered, but walked toward him.

He pushed his thick glasses higher on his nose, eying her every step. "Well, I didn't think I'd see you again."

"I'd like to see Mr. Klaw. He invited me to return. I would like some photos taken of me."

His eyes widened as his eyes glided over her body. She was glad she was wearing a thickly padded jacket. "Mr. Klaw isn't here now. But he'll be back soon."

Perfect, she thought. "I don't mind waiting. In fact, if you have a storeroom with some photos, I'd love to look at them to find a style or pose that I think will suit me. If you don't mind, of course."

He frowned. "I don't know about that."

"Also, if I find a movie that sounds interesting," she said, lying through her teeth, "maybe we could watch it together, and you could give me some pointers on acting in these videos."

"Oh?" He gulped, but then a grin slowly spread over his face. "Yeah, why not? Okay, come with me."

"Do you have a catalogue?" she asked as they walked into the studio.

"No."

"No? You just keep canisters of film lying around without knowing what's in them?"

"Film? No way. Everything's on computers now, and some of the older stuff's on DVDs. You can see outtake photos."

"That sounds fine. I'll look at those."

"You can hang your jacket on this hook," he added. "I want you to be comfortable."

Angie quickly unbuttoned it and hung it. She had put on a black, very well-fitting jumpsuit with a wide and long gold zipper down the front. She had no idea why she ever bought the jumpsuit, and had never worn it... until now. The way Whiskbroom Head's eyes—huge behind his eyeglasses—gawked at the zipper, she realized why she'd never been comfortable wearing it before.

As he led her to a dark, dusty, back room filled with file boxes of folders. The folders were all labelled with six-digit numbers similar to the one she found on Wielund's recipe.

"Here you go," Whiskbroom Head said.

Angie looked over the room. The good news was that she'd been right about the number being part of a catalog. The bad news was that there were so many file boxes in the room.

Paavo knew a waste of time when it kicked him in the face, and this was a waste of time. The accounting books from Sorrento were spread over his desk. Leaning back in his chair, he rubbed his eyes. Clearly, Chick hadn't been cooking his books, and from the profits he saw coming in, plus his personal finances, Chick hadn't needed to.

His gaze moved from the accounting books to a stack of folders from files about cases that had been closed out, plus a few magazine articles. His review of the Sheila Danning case led him into general reading about the world of pornography from both sides of the camera as well as a number of case studies from Vice, Homicide and Missing Persons.

The women in these stories were universally so incredibly naïve he had trouble believing they were real until he remembered that a certain miss he had been close to also surprised him with her naïveté. Even the hard ones, the ones who grew up with abuse and drugs and sold their bodies from the time they learned they were salable, still seemed to have some hope that these films could offer them a way out, a way to riches or an escape to the kind of life they could only dream of. They were in it for the money, only to find that the money was hardly enough to buy the escape offered by drugs.

The men who took part in these films, on the other hand, Paavo found to be a complete enigma. He couldn't begin to comprehend what kind of sickness might lead a man to perform on camera like that.

His telephone rang.

"Smith, here."

"Officer McGifford, Berkeley. We just spotted afore-mentioned female going into the building at 9699 Dwight Way. Reporting as instructed, sir."

Paavo froze. "The woman with the Ferrari?"

"Yes, sir."

"She's there now?"

"She just walked in."

"Thank you."

Paavo hung up the phone, simultaneously gripped with outrage and worry. *I cannot believe her!* He'd told her not to go back to that place. Warned her about it. Did she listen to him? Did she *ever* listen to him?

He looked at the horrific files he'd been reading and a cold shudder went down his back. "Yosh," he called. "Time for a field trip."

As soon as she was alone, Angie started to look through the files. They were sort of in numerical order, though someone did a pretty sloppy filing job. She went through them until she found the one labelled 911,394, the number in Karl's cooking notes.

She opened it, stared, then quickly shut the folder. Her body trembled as her mind had trouble accepting the face she'd just seen. Trying to control the sudden shaking of her hands, she opened the file again, quickly perused the photos and then pulled out one, turned it face down, and shoved the folder back into its spot in the file.

She left the room to head back to the front counter when she saw Whiskbroom Head approaching her. "I believe I'll simply buy this one shot," she said, holding up the photo she had found. "I want to show my boyfriend and see if this is the kind of pose he likes."

"Wait a minute," he said with a scowl. "We were supposed to watch those films together."

"I'm sorry. I've changed my mind."

She tried to continue to the entry area when he stepped in

front of her, blocking her path. "You don't get to just waltz in here and look at all this for free, you know. You got to pay... one way or another."

She looked him straight in the eye. "I will. For this one photo. How much?"

Whiskbroom Head glanced at her clothes, her shoes, as he stroked his beard. "Three hundred bucks."

"Three hundred! That's outrageous!"

"It's a bargain. Less than the shoes you're wearing, for sure."

"Oh," she glanced at her feet. "Well, if you put it that way. Do you take plastic?"

He walked her back to the reception area. "A personal check will be fine. I'll trust you." He then sat at the counter and gave her a wide smile, the green on his teeth turning Angie's stomach.

As she filled out the check he said, "Make it out to Dwayne Cartwright."

"Wrong, Dwayne," a deep, booming voice said.

Angie spun around. "Mr. Klaw," she said, and then forced a smile. That day he wore lots of heavy gold jewelry around his neck, wrists and fingers. He had on a thin, almost see-through cotton tee-shirt and over it a light blue jacket with silver sparkles.

"You can call me Axel."

"Shall I write the check out to you?"

"Sure."

She gave him the check, took the photo, and started for the stairs.

"Not so fast." Powerful fingers gripped her wrist firmly as he glanced at the name and address on her check. "Tell me, Angelina Amalfi of Green Street in San Francisco, whatever makes a sweet young thing like you interested in this stuff?" He stuffed the check in his pocket.

A long moment passed before she could find her voice. "My... my boyfriend—"

He released her wrist, but slowly shook his head as she spoke. "Uh, uh. You aren't the type for boyfriends like that."

She blanched. "Bad taste in men, I guess." Her laugh was hollow. She stepped back from him. "I've got to go. Thank you for your help."

Klaw grabbed the picture from her.

"Hey!" she cried

He turned it over, his eyes narrowing as he glanced from the picture to Angie. "Why this one?"

"I don't know. I looked at a bunch and liked that one."

Klaw grimaced. "You know her, don't you?"

The world seemed to shift, and she was careful not to look him in the eye. "Me? No. Should I?"

Klaw chuckled. "Maybe."

Angie kept her face immobile. "Well, I have no idea what you're talking about. And on second thought, I don't have to take that photo. Anyone will do, as long as it's old. 'Oldies But Goodies,' that's what my boyfriend says. But then, he's sixty-five, so that's probably why he feels that way. I don't care myself. Any age is--"

"Shut your trap!" Klaw turned to Dwayne. "Why were you helping her?"

Dwayne's Adam's apple bobbed a couple of times before he found his voice. "I... she... I... she said she wanted to be in a movie."

"Be in a movie?" Klaw looked her up and down, then burst out laughing. "Don't that beat all? I get it, *Angelina*. Guess you aren't quite the 'little angel' you pretend to be, are you?"

Angie blanched. "On second thought, I changed my mind. My boyfriend's a big fan of these movies, that's all."

"That so? And what's this boyfriend's name?"

Her mind went blank. "Steve," she answered.

"You're lying," Klaw said. "All this boyfriend jazz is nothing but an excuse."

"An excuse?" Her voice was tiny. Klaw couldn't possibly know about Paavo, or her restaurant background. Could he?

He folded his arms. "You're just some rich bitch who wants a little fun. A thrill. You want to make one of these movies but you don't have the nerve to come right out and say it. I've seen your type before. Plenty of times. And I can be *very* accommodating."

She felt a chill down her back. "It's not true."

Klaw laughed, then wrapped his arm around her waist and directed her once more through the door behind Whiskbroom Head. "Women come here and then get cold feet. Don't worry. I'll hold your hand along with anything else you'd like held. And I like your outfit—swanky and seductive. The kind of outfit that gives a man ideas. You got class. Something lacking in a lot of these films. Let's see how you do on camera."

Angie couldn't believe this man was touching her, let alone taking her anywhere. Panic filled her, but she did all she could to hide it. Digging in her heels, she pushed him away from her. "Let go of me! I said I've changed my mind."

He chuckled. "So, you want to get rough? I can oblige you in that, too."

She was shocked. "This is no game."

"You're good. I like the tone. You'll be great on camera. Freddie will take you to the 'studio.' I'll be right behind you." He snapped his fingers.

Out of nowhere, a mountain of a man stepped up behind her, between her and the exit. He looked like a bouncer at some of the clubs Angie's friends liked to go to. Her heart beat so hard she felt her whole body tremble. "You can't do this to me!" she yelled at Klaw. "I'm going home!"

Klaw grabbed her arms and yanked her in front of him so hard and so fast she nearly stumbled into him. She felt trapped as he gripped the back of her neck with long, hard fingers. Dread and confusion filled her as she stared into gray eyes as flat and devoid of feeling as those of a dead fish. She pushed hard against him, but it was like trying to shove her way past a steel door. Suddenly, with an evil grin, he relaxed his grip. "To think, I expected today to be boring."

She drew in deep, gasping breaths as her fear grew. Somehow, she needed to get free of him, but how? He was stronger than she'd expected and, instinctively, she knew pleading would do no good.

He waited a mere second or two before he cupped her jaw in his hand and roughly lifted, forcing her head back, her face upward. Unwanted tears filled her eyes, and she tried to blink them away, scared of his reaction at seeing her weakness. He leaned forward, his nose almost touching hers. She felt his breath against her face as he spoke. "First lesson in film. I'm the producer. That's like God around here. Life and death are in my hands." His fingers ran along her neck, then dipped lower to stroke her collarbone. She recoiled, but was too petrified to dare to stop him. "So remember, I can do anything to you I damn well please."

He grinned at her again, as if relishing her reactions to him, then stepped back. "She's all yours, Freddie."

Klaw pushed Angie into the bearlike arms of his personal mountain man. She tilted her head back to see a man about her age with curly brown hair, dark eyes, wearing a white sports jacket, and a red shirt open to show off his numerous chest hairs and a thick, gold chain. The smell coming off him was an acrid mixture of a cheap men's cologne and sweat. A scar across his top lip caused it to pucker at one side, as if he had a perpetual sneer.

"Let go of me," she demanded.

Klaw smirked, and with a waved of his hand directed Freddie to take her away. The big man did let her go, but then gave her a push forward. When she refused to keep going, he took her arm and dragged her along as if she weighed no more than a rag doll. She yelled at him to get his hands off her, but he paid no attention.

He gave her what he called a "tour" of the various cubicles and all that was going on within them, so she would "know how things work around here," he told her. Then he pushed her into the cubicle where they'd been filming the last time she'd been here and flipped on the light switch.

Angie faced Freddie. A camera stood at the edge of the room, while tall spotlights pointed down at the big, brass double bed.

"You've got to be joking," Angie said, hands on hips, doing all she could to sound strong and masterful, despite the raw terror building within her.

"Mr. Klaw never jokes," Freddie answered, his words slowly spoken.

So, the man could speak without drooling, she thought, as fear turned to blind hatred of him and everything he and Axel Klaw represented. "Sorry, Freddie, but I get stage fright. I'm leaving."

"You can't go until Mr. Klaw says."

Her eyes narrowed. "Watch me."

She tried to walk out of the cubicle, but Freddie stepped in front of her, his arms folded.

She took a side-step.

So did he.

Quickly, she glanced around and saw that the back partition had a door. She sprinted toward it. Freddie ran after her.

She grabbed the doorknob just as Freddie's hands took hold of her waist. She turned the knob, but the door didn't open. Freddie tried to drag her away. Putting both hands on the knob, she pulled harder. So did Freddie. Clutching the knob with all her might, she tugged at the door refusing to let go. She felt the partition move, convincing her it could lead to freedom.

Freddie wrapped his arms around her waist, trying to haul her away. Her feet lifted right off the floor. But she wasn't called stubborn for nothing.

29

A short while earlier, Paavo and Yosh had hurried up the wooden stairs to the porno studio. A dark-haired man sat behind the counter talking to a blond man whose back was to them. Then the blond man turned around.

Paavo felt as if someone had plunged him into an ice bath. For an instant, time stood still, and he was fourteen years old again. Afraid, grieving, and filled with cold, black hate.

It had been too many years, Paavo told himself. His eyes were playing tricks on him. Or, his imagination was.

His memory had to have faded from the time he first searched for this man. No, not *this* man, but someone who resembled him. The flat gray eyes weren't really the same, were they? Nor was the big, black mole on the man's cheek. Before him, now, couldn't be the man he'd searched for, for so long.

He was stockier than Paavo remembered, and his hair was a little thinner, a little shorter, a lot blonder, but that was all. The protruding lower lip, the heavy-lidded, darting eyes, the mole...

They were the same.

"Axel Klaw," the man said, holding out his hand. "What can I do for you?"

Paavo tried to shake off the feeling, but it was as if he were looking at the man through a microscope, and all his features were enlarged and overwhelming. Paavo could barely stand the thought of touching the offered hand. "Paavo Smith, Homicide, SFPD. This is Inspector Yoshiwara."

Klaw shook hands with both. "What seems to be the problem?"

Suddenly the past vanished, and blood rushed to Paavo's head, throbbing and pounding its way through him. Angie! She was here, with this man! Klaw stepped back from the icy force of the blue eyes focused on him.

"A young woman was seen entering these offices. We're here to pick her up," Paavo said. The chilled, unemotional voice seemed to come from someone else, not him.

"Many young women come in here."

"She's little--"

"Most of my women are short. They aren't your typical models, you see."

"Dark hair—"

"More common than blonds."

There were more questions, lots more questions that he wanted to ask, that he would ask. Someday. Soon.

"Her name's Angie."

"Doesn't ring a bell, Inspector."

The same smirk. Years ago, he hadn't been able to stop his sister from going off with this man. The coincidence was almost too much, yet he'd known every minute of his life that someday his path would cross this man's again. He just never bargained on Angie being in the middle when it did. It was like being caught in a nightmare.

Paavo snapped. Despite all the years of training, he gripped Klaw by the lapels of his sparkling blue jacket and jerked his face nearer. "You damn well better get some bells ringing." Each word was spoken with chilling exactness.

"Paav," Yosh cautioned, his hand on Paavo's back.

Klaw raised his arms."Hey, there, copper. I ain't done nothing. You've got no right—"

"I got every right, Klaw." Still seething, Paavo let him go. "She came in here. I want her *now*."

Klaw tried to schmooze. "Look, inspector, these broads, they all change their names, anyway. I mean, none of them come here and tell the truth, so I don't pay attention to what they say. If a young woman wants to come up here, to work for me,"—he smiled—"*with* me, I got to be a most obliging fellow."

A muscle in Paavo's face twitched at Klaw's words. "You get her now or you won't be able to jaywalk without doing time. Is that clear? You want to be shut down, Klaw? It's the easiest thing in the world."

Just then they heard a loud crash. Screams and shouts rang out, then another crash. It sounded like a filming of *Debbie Does the Terminator*.

Paavo and Klaw ran to the door, pulled it open, and stopped, their mouths gapping at the scene before them.

What had once been a movie studio, all carefully partitioned off, looked like the set of a biblical epic—Jericho, after the walls came a-tumbling down. Partitions had fallen, lighting equipment was strewn on the floor, and cameras knocked off their stands lay broken. A bewildered jumble of voices filled the dusty, poorly lit room. Paavo and Klaw glanced at each other briefly, as if each expected the other to offer an explanation.

Dazed, naked actors scrambled to their feet, using their hands to cover and protect their professional assets. Shrieking actresses sat bolt up-right on the beds and couches they'd been performing on, holding sheets and clothing under their necks, either because of newfound modesty, or to keep the dust and dirt off their well-oiled bodies. Cameramen and stage-hands stood stupefied, as if wondering how to begin to put everything back in order.

A bruising hulk of a man pushed a partition off himself, and struggled to his feet. He brushed off his once-white sports jacket and reached up as if to be sure the thick gold chain still dangled from his neck.

"Freddie," Klaw thundered. "What the hell's going on here? How'd this happen?"

"Me? I didn't do nothing! That dumb broad tried to go through a phony door, for Chrissake. She wouldn't let go, and pulled down the whole goddamn set. Then everything started falling."

Klaw turned purple. "Can't you do anything right?"

"Where is she?" Paavo demanded.

"What?" Freddie frowned at Paavo.

"I said *where is she?*"

Freddie turned and looked at the mess around him, and scratched his head. "I don't know. I kinda lost track of her."

"Goddamn!" Paavo ran to the area where Freddie had been. "Angie!" he shouted, anguish at what he might find filling him as he tore through partitions, lighting structures, and broken, tumbled furnishings, searching for her, needing to find her.

"Look at this mess," Klaw bellowed. "She's done a *Thelma and Louise* on me."

"They make films for us?" Freddie asked.

"Shut-up, jerk. Do something about this."

"Let me shoot her, boss," Freddie pleaded.

"You don't know where she is."

"I could find her."

Klaw told Freddie he couldn't find an intimate part of his own body.

"Paavo," Yosh called. "Stop. I've got her."

There in the doorway, beside Yosh, stood Angie. Relief

surged through Paavo, as he stepped over the debris to reach her.

"She snuck out the back," Yosh said. "And would have been long gone except that I told her you were in here looking for her."

Paavo grabbed her shoulders, studying her, and swallowing hard at the outfit she was wearing. "Are you okay?"

She nodded, then stared without expression at the warehouse. "Now I know how the domino theory works."

Paavo saw that despite her flippant words, she was more than a little shell-shocked and frightened. He touched her arm. It was ice cold. His throat tightened so he could scarcely speak, and couldn't help but wrap his arms around her and thanking God she was safe. "Come on. Let's get out of here."

"That man is crazy," she said, trembling as she looked past Paavo's shoulder.

Paavo turned to see Klaw marching toward them. The thought of Angie's reaction to the man made Paavo murderous. He held her closer.

"These broads." Klaw chuckled at her. "They all think they're gonna be Linda Lovelace, but then they get scared and freak out. Too bad. I thought this one showed a real talent."

Paavo led Angie to the top of the stairs, but before leaving, looked back at Klaw. "You're going to wish you'd never said that."

Klaw shrugged and walked away.

30

"Is she all right?" Yosh asked when they were on the sidewalk.

"She seems pretty woozy. I'll take her to the hospital," Paavo said.

"No, Paavo," she said, doing her best to pull herself together, even while rubbing her wrists and fingers. "It was scary when all that stuff started to fall, but luckily, most of it landed on Freddie's big body. He made a good shield. I'll be all right."

"I want to be sure."

Angie began to chuckle, then her laugh grew harder until she couldn't stop the tears that suddenly ran down her cheeks.

Paavo held her close, a worried frown on his face. "Calm down, Angie. You're all right now."

"I'm not hysterical," she said, her arms circling his back as she looked up at him. "At least, I don't think I am. It's just that when the partitions started going down I saw..., well, let's just say I didn't think the human body could do the things going on in there." She shook her head. "Then I started running."

Paavo arched his eyebrows.

She leaned against his broad chest, her head on his shoulder, luxuriating in the security and goodness he offered her, so completely different from the sick hell-hole she just left. "I'll tell you about it someday. But you'll think I was hallucinating."

Yosh whistled softly. "Remember, Paav, it's standard procedure to share what you learn with your partner."

"Yeah, right," Paavo said handing Yosh his car keys. "I'll use Angie's car for now. In the meantime, why don't you start the paperwork for a search warrant on that place? I plan to go through it with a fine-tooth comb."

"No sweat, partner. Take care of her, and I'll call you soon as I get the warrant. And don't forget to tell me whatever you learn. I mean, I'm always eager to help."

Flashing his badge, Paavo by-passed the usual mountain of paperwork at San Francisco's Emergency Hospital to get Angie into a doctor as soon as possible. When the doctor finished his examination, he told Paavo she had a few bruises, several sprained fingers, and sore hands and wrists when she wouldn't let go of the doorknob, but she'd be okay. He saw that she was pretty shaken and gave her some medicine for the pain of the sprains and a sedative to help her sleep.

"Paavo," she said, her brow furrowed, when they were back in her car, "Klaw knows my address. I gave him a check. You don't think he'd..." She bit her bottom lip.

Paavo placed his hand over hers, trying to soothe her despite his own fears for her safety. "He won't bother you. He thinks you were someone who was too curious and too foolish for your own good. That's all."

"Let's hope," she said warily.

"But it'll be a good idea for you to stay at my house tonight," he quickly added.

"You just said I'll be all right." Her voice was tiny and fearful.

"Yes... But I don't like the idea of you being alone after the doctor gave you that sedative."

"I see." She glanced over at him. "Okay."

The fear in her voice hurt Paavo more than any physical blow could. He understood what was happening to her. Even though she'd gotten safely away from the man who now called himself Axel Klaw—the same man Paavo knew as Alexander Clausen—her mind was assailing her with thoughts and images of what might have happened had she been trapped there.

Men like Klaw and his henchmen were common in Paavo's world, but Angie had never before had to deal with people who made a mockery of the morals and balance that shaped her life. With them, it hadn't mattered who or what she was. They operated on base animal instinct where the scent of fear was as powerful an aphrodisiac as power and money.

The thought of Klaw anywhere near Angie sickened him.

Paavo drove straight to his house. As he opened his front door, he was greeted by the thudding feet of Hercules, who then hurled himself against Paavo's leg.

"This cat is so damned spoiled," Paavo muttered.

"Feed Hercules, Paavo," she said.

She refused to lie down on his bed. Despite the medicine the doctor gave her, the thought of closing her eyes and trying to sleep made her uneasy. The memories of Klaw's lurid face and Freddie's strong hands were too sharp and frightening.

Paavo settled her on his sofa, gave her a pillow and covered her with an afghan, then hovered near to pat her shoulder or brush back a wayward curl from her forehead. He wondered what had caused her to go back to Axel Klaw's studio, but knew she'd tell him when she was up to it. For now, he was content just to have her near.

When he returned from feeding Hercules, he thought she was asleep when she said softly, almost calmly, "I looked through Karl Wielund's notebook." She then shifted so he could fit on the sofa beside her.

"Notebook?" He sat where she indicated.

"He used to keep notes on his recipes—what he cooked, when and why he changed the ingredients, the temperatures, all that. Mark Dustman had Karl's notes and brought them to LaTour's with him. In Karl's notebook, I found a number just like the ones on the DVDs that you had in your briefcase."

"You remembered the numbers?"

"Kind of." Drowsily, she rubbed her eyes. "Anyway, I talked my way into the storage room where films and photographs were kept."

"You're kidding."

"I'm not. And there, I found the folder with the number Karl had written in his notebook. In it were some stills, outtakes, from a film. The photos were nearly twenty years old, but I still recognized the woman in them. Lacy LaTour."

He let that sink in a moment. "You're saying Henry's wife made porno flicks?"

"I saw more of Lacy in those photos than I ever wanted to see of her. They were sickening."

Hard though it was to imagine, what Angie was telling him tied many pieces together—Karl Wielund, Sheila Danning, and now, Lacy LaTour. All were connected through the photos found in Wielund's place. But Chick Marcuccio and Hank Greuber, also killed, didn't seem to be linked to the porn palace at all. Paavo rubbed his chin. "So, if this porn studio is a connection, what about it caused the death of four people?"

Angie shook her head wearily.

Paavo stood. "Get some sleep, Angel."

"Don't leave." She pulled herself to a sitting position, curling her legs under her.

He gave a halfhearted smile and then sat again. After a moment, he said, "Wouldn't you rather be lying down? You can take my bed. I'll sleep here."

"I'm quite comfortable." Then she reached for him and guided his head to her shoulder. He was surprised at first, but then put one arm behind her back and let himself sink into the warmth she offered. She gently stroked his hair and his shoulder. He felt himself relax and soon, his free arm rested across her hips. As much as she needed him now, so he, too, needed her. She was his peace, his refuge.

"Good," he murmured, as his eyes shut. "I'm comfortable now, too."

31

ngie awoke the next morning to a light knock on the front door. She sat straight up.

She was in Paavo's room, in his bed, under the covers.

She was still dressed, except for her shoes. Paavo lay beside her on the bed, on top of the covers, also still dressed. Somehow, she guessed they'd both decided the sofa wasn't comfortable enough, and she vaguely remembered insisting he not leave her alone.

He stirred, the knocking waking him a bit, and she hurried from the bed and ran to the door, hoping to open it before whoever was out there knocked again.

At the door, she looked through the peephole, then swung it open. "Inspector Yoshiwara."

His eyebrows lifted in surprise at seeing her, then he smiled and bellowed, "Hey, there!" The way his voice thundered she was surprised it didn't set off a sonic boom. "Can I come in?"

"Paavo is still asleep."

He remained on the front stoop, looking uneasy. "Hope you're doing okay after all that yesterday."

"Yes. A doctor gave me a sedative, so I was able to sleep like a baby. I suspect Paavo stayed awake watching to make sure the bump on my head didn't cause any problems." She tried to downplay, as much as possible, any ideas Yosh might get about her having spent the night there.

"Listen, Angie, I'm really sorry to bother you both, and I wouldn't be here if it wasn't an emergency, but I've got to get Paavo down to the station. There's going to be a live press conference on TV. The newsies are all over Hollins like flies in a cow pasture, and he needs Paavo there to bail him out."

She frowned. "I just told you, Paavo worked all night. He's exhausted."

"I understand! I do, and I just learned about the press conference this morning when I went in to work. I couldn't believe it! That Paav, he's a great guy. And he's real good with the press. They eat up what he says like hot buttered popcorn and when he tells them he can't say more, they don't even yell at him! I couldn't do that. And Hollins gets mad and makes things worse."

She folded her arms. "I don't think he should be disturbed. You and Hollins need to put on your big-boy pants and learn to deal with a few reporters. That's all."

"Angie, we really need him. The Chief wants him at the Hall. Pronto."

Angie realized that what Yosh had under his Tickle Me Elmo façade was the stubbornness of a mule. Well, so did she. "He's not fully recovered yet from the bullet wound he suffered, and he needs his rest. I don't care what the Chief wants. I know what's best for him."

"Look, I came out here because I figured he'd be tired and upset after... well, you know, about yesterday. Anyway, I'll drive him down there and I promise I'll get him back here just as soon as possible. I'll even tuck him in if that'll make you happy."

She took hold of the door knob. "If you'll excuse me, Inspector Yoshiwara. I really can't help you."

"You can call me Yosh."

She started to shut the door. "Good day, Inspector Yoshiwara."

He put out his hand, stopping the door from moving. "Look, Angie. You've got to understand—"

"I understand. You don't. I said 'leave.' Is that so difficult to do?"

"But, Angie--"

"Say, you two." They both turned to see a sleepy-looking Paavo standing a few feet behind Angie. "This stand-off is real interesting, and I'd love to see how it ends, but I don't think I want to see any more bloodshed. Let me just take a shower and put on fresh clothes, Yosh, and I'll go with you. Ten minutes, okay?"

"Sure, Paav." Yosh heaved a sigh of relief as Angie finally allowed him into the house. He walked over to an easy chair and sat.

"Please excuse me," Angie said, not even trying to hide her frustration. Then, nose in the air, she swept into Paavo's kitchen. "I'll make us all some coffee."

———

Paavo was quiet when he returned from the press conference, but she hadn't expected him to be otherwise. She looked at him in amazement as he'd called work and said he wouldn't be back until later that afternoon.

She had told him as he left that she'd have breakfast for him when he returned. At a local grocery store she bought ingredients to make him a Belgian waffle, to be topped with butter and his choice of real maple syrup or homemade boysenberry jam, plus bacon, scrambled eggs, fresh-squeezed orange juice and strong, Italian roast coffee.

He took off his sports coat, loosened his tie and rolled up his sleeves as he looked at the feast, then glanced at her uncertainly. "Looks good enough to eat," he said, then smiled awkwardly.

Paavo rarely smiled. She knew he was uncomfortable, unsure of what to make of their closeness last night, or of their pure, uncomplicated joy at being together after he'd gotten her away from the porn studio. She knew what it had meant to her, but not to him.

"Don't let it get cold!" She tried to make her voice light, then quickly sat to join him, knowing he was too much of a gentleman to start to eat while she was standing.

He sat across from her and busied himself with the meal. She watched him instead of eating.

"Aren't you hungry?" he asked.

"I am." She grabbed the syrup and poured it on top of her waffle before she realized she'd already added some. The waffle floated in the sticky mess.

They had just finished eating and moved into the living room when Paavo heard a car stop in front of his house. He stepped to the side of the front window and looked out.

"Who is it?" Angie asked, suddenly fearful.

"Your father," he said, surprise filling his voice.

"It can't be!" she cried.

"It is. And he's got Police Commissioner Barcelli with him."

"The police commissioner?" Bewildered, she peeked out the window, hoping Paavo was making an extremely rare joke. He wasn't. "Don't tell him where I went yesterday, Paavo, please! Promise me."

Paavo gave her a sharp look, then opened the front door. "Hello, Mr. Amalfi. Commissioner Barcelli."

"Where is she?" Sal's look was withering. He pushed the door wide and stepped inside, but halted abruptly as he stared at Angie's pale face and her disheveled state in a too-tight, too-wrinkled jumpsuit. "Angelina, what are you doing?"

Angie felt her throat tighten. No words would come to mind or to her lips. She looked to Paavo.

"She's fine," Paavo said.

"Angelina?" Sal barked.

All she could think of was her father's reaction... and his bad heart. "I'm all right. Why are you here?"

Sal's gaze fixed on his daughter. "I heard that you went to a pornographic theater, or worse. Someplace where they make the films. Those people are the worst kind... drugs, diseases, guns. I can't believe you'd go somewhere like that. That's not like you, not my Angelina." With each word, Sal's fury grew. "I can only imagine you did it because you've been seeing this man! His influence is no good for you, no good at all."

"Papà, calm yourself, please!" She stepped closer to Paavo, touching his arm. "It's not that way."

Sal glared at her. "No? Then why were you there?"

"It was nothing, Papà, a mistake on my part," she whispered, slowly shaking her head as she walked toward him.

At the same time, Sal moved toward her, twisting his hands with worry. "When the Commissioner heard where you had been, he called me. I went to your house, and you weren't there. He was able to track you down. I couldn't believe it. My baby, first in such a filthy place in Berkeley, and now spending the night with... him. I don't understand you at all. I want you to come home with me this minute."

Stricken, Angie turned to Barcelli. "You have it wrong."

"You're the daughter of one of my best friends," Barcelli said. "And you're going out with someone in the department. I feel a certain responsibility." He glanced quickly at Paavo. "We'll discuss this tomorrow, Smith."

"No, please Commissioner," Angie said. "Paavo did nothing wrong. I went to that... place... on my own. I wanted to find out something, and I did. But the people there were scary, and then Paavo came and helped me get away! He helped me!"

"It's all right, Angie." Paavo's voice was soft, his gaze despondent but accepting. "They have a point."

She glanced at him and shook her head. "No."

"The question is, Angelina," Sal said, recapturing her attention, "why would you go there in the first place? It's got to be his influence. We know nothing about him, about his family."

"One of my detectives," Barcelli said, "should have taken you home, not to his house! I don't like it." He turned to the door. "Sal, *andiamo.*"

"Paavo." Angie turned to him, her hand tentatively reaching for him.

But Sal took hold of her arm. "*Non importante, Angelina.* The Commissioner is waiting for us. *Andiamo!*"

Her father's flushed looks scared her. It'd been too soon after his surgery for him to become so upset. She was no longer a child that he could order around, but at the same time, she was scared that he might get so upset he would end up in the hospital again. She couldn't see that she had any choice but to go with him, to try to calm him, at least for the moment. She glanced at Paavo, not knowing what to do.

She guessed he saw the hesitancy in her eyes and decided to make things easy for her, which was so like him. He took her jacket from the sofa and held it as she put it on.

"Go home with your father, Angie," he murmured. "It's where you belong." He then, lovingly, tucked a curl behind her ear.

She wanted to throw her arms around him and stay right there, but with her father waiting for her, she hesitated to do that.

"Go," Paavo urged.

Sal took her arm and started to pull her toward the door. She faced Paavo, "I'll make sure Barcelli understands," she said as Sal led her out of the house.

Paavo quietly shut the door behind them. His house never felt so empty.

32

Paavo's frustration with the case went right over the top that afternoon as he returned to work and was called into Lt. Hollins' office. "Doesn't Barcelli have the brains to figure out that I was trying to get Angie *out* of that place? I've come across Axel Klaw before in my life. His real name, the name I knew him under, is Alexander Clausen. Believe me, if he has her address and wants to make trouble, it could get very dangerous for her."

"I'll fill Barcelli in on the case," Hollins said, trying to calm Paavo down. "I doubt he knows anything about what's really going on. He's not a cop. He's a politician."

"Don't I know it!"

"Look, if you can get Angie to talk to Barcelli, the heat'll be off you."

"It's between him and me. I don't want her involved."

Hollins shook his head. "You got it bad, don't you? Why don't you just marry the girl?"

That stopped Paavo in his restless pacing. For a long, silent moment he stared down at the floor. Considering how Angie left that morning, he wondered if he'd even see her again, let alone anything more. But he wasn't about to go into all that with Hollins. When he lifted his head, his expression was almost savage. "She'd be in danger every time I got a case she was interested in."

"Just keep her out of them."

Amusement eased some of the grimness from Paavo's face. "You don't know her very well, do you?"

Hollins nodded. "Can't say I do."

"The trouble is," Paavo continued, "her poking her nose around works. She's found the connection between the porn studios and the restaurant owners. Henry LaTour's wife, Lacy, was an actress in at least one of Axel Klaw's film."

"Crap!" Hollins muttered.

"That's right. And Karl Wielund knew about it."

Paavo went to Vice to learn as much as he could about Axel Klaw. Klaw was associated with drug dealers and gamblers as well as pornography operations, but Klaw was called the Teflon King of Porn. Nothing stuck to him, no matter how big or small the charge.

He found that Vice had, in fact, connected "Axel Klaw" to his birth name of Alexander Clausen. Unfortunately, they hadn't annotated the reverse connection, from Clausen to Klaw. But Paavo did find that Vice had records going back twenty-one years when Clausen was first picked up for selling drugs, but let off due to a technicality.

As Paavo turned the pages in the Klaw/Clausen file, suddenly, there, in front of him, was the story he'd wanted, yet dreaded, to see.

The record showed that a man named Alexander Clausen had been investigated in connection with the death by an overdose of a nineteen-year-old woman named Jessica Smith.

Witnesses said they'd seen Jessie go into a friend's apartment with him, but a number of others swore Clausen had been seen in other places throughout the night. Jessica was found dead, and no one ever proved who was or was not with her.

The investigation to Jessica Smith's death went nowhere, and the police determined the overdose was an accident.

But Jessica's little brother knew there was more to the story. He'd seen his older sister go off that night with the man named Alexander Clausen. And he remembered how Clausen had frightened him. He had a hard, mean look about him. But Jessie had said her friend, Alex, was fun.

Fun! Damn the man, Paavo thought.

He had gone in search of his sister when she didn't come home after her date with "Alex." He'd managed to find her, but she was already dead. Paavo was only fourteen at the time; he was now thirty-four. For years after he joined the SFPD, and particularly when he became a detective, every chance he'd gotten, he'd searched police databases for Alexander Clausen. But Clausen stopped showing any activity, any movement at all, about ten years earlier. Finally, he knew why.

I've spent a lot of years looking for you, Clausen. Now, you've fallen into my lap, and I won't let you go again.

33

After two days hiding at her parents' house, afraid of everything around her, Angie wanted to go back to her life, back to her job at the radio, her history class, even to her so-called apprenticeship at LaTour's Restaurant.

That morning, as the sun was just peeking over the hills of the East Bay, Angie forced herself to get into her car, and go for a drive around the city... alone.

She drove first down to the Marina Green and along the boulevard of homes along the bay. Yachts and sailboats rocked peacefully in the harbor. She parked the car at the edge of the Green near the Presidio and gazed at the water.

Since her encounter with Klaw, she'd learned more and more how to block out thoughts and sensations. If she hadn't, she didn't know how she'd have gotten through these past days. At first, thoughts of the afternoon with him would make her physically ill. She told her parents that she'd fallen on some stairs, and that's why her body ached and she had some black-and-blue marks, as well as aching hands and sprained fingers. They didn't quite believe her, but didn't press her, either.

She then drove to Fisherman's Wharf, where early morning

meant that the real wharf, where fishermen brought in their daily catches, was astir. The aroma of baking sourdough bread mixed with salt air gave the area its distinctive smell... one that tourists rarely knew. Angie breathed deeply, trying to calm the turmoil within her.

She wanted to go back to her apartment. Axel Klaw shouldn't have any reason to go after her, should he? To him, she shouldn't have been any more than a play thing, someone who had brought him a lurid diversion in an otherwise boring afternoon.

To her, though, he was the bogeyman she'd feared as a child come to life. He was the monster living in the back of the closet, or lurking in the hallway between her bed and the bathroom in the middle of the night when everyone else was asleep, or the faceless man who would lure little girls into his car with promises of candy and big, pretty dolls.

Finally, she drove up to Telegraph Hill. The circular parking lot surrounding Coit Tower was empty, so she parked and got out. Climbing over the low railing, she sat on the hilltop, looking out on the city as the late morning sun now brightened the sky. Despite everything going on in her life, she did love this city, loved seeing the beauty of it spread out before her.

The one comforting memory during this time was being with Paavo. She had felt safe with him, and somehow complete —as if she were where she wanted, and needed, to be.

Yet her father had told her Paavo didn't want her with him —that she was a bother. Her father wouldn't lie to her, would he?

But he might have misinterpreted something Paavo had said.

At least she had explained to Commissioner Barcelli what had happened in Berkeley and why she ended up at Paavo's house, explained that he had helped her, and was to be commended, not reprimanded. Her father had listened to everything, but he clearly didn't like what he was hearing.

From her hilltop perch, she gazed out at the city. Paavo was out there, and Yosh, and all the others. As she sat, thinking, feeling, absorbing, it was as if a cloud lifted from her mind.

Even though Paavo hadn't called, hadn't tried to see her, she knew there was a reason, a good, probably very Paavo-like reason. No matter what her father told her, Paavo wouldn't toss her aside. The warming realization came to her that she trusted him. She trusted that when he was ready, he would see her again.

As noon approached, she thought about *Lunch with Henri.* She had taken "sick days" and apparently, Lacy was filling in for her.

Angie didn't want to see Henry LaTour or Lacy, especially after what she'd seen of Lacy at Axel Klaw's studio. To tell the truth, she didn't care what Lacy did to make a living, but she simply didn't want to face the woman in person until she could get those images out of her head.

But she did want to check in at LaTour's restaurant as an "intern." Going there at noon, when she wouldn't run into Henry or Lacy, seemed like a good idea.

At LaTour's, Mark Dustman greeted her warmly, and immediately put her to work helping him make an enormous pot of bouillabaisse.

Angie waited until Dustman and his assistants were busy then went into the office. She picked up the landline telephone receiver and, wanting to look as if she was making a business phone call if anyone caught her there, she dialed the IRS since she knew she'd be put on hold for hours. With the phone against the crook of her neck, she began flipping through print-outs of the restaurant's financial records.

LaTour's was doing worse than she had imagined. Each month had ended with a negative balance. She ran her finger up and down the spreadsheet columns, looking at headings and amounts to see if anything looked out of line. Not that she could see. It was just a very expensive place to run, apparently.

She flipped back some pages to quickly scan detailed lists of income and outgo. It was the beluga caviar that stopped her first. Two pounds of it? Being sold at *LaTour's*? She didn't think so. Why on earth would LaTour have bought so much of the stuff? Then her eyes jumped to five hundred grams of saffron. Did LaTour plan to season all the rice in Spain? Real saffron was so costly it was sold by the quarter ounce! And lobsters. LaTour didn't have lobsters on his menu. His was a meat and potatoes restaurant, and she wasn't talking filet mignon. Plus several pounds of Perigord truffles. What was going on here?

She hung up the phone—still on hold—and went back into the kitchen to help Dustman.

LaTour came in after his radio show. He looked over the items cooking on the stove and in the oven, harrumph that the food looked passable, and then left.

Angie stayed at the restaurant until the ten p.m. closing time and helped the staff clean-up. Throughout the evening, she racked her brain to come up with any rational explanation for the large quantities of expensive foods she'd seen in their books. There was no caviar, saffron, or lobsters to be seen, and the only mushrooms were the button variety.

So why did LaTour purchase such expensive ingredients? And why in those quantities?

There was something fishy here... besides the caviar. She really ought to let Paavo know what she'd found out. Earlier that day she'd decided to patiently wait for him to contact her, but sometimes patience, like virtue, was not its own reward.

She pulled out her cellphone, then put it back in her hand-bag. The hurt she felt whenever she recalled her father's words about Paavo not wanting her to "bother" him, hit her once more, despite her resolve that there was more to the story. She pulled out a chair and sat.

Memories filled her of Paavo taking her to the hospital, doctors and nurses surrounding her, then Paavo holding her, and feeling safe and secure, peaceful... and then, her father telling Paavo it was his fault she'd been hurt. His fault...

Of course, he wouldn't contact her. Well could she imagine Paavo thinking what had happened to her *was* his fault and blaming himself. He was like that.

She ran from the restaurant to her car.

"I can't believe this," Paavo said when he opened his front door and found Angie standing on the front stoop.

"Hi, there!" She heard the nervousness in her voice, unsure if she'd been right about his reasons for not seeing or contacting her the past few days. She forced a smile.

"Hi, indeed." He stuck his head out the door and looked up the street, then down. "Is your father nearby? Or, maybe the Mayor is lurking in the bushes this time? Thank God your father's not friends with the President or I'd probably have Air Force One circling overhead."

She could tell he'd been hurt by her father's actions, and by being made to feel inferior and responsible. She wasn't about to let him wallow in guilt or self-pity, but brushed past him and went into the house. "Nope, I'm all alone."

"What are you doing here?"

She reached into a paper sack she carried. "Look. Coffee filters, and a fresh pound of Graffeo's Italian Roast. And crème brûlée from LaTour's." Without another word she went into the kitchen and put on the Melitta. He followed her in there.

"What's this about?"

"I wanted to see you. What else? Now go sit down. This will just take me a minute."

He gave her a cautious look, but deep inside she saw... or hoped she saw... a teensy-tiny flicker of happiness that she was there.

Once the coffee was made, she poured them each a mug and brought them and the crème brûlée ramekins out to the living room. Placing them on the coffee table, she sat on one end of the sofa while Paavo sat on the other. She turned to face him, her elbow on the backrest.

He gave her a cautious look. "How are your fingers?"

"Coming along. I only go half-way to the ceiling instead of all the way when I bump them."

Paavo winced. "That's good, Angie. It's progress."

She smiled. "I did want to tell you about something that might affect your case. I saw something most peculiar today at LaTour's restaurant. It probably doesn't mean anything, but you mentioned looking at Wielund's and Sorrento accounts, and I know you had no reason yet to go over Henry's, so I thought I'd check it out for you."

For a moment, he looked as if he was going to protest, but then his expression changed, and he simply nodded. "And you found something peculiar, you said?"

"That's right!" She leaned conspiratorially closer, and told him all about finding the extravagant food purchases that didn't have anything to do with the recipes used, the size of the customer base, or LaTour's menu.

As she talked, Paavo was on his feet and pacing, his usual stance for thinking through the implications of what he was hearing.

"Could these purchases have come anywhere near ten-thousand dollars in a month?" he asked.

"Ten thousand?" She tried to mentally add up the size of the purchases she'd seen over the course of a month. "Easily. I only know the retail prices, and they would get the goods wholesale, but you can easily spend $250 an ounce for Beluga caviar and double that for real saffron. Why?"

He again sat on the sofa. "Karl Wielund was getting a payment of ten grand a month transferred in a round-about way into his account in Germany. It's untraceable, so far. But without that money, Wielund's would have either closed, or toned down their menu considerably."

She stared at him. "Wait, are you saying Henry might be buying those fancy ingredients to give to Karl Wielund for his restaurant?"

"No. Wielund is getting ten grand in cash, not fancy foods. He buys expensive delicacies, but not in the quantities you just mentioned."

She pondered this a moment. "So, you think Henry might be pretending to spend ridiculous amounts of money on caviar and such so he can withdraw a lot of money... and give it to Karl Wielund? Why?"

"It looks like a payoff," Paavo said.

"Wait. If Henry was taking ten thousand dollars a month out of his restaurant to give to Karl..." Angie stopped speaking as the full implication of all this struck, "that means LaTour's low net profits weren't really all that low. That's incredible! LaTour's might not be the disaster everyone thinks it is. And Wielund's very expensive entrées and wine selections might be hurting its bottom line, and could explain why his prices are considered low for the quality of the food he's serving."

"I can't help but think Wielund was blackmailing LaTour," Paavo said. "I wonder if it didn't have to do with Wielund learning about Lacy LaTour's adventures in pornography. It wouldn't be the first time photos and films like hers turned up in the hands of a blackmailer."

"But I can't see Henry or Lacy hurting anyone," Angie said.

"And we're talking about four people. That's serial killer territory."

"At least it's a motive," Paavo said, "and one we'll definitely look into, although I agree. It's hard to believe blackmail alone would cause four murders. Still, you never know about people. Until this is resolved, I'm asking you to keep away from the LaTours—people and restaurant."

"I never take chances."

"Not much." His gaze met hers and she couldn't help but grin—and to her surprise, he actually grinned back, along with a shake of his head. "In any case," he said, "it's late, and you've got a long drive back to your parents' house. Thank you for the coffee, dessert, and very useful information."

"Thanks?" she repeated.

He stood.

So did she.

He took her arm and turned her toward the door. "I'll be seeing you, Angie. It's late and I don't want to keep you any longer than necessary. I really appreciate all you found out about this case, though. You did just great."

"Great?"

"Bye." He opened the door, patiently waiting for her to go through it.

She stiffened her shoulders and, head high, left the house. "Bye," she murmured with a weighty sigh. *Someday, Inspector, you'll want nothing more than for me to stay with you.*

34

Angie had fully intended to keep away from the LaTours, claiming she was still sick, but two mornings later, Lacy telephoned her, sobbing so hard and sounding so drunk she could hardly speak. "Angie, it's so terrible. Henry's been arrested!"

"Lacy, have you been drinking?"

"Only to settle my nerves. I can't take it, Angie. Not another second! What will I do if Henry's in prison?"

"What was he arrested for?"

"I don't know. The police all but raided our restaurant yesterday, looking at all our books, and taking things, and this morning, they showed up and said they want to question him at the police station! Oh, Angie, you've got to help me." She hiccoughed loudly. "It was that detective, the one you brought to Karl's memorial service. I thought he was a friend, and now! I don't know what to do. Maybe if you talked to him... told him that Henry would never hurt Karl. Henry's a darling! You know that." She started crying loudly into the phone.

So, Angie thought, Paavo hadn't actually arrested LaTour but was questioning him—probably about the extravagant purchases she'd discovered. Good! "Pull yourself together, Lacy. Drink some black coffee. I'm sure Paavo's just talking to him about something. Did you call your lawyer?"

"Yes. He said he'd handle everything, that I shouldn't worry."

"He's right."

"But... but, what about the radio show? How can I handle Chef Henri's part? I don't know anything about cooking! People will laugh and I could ruin Henry's career."

"I'm sure you can handle it. And callers will be understanding."

"But I can't do it! The thought of speaking on the radio scares me to death. And... and I had a little vermouth. Just a thimbleful, mind you. But since I never drink, it's gone straight to my head."

Godzilla's thimble, Angie thought.

Lacy continued rambling. "What if I say something foolish, or something that upsets Henry? What if the police keep him and I have to go on, day after day, trying to answer questions from callers, trying to be witty like my Henry, to keep his listeners..." An onslaught of sobs got in the way of her words for a moment, and then she blurted out, "I need you to do it for me. Please, Angie. Take over as Henry's substitute today. And maybe tomorrow."

Angie drew in her breath. "Me?"

"You'd be great at it!"

It was oh, so tempting! But then a vision of Paavo waggling his finger and warning her to be careful and stay away from the LaTours flashed in front of her. "I just don't know."

"You're good at all this stuff, and I'm not," Lacy said with a sob.

Angie couldn't help but visualize the joyful expressions of the station executives after listening to her witty, knowledgeable, fast-paced, exciting radio show! Just the thought of it made her whole body tingle with excitement.

Paavo had warned her to stay away from the LaTours, but not the radio station. An idea came to mind. "If I do this," she began, "you know I can handle the show by myself, right? Along with the engineer, of course. But I don't need a call-screener or anyone else."

"Okay, if you say so." Lacy sounded surprised and even cautious.

"So, if you promise that you'll stay home and rest, I'll handle the radio show for you. How's that?"

"What would Henry and I do without you?" Lacy cried.

"It's my pleasure." Angie soon ended the conversation, her head filled with thoughts about her debut performance on the radio. She couldn't help but smile. "Showtime!"

"Homicide Department, may I help you?" the nasal voice intoned.

"Inspector Paavo Smith, please," Angie said. She had tried to reach him on his cellphone, but he wasn't picking up and it was getting close to noon. "This is Angie Amalfi."

"One moment."

It didn't take long for the woman to tell Angie that Paavo wasn't available. She asked if Inspector Yoshiwara was there.

"He's with Inspector Smith. They can't be disturbed at the moment. Oh, wait, he just stepped out of the interrogation room. Let me see if he can take the call."

"Hey there, Angie," Yoshiwara's voice boomed into her ear. "How's it going? How's the hand? Guess you're not doing 'this little piggy went to market' these days, huh?"

She winced. "I'm okay. Look, I'm trying to reach Paavo. Any idea when he'll be available?"

"It'll be awhile. Things are going kind of slow. Can I take a message for him? Hey, the big P.S. told me about you finding out that someone's been skimming the take at LaTour's. Good work, Angie. You might be going into the private eye trade before you know it."

"I don't think so. Is he with Henry LaTour?"

Yosh hesitated a moment, then said, "You guessed it."

"Thanks, Yosh. Would you do me a favor and tell Paavo that I'm doing Henry's radio show for him? Lacy called. She's so upset she's gotten herself drunk, and now she's in no condition to go on the air. So I volunteered to go on for her."

"The radio show, huh? Pretty brave Angie, to talk on the radio that way."

"Or pretty foolish."

"Anyway, I'll let him know. Let's see, that's a twelve o'clock show, right? I'll try to listen to it. Paavo, too, if he's free."

"Great. I'll give you guys a special hello."

35

Paavo sat on one side of the table in the interrogation room and faced LaTour. "I appreciate your willingness to discuss your accounts with me," he said. The day before, Paavo and Yosh had a search warrant for LaTour's restaurant. Using its financial data, the SFPD's financial crimes unit investigator was able to tract payments from the LaTour's account through Cyprus to Karl Wielund's German bank.

"No problem," LaTour said. "Anything I can do to help find our fellow chefs' murderer is fine with me. Especially since, I hasten to remind you, I was also threatened."

Paavo studied LaTour as he spoke those words. The man looked and sounded surprisingly sincere. Of course, Paavo had also witnessed more than one murderer declare their innocence in equally compelling terms. And, he could have easily paid someone to threaten him on the air. "I remember, Mr. LaTour. Now, before hiring Mark Dustman, were you the head chef at your restaurant?"

"I still am, actually. But much of my time is spent on my radio show and promoting the restaurant."

"Who orders the food for the restaurant?"

"I do...er, did. Now, I leave it up to Mr. Dustman."

"Now, but he only started working for you recently, right? So who ordered before?"

"I did. Why, is there a problem?" LaTour asked.

"You tell me." Paavo opened a file with computer printouts and then turned it so LaTour could read them. "For each of the past three months, your expenses have exceeded your income."

LaTour put on his reading glasses and still had to hold his head back abnormally far in order to read the columns. "It's the economy. We'll pull out of it, I'm sure."

"Of course." Paavo said. "It's interesting, isn't it, how your gross income each month has been surprisingly consistent."

LaTour looked over the printouts. "Ah, that's the sign of strength for our brand, isn't it?"

"So, if you're now losing money, it must be that your expenses have increased."

LaTour's brow knitted. "Not at all! If anything, we've been doing all we could to economize. I've even taken to going to..." he shuddered, "places like Costco to get some standard supplies. Please, don't let word of that get out!"

"Generally, you deal with a set group of food and restaurant wholesalers?"

"Of course." LaTour glanced down at the next printout Paavo turned to. "Yes, right here are our food expenses. I haven't changed my menu in months, so my purchases should be..."

He stopped short.

"What is it?" Paavo asked.

"Just a minute," LaTour said, light beads of perspiration glistening on his forehead. "There's something wrong here."

Paavo sat back. "For the past three months, your expenses have jumped over ten-thousand dollars higher than the previous months. Why is that?"

"I... I'm not sure. Normally, everything is so simple in a restaurant. You buy raw ingredients cheap, cook them, then sell them for a lot more money. That's it. But..." LaTour's fingers covered his mouth, his brow furrowed, as he studied the figures. He flipped to the expenses two months earlier, and then three months ago.

LaTour was sweating profusely at this point. "I don't know what's going on."

"Do you keep these books, Mr. LaTour?"

"Well, not exactly. I don't have much of a head for figures. My wife does the bookkeeping."

"Your wife?"

LaTour nodded so quickly his jowls jiggled like jello. "Yes. She's a regular wizard at numbers. Can do a lot of math in her head even."

"Does she also do the banking?"

LaTour wiped his forehead with his handkerchief. "Yes." He flipped to the back pages where Lacy had listed out details of the various columns. "Saffron... truffles..." he muttered, moping his brow. "Beluga... oh, my..."

"Mr. LaTour?" Paavo called. The restaurateur looked ready to faint.

"I... I'm sorry, I just..." He swallowed, staring glassy eyed at the books.

"Did you authorize the purchase of those foods?"

He shook his head, nearly on the verge of tears. So Angie was right.

"What happened, Mr. LaTour," Paavo asked then, "to make the past three months different from the prior months?"

He looked ready to faint. "I have no idea."

"No?"

"None! Believe me. I don't understand it myself."

"You never checked these books?"

"No. I trust my wife."

"Do you realize, Mr. LaTour, that the way these books are written, it appears that phony expenses of food were placed in the accounts books to syphon off ten thousand dollars each month?"

LaTour's voice squeaked. "Yes."

"Does anyone besides Mrs. LaTour work on these books?"

"No."

"No accountant?"

"None."

"Tax preparer?"

"Lacy does our taxes."

Paavo looked at him skeptically.

"She saves us lots of money."

"I'm sure she does."

LaTour ruffled the pages back and forth, leafing madly through the pages in front of him one more time. "I don't understand it. I just don't!" He looked frightened and confused. "I don't know what to tell you. You can't think she was taking this money. She wouldn't! What reason would she have?"

"We have reason to believe this money was going to Karl Wielund," Paavo said. "We suspect he was blackmailing her. Now, he's dead. Which means, if you didn't kill him, there's only one person who had a serious motive."

LaTour looked faint. "No. It's not possible."

"Is Mrs. LaTour home?" Paavo asked.

"No. She's at KYME. She's going to host my radio show."

Hearing that, Yosh stood up. "What? Not Angie?"

"Angie?" Paavo said, surprised at Yosh mentioning her.

LaTour looked at Yosh as if he were crazy. "Of course not Angie! Lacy's handled it before plenty of times. She can do it again."

Yosh faced his partner, his gaze severe. "Paavo, let's go. I think we have a problem."

As Angie entered the KYME studio, she'd never noticed it before, but the call-letters looked distinctly like "cwyme", as in the way Elmer Fudd would pronounce "the scene of the cwyme."

Angie had arrived early to have plenty of time to tell the station manager and the engineer that she'd be doing Henry's show that day, and possibly several days in the future due to a personal problem. They looked completely uninterested in her exciting news, and concentrated instead on their Big Macs and fries.

Well, she wouldn't let them dim her excitement. Since *Lunch with Henri* was nearly the bottom ranked radio program in the greater Bay Area, she figured the station didn't much care who hosted it. The last time she saw the ratings, only the *Let's Learn Khmer!* broadcast was lower.

Angie picked up her reference cookbooks and waited outside the studio booth for the show ahead of Henry's to end. A man whose name Angie could never remember talked about fly-fishing. The fact that almost no one did fly-fishing in the Bay Area didn't seem to bother him. Maybe it wasn't Henry's fault his show did so poorly. Maybe the show before his put the audience to sleep.

Since she wouldn't have any call-screener, she realized she would have to take the phone calls blind. She just hoped she didn't get the funny little man who called at least three times a week to ask if he'd reached Marvella's French Laundry.

Ten minutes until showtime.

At five minutes before the hour, Angie began to hyperventilate. She took several deep, deep breaths, and then felt a little dizzy.

Just then, the fly-man left and Angie hurried into the studio booth. She plugged in her cellphone—she didn't want to take the chance of her battery running out—and hit the "Record" button. Better too early than to get nervous and forget to start the recording. She wanted a complete record of her very first radio show.

Sitting in Henry's chair, she tucked her hair behind each ear, put on the headphones and watched as the clock's minute hand pointed straight up, then the seconds hand ticked off the remaining time until noon. She pressed the earphones close against her ears, but she couldn't hear *The Teddy Bear's Picnic.*

"There's no music," she whispered to the engineer.

"That's because it's Henry's music, not yours. Talk!"

Angie looked stricken. She glanced at the clock. Not only was it time to start talking, it was past time. And she knew that the absolutely worst thing you could do on radio was to have dead air. She sat up in her chair, feeling badly rattled, as all the great opening lines she'd practiced suddenly flew right out of her mind as she flicked on the microphone. "Hello, ladies and gentlemen. I know I don't sound like Chef Henri,"—she was proud of the way she'd managed to roll the "r" when she said "Ahnree"—"and that's because I'm not." She glanced at the engineer who was busy dipping a French fry into catsup.

Angie licked her lips, then began to speak.

"My name's Angelina Amalfi, sitting in for Chef Henri who's having a very special lunch today. I've spoken to many of you in the past when you've called in to ask Chef Henri about food preparation..." For some reason, she glanced at the microphone. Just as they tell mountain-climbers never to look down, seeing that microphone made the full impact of what she was doing hit her.

There she sat, with every word she spoke going out over air waves all over the greater Bay Area. Suddenly, her mouth grew dry, perspiration beaded on her forehead, and her mind went blank. "So... so now... instead of talking to you on the phone, I can sit here and talk to myself like Chef Henri does. I mean, talk into this mike... without any feedback... I don't mean talk to *myself*, of course...."

Angie swallowed hard. She'd never, ever make fun of Henry LaTour again.

"Well, why don't we go to the phones?" She glanced at the monitor. Not a single call had come in. She wiped her forehead. "Let me give you those numbers, first. Today, why don't we talk about all the good things we can get right here in San Francisco? Being a port city and all... I mean, I've met people from other parts of the country who've never eaten an artichoke. Can you imagine? Probably, not even a kiwi. Now, on the east coast, there are a lot of *different* kinds of fruits and vegetables... at least, I guess there are." Oh me, she sighed. Should she slash her wrists now or later?

A telephone line suddenly lit up. "Oh, a caller," Angie said breathlessly. At least someone was listening. She hit the open-line button. "Welcome to *Lunch with Henri*, this is Angie. How can I help you today?"

The light on the line went out.

"Hello," Angie said once more, then looked again at the microphone. "I must have hit the wrong button, folks." She gave a half-hearted laugh. "Whoever it was, be sure to call back and we'll put your call *right* to the front of the line! No waiting for you. No sirree." *Please someone, phone me! E.T., where are you?* The line remained empty.

Now what? Maybe a commercial break. She looked up to signal the engineer, but to her surprise, he and his lunch were no longer at his desk. She stood. Who was running the show?

"Angie."

Angie jumped at the sound and turned around. Lacy stood at the door of the recording studio. The woman looked awful—almost as bad as she'd sounded earlier on the phone. Her hair was uncombed, her make-up smeared and caked, and she was wearing sweat pants, a stained, wrinkled t-shirt and... slippers? "What are you doing here?"

Lacy stepped closer, her eyes wild. "No one's going to call."

Angie took off her headphones. "What do you mean? What's going on? Where's the engineer?"

"I changed my mind about you doing Henry's show. I told the engineer to put on 'Golden Oldies,' and to forget about commercials. I gave him the hour off."

Angie stared, not wanting to believe what was happening. Not Lacy. It couldn't be Lacy, she told herself. "I don't understand."

"But you will. Karl Wielund phoned me—asked me if I know who you are. I sure do. And I realized you would soon figure it all out."

37

Angie stared at Lacy, her mind racing.

"I had to find a way to get you alone," Lacy said, "because of this." She took a gun out of her purse.

Angie backed up until she bumped into the studio wall. "Lacy, no!" Her gaze darted between Lacy and the gun. Lacy's hands were shaking worse than glass in an earthquake. Taking a deep breath, Angie tried to calm herself. Somehow she had to take control. "Tell me what this all about."

Lacy glanced down at the gun, letting the barrel drop so that it was pointed toward the floor, then shook her head. "It's all falling apart." She gave a harsh sob as tears filled her eyes.

Angie fought her own nerves and quietly asked, "What is? What do you mean?"

Lacy shook her head, still staring at the gun. "Axel promised me everything would be all right. But it isn't." She raised her gaze then shrieked at Angie. "Why couldn't you leave us alone!"

Angie's heart nearly stopped. "Lacy, I didn't do anything to you!"

Lacy stared at her, and slowly her expression changed from anger to desperation. She sat where Angie had been sitting, looking exhausted, and placed the gun in front of her on the desktop, as if holding it had become too much of an effort for her. "Karl Wielund was a horrible person, evil! " she cried. "I didn't care when he died. He deserved it!"

Angie inched forward a step. If she could just keep Lacy talking, perhaps she could grab the gun. "Why did he deserve to die?"

"He was blackmailing me!"

Angie's pulse beat harder. So she and Paavo had been right. "So you had Henry get rid of him?"

"Henry? Of course not! I couldn't tell Henry what I'd done."

Angie's head was reeling. "Is all this because of the films you made years ago? I don't think people care much anymore." She tried to make her voice soothing. "You'll be all right, Lacy."

Lacy sneered. "People care. They always do. And Henry would definitely care. I was his 'lambikins,' his precious bride. Finally, with him, I had it made. Money, prestige. Now, it's all gone."

Angie could see the hysteria building in Lacy again. "That's not true—"

"What do you know! You have no idea about having to claw your way to make money, to get attention, to find someone who treats you well. And then, what a struggle it is to keep them!"

Angie was horrified, both by Lacy's words and the way she looked and acted. "I'm sorry, Lacy," she said and then realized what might have happened... some four months earlier. "It was Sheila Danning, wasn't it? She recognized you. She must have told Karl Wielund."

Lacy's head swung from side to side as tears rolled down her cheeks. "That damned Sheila Danning. I should have known she was trouble. Lousy, stupid little bitch!"

Angie glanced from the gun to the glass that looked out beyond the studio booth to the radio station. Still, no one was there. She, again, eased herself closer to the gun. "I don't follow."

"Karl Wielund needed money to get his restaurant going, to buy the fancy ingredients he had to have to serve the kind of food, attract the kind of clientele he saw for himself. That takes money, and somehow, Wielund learned there's a lot of money in pornography. He and Sheila were made for each other. She wanted to be in films. Somehow, they ended up working with Axel Klaw. Sheila had her films, and Wielund had money for his restaurant. He was actually making a go of it. But then she came across one of my old movies."

Angie drew in her breath. "I see."

"She confronted me at the restaurant and asked for money —a lot of money! I was scared, horrified at what she threatened to do to me, my reputation, even to Henry. I asked her to go out back, where I was parked, so we could sit in my car, in private, and discuss it. I was willing to go along, but her demands were outrageous. And the way she looked down her nose at me—at *me!* I couldn't stand it. I couldn't stand her. She was wearing a scarf around her neck, and... she just made me so damned angry! I didn't know my own strength. I didn't mean to hurt her, just to scare her! It was an accident!"

"I'm sure it was," Angie murmured, sad and sickened by Lacy's tale.

Lacy rocked back and forth as she continued. "Karl guessed why Sheila had been found murdered. She had told him everything, and his demand was even worse than hers! But I had no choice! I paid him and paid him and paid him until there's no money left. He was destroying LaTour's restaurant. I couldn't let him do that."

"Then you served him the quiche that killed him," Angie said softly.

She smiled. "I did."

Angie couldn't stop herself from asking, "How in the world did you get him to eat it?"

Lacy's lips twitched into a small smile. "I knew his arrogance. On Sundays, Wielund's is closed and we close early. But I knew Karl would be in his restaurant for a later meeting with Dustman. So I dropped in and told Karl I'd be able to pay his next blackmail 'installment' because LaTour's had a new recipe, one that would make our brunches world famous. He laughed at me. I said it was because of our secret ingredient, and then told him he'd find out all about it, once it was on our menu. He didn't believe me. I said fine, don't. I then told him I had to go back to LaTour's since I had it in the oven right then. I didn't want the rest of the staff to see it or they might give away the secret. I knew he couldn't resist such a story!

"Sure enough, I wasn't back at LaTour's ten minutes when he showed up. When he saw it was a quiche, he laughed hard that a quiche could ever make us 'world famous.' I simply said, 'You'll find out.' I then cut a piece for myself and plated it, as if I was going to eat it. 'Secret ingredient?' he said, 'I'll show you how secret it is!' He then grabbed the plate from me and ate a mouthful, then another. He admitted the quiche was above average, but the secret ingredient eluded him... until the poison began to work.

"I pretended not to know why he was feeling sick. He blamed it on the quiche—he at least got that right! I got him into his car, but instead of taking him to a hospital, I took him to the Sierra Nevadas, where he and his car had a terrible accident. Whoopsie!" She shrugged. "The hardest part was walking in that cold to a truck stop and finding a friendly trucker to drive me back to the city."

"Oh, my," Angie murmured.

Lacy nodded. "It should have been the perfect crime, and I have no idea how it failed."

Angie nodded, then took a deep breath, "And Chick?"

She shrugged. "He heard Henry read one of Karl's recipes on the air. It made him suspicious of Henry—as if Henry would kill anybody! He wouldn't back off, but kept coming around, questioning Henry about where he got Karl's recipes."

"Where did he get them? I thought Mark Dustman had Karl's notebook."

"Yes, but Karl also had recipes at his house, those he was perfecting—poor boy was such a perfectionist! I went to his house looking for something else, and found them." She gave a heavy sigh. "I couldn't allow Chick to cause people to question how Henry ended up with Karl's recipe from his house!"

Angie found Lacy's tale became more repugnant with every word she spoke. And then, she realized why Lacy had gone to Wielund's home. "You knew Wielund had a lot of pornography in his house, didn't you? And that, once the police ruled his death a homicide, they would go through it looking for clues to his murder. You had Wielund's keys to drive his car, and must have kept his house key so you could search the place."

Lacy nodded. "I knew you were smart. I never expected the police to show up at his home so quickly. I was hiding when they arrived, and as I tried to sneak away, that idiot landlord saw me."

As Lacy said that, she shook her head and stared at the floor a moment.

Angie lunged for the gun.

38

As Paavo, Yosh, and LaTour stepped off the elevator to the KYME station offices, a woman's shriek of raw fury pierced the air. "Lacy!" LaTour cried and ran toward the studio.

"Stay back!" Paavo ordered.

LaTour didn't listen, but burst into the recording studio, Paavo at his heels.

Paavo's gaze first went to Angie, shocked to see her and Lacy fighting over a handgun. It appeared to be in both their hands, but the way they were twisting and turning, he wasn't sure who had more control of it.

Paavo grabbed the back of LaTour's suit jacket and yanked him back. LaTour landed hard against Paavo's bad shoulder. A mind-numbing pain went through him, momentarily stopping him.

Suddenly, the gun went off. Plaster fell from the ceiling. Both women froze. Paavo was about to join the fight, when Angie shoved Lacy from her and stepped back, the gun firmly in her hands. She pointed it at Lacy. Paavo stepped behind her and gently took the gun away.

Yosh grabbed Lacy while doing his best to keep a terrified, wailing LaTour from her.

Now, with Lacy in handcuffs and LaTour subdued—he'd been brought there in hopes he could calm Lacy before any violence happened—Paavo's eyes caught Angie's. His heart was still in his throat as he thought of the chance she'd taken fighting with the killer over that gun. "Good job," he said, hearing the tension in his voice.

"Thanks." Her voice quivered. He watched her gaze go from him, to Lacy who was swearing at him while trying to pull her hands out of the cuffs, to LaTour who was leaning against a wall, tears streaming down his face.

Angie's felt woozy as her head began to spin. Paavo helped her sit and lower her head to her knees so she wouldn't pass out.

Angie remained quietly seated in the main room of the KYME studio and watched the proceedings. When the Crime Scene Unit came in to pick up evidence, she was able to give them something that made the case against Lacy easy: the recording on her phone of everything that had taken place in the studio.

As soon as all the details were taken care of and Lacy was turned over to uniformed police to be taken to the county jail, Paavo walked over to Angie and held out his hand. She took it, and he led her out into the hallway, his large frame shielding her from the curiosity seekers in the building who had come by to watch the police activity. His hands traced over her arms and shoulders. "You're still so pale," he said.

"I'll be okay," she answered softly. "I thought she was a friend. It's hard..." She bowed her head, unable to say more.

He wrapped her in his arms and she buried her face in the crook of his neck. He held her close until some warmth once again flowed through her veins, and the shivering he suspected she hadn't even been aware of, ceased.

A slight cough, then another, caused him to look around. Yosh stood in the corridor. "We just called the paramedics for Henry. He looks like he's on the verge of a heart attack. And the engineer is ready to give his statement about Lacy's activities."

"I'll be right there," Paavo said as he stepped away from Angie trying, unsuccessfully, to appear nonchalant. "I'll also get Angie's statement."

Yosh nodded. "Seems you're doing that already, buddy," he said, one eyebrow lifted, as he turned and went back inside.

Paavo smoothed his tie, then led Angie, who couldn't help but smile at Yosh's comment, back into the radio station.

Angie insisted on going to Homicide with Paavo when his work was completed at the studio. The way her adrenalin was pumping, going back to her parents' home and pretending nothing had happened was the last thing she wanted to do. She expected that she might even think of something more to tell him and wanted to be there.

Instead, she spent two hours sitting alone in the reception area. After a while, she walked over to Yoshiwara's desk.

Yosh glanced at her. "I guess Paavo will be through with the paperwork and his reports sometime soon. I'll sure be interested in hearing why Lacy killed all those people."

"I think it boiled down to vanity and jealousy." Angie sighed.

Yosh nodded. "Two of the cardinal sins—pride and greed. It's always something like that."

"I'm not surprised," she murmured, and then looked toward the interview room where she suspected Paavo was concentrating on his report. "I wonder why Paavo's taking so long?"

"I don't know. It can't be much longer. I suspect he'll be back any minute."

"Okay."

"Why don't you go home, Angie? I can have him call you."

"I'll wait here a little while longer," she said, and then walked over to Paavo's desk and sat in his chair. "Sitting here, I can see what it's like working in Homicide. Maybe it'll help me understand him a little, right?"

Yosh smiled. "I think you understand him a lot better than you realize. Better than he realizes, too."

Angie looked at the papers on his desk. Most were carefully placed in manila folders. A glance at Yosh's desk told her that not all detectives did that. Yosh's desk looked like a blizzard had struck it. She should have known Paavo was a neatness fanatic. Organized and orderly. Maybe that was why she drove him so crazy?

She thumbed through the carefully labelled, alphabetized folders on a stand-up rack on the side of his desk. Danning, Greuber, Klaw, Marcuccio, Wielund... Klaw? The others were all murder victims. But Axel Klaw was still alive. She pulled the folder out of the rack.

"That's all confidential, Angie," Yosh said. "Not for the public. Sorry."

"Oh, of course." She pushed the folder aside, away from her, then folded her hands, waiting.

A few minutes later, Yosh turned to her once more. "Would you like some coffee?"

"Love some."

He went out to the coffee machine. Quickly, she opened Axel Klaw's folder and started to skim through it, particularly curious about Klaw's prior arrests.

Klaw had been arrested a few times, but only convicted once—heroin possession—and was given a suspended sentence. She glanced through the file until her eye caught a name and then a date... twenty years earlier.

Carefully but quickly she read that Axel Klaw, who at the time was still using his real name of Alexander Clausen, was questioned concerning the death by heroin overdose of nineteen-year-old Jessica Smith. Angie gasped, her heart pounding.

That was Paavo's sister's name... and her age at the time of her death. She knew how Paavo felt about his sister.

Clausen, she read, age twenty-five, was suspected of being a drug dealer and introducing young people to drugs. But the police couldn't find anyone willing to testify against him. Clausen had been seen with Jessica at local bars throughout the evening, but he swore she was fine when he left her at a friend's apartment.

Jessica's family, a step-father and young brother, swore she'd never used drugs before. She was found by her young brother the next morning. Others in the apartment were passed out, but Jessica was dead. For lack of evidence, the district attorney dropped the charges against Clausen. A reference was made to Jessica Smith's own file where more detail of the investigation into her death could be found.

Angie carefully slid the report back in the file, then sat unmoving, scarcely believing what she'd read, as Yosh came back with coffee for both of them. "The machine was cranky," he said in his booming voice. "Sorry for the delay."

"No problem," she murmured.

He gave her a strange look, but put down her coffee cup and went to his desk.

After a moment, she picked up the coffee, leaned back in her chair, then spun it around so that she could stare out the window, lost in thought.

The report said that Jessica had been found by her younger brother. Paavo had told her a little about that, but the police report made it cold and brutal. Angie couldn't imagine how horrible it had to have been for Paavo. Such tragedy, at such a young age.

She suspected Paavo didn't believe the accidental overdose

conclusion. And from what little she had seen of his reaction to Axel Klaw, he could well believe Jessica's death was Klaw's fault.

"Well, well, why do we have the honor of her presence?"

Angie looked up to see Inspector Luis Calderon stroll into the room and address his question to Yoshiwara. She'd encountered him when she first met Paavo, during the time someone was trying to kill her. Yosh cast a reassuring glance at Angie before answering. "She's waiting for Paavo. I think he's wrapping up some paperwork in the interview room. He went off to find a place he could write and not be disturbed."

Calderon snorted. "She's gonna have a long wait. I passed him driving down the street as I headed back here. He turned onto the Bay Bridge approach."

Angie jumped to her feet. The Bay Bridge led to Berkeley... and Axel Klaw. Panicked, she said, "Yosh, will you come with me? I think I know where he's gone."

"You can't let her drag you around, man," Calderon argued. "You got work to do. Paavo's a big boy. He can take care of himself."

Yosh looked at Angie, saw her distress. "She's not dragging anyone anywhere, Luis. She did a damn fine job today for all of us. I think you owe her an apology. And I think you owe Paavo one as well."

Angie wasn't about to wait, though. The thought of Paavo going off alone to face Klaw made her nerve endings raw. Grabbing her purse, she ran to the elevator and pushed the down button again and again. Before the elevator arrived, Yosh was at her side.

39

Paavo sat in Axel Klaw's office. With him, was Lieutenant Bert Janosky of the Berkeley Police Department.

Klaw sat behind an enormous polished mahogany desk, a poster-size black-and-white photo of a woman's naked torso on the wall behind him. The walls of the office were painted black, and the upholstered furniture was red leather.

"Thank you for your cooperation, Mr. Klaw," Lieutenant Janosky said. "Since you know nothing about Karl Wielund, Chick Marcuccio, or the others killed in the strange crime wave in San Francisco, it won't be necessary for you to come to the station at this time. And we've denied the SFPD's request for a search warrant against you."

Klaw smiled at Janosky, ignoring Paavo, as he then stood. "My pleasure. I always cooperate with the police."

Janosky also stood and looked at Paavo, who remained seated. "Shall we go, Inspector Smith?"

"You go ahead. I'd like to talk to Mister Klaw about something."

"What's this?" Klaw demanded "Haven't I cooperated enough?"

"This isn't your jurisdiction, Smith," Janosky warned.

Paavo smiled coldly. "Let's just say I might be here as a customer."

Janosky eyed him skeptically.

"Fine." Klaw shook hands with Janosky. "It's been a pleasure, as always."

Janosky left without even a glance at Paavo.

Klaw eased himself back in his chair, his hands clasped behind his head as he regarded Paavo. "You want to talk. I'm waiting."

"I want to talk about Alexander Clausen."

Klaw stiffened, but then smiled mirthlessly. "I don't."

"I want to talk about a string of murders Clausen was involved in. Starting with Jessica Smith and ending with Sheila Danning."

Klaw blinked; then recognition filled his eyes. "Smith. A common name. Most Smiths aren't even related."

"But some are."

Klaw studied Paavo, then nodded. "So that's it. The little brother grows up to become a hotshot cop, to right the injustices of the world." When Paavo remained silent, Klaw lifted his hands, palms up. "I don't know anything about anything. I'm clean, like Janosky said."

"And I've got Lacy LaTour, who I'm sure will be quite willing to say otherwise."

Klaw's mouth tightened. "I don't think so."

"Lacy knew Sheila Danning. Sheila wanted to blackmail her, working with someone who knew a lot more about Lacy's history than Sheila ever could have stumbled across on her own. Lacy killed Sheila because of that knowledge. That case will be going to trial. A lot will come out during it."

Klaw removed his hands from the desktop and placed them in his lap. "You're just bluffing, Smith. You don't have anything on me, and you won't get anything."

"You never know."

"You don't know me, the new me. You knew a young guy who might have gotten into things he didn't know much about. That kid grew up."

Something about the look in Klaw's eyes, the tightening of his jaw, warned Paavo. He pulled out his gun. "Don't try it, Klaw."

Klaw's eyebrows lifted, then a malevolent grin spread over his face. "How'd you know I had it?" Klaw slowly lifted the gun he'd been concealing under his desk. It was pointed at Paavo. "Put the gun down, Smith." His tone was icy. "And leave. If anything else happens, my boys will make sure you don't get out of here alive."

The door swung open and Dwayne from the front counter burst into the room. "Mr. Klaw, a cop outside—" He then froze at the sight of the guns.

Paavo didn't dare take his eyes off Klaw.

"Holy Christ!" The voice sounded like Yoshiwara's.

Klaw's eyes held Paavo's as he slowly lay his gun down on the desk, then pushed it forward, out of easy reach. Cautiously, Paavo did the same. Then Klaw turned to the people who had entered, and Paavo, for the first time, glanced their way. Dwayne still held the doorknob, his mouth agape. Yosh had his hand on his holster, and behind him, Angie was peering around his bulk.

Klaw chuckled, then smiled at the audience. "We were just showing off our revolvers. No need to look so startled, folks. No danger."

Paavo stood, placed his gun in his holster, and walked toward the door. "You haven't seen the last of me, Klaw," He left, not before seeing the fear behind Klaw's bravado, but even that gave him no satisfaction.

He walked by Angie who still stood in the doorway. He was

surprised when she stuck her head into Klaw's office. "You know what else, Klaw?" she said

Klaw lifted one eyebrow.

"I plan to be your worst nightmare." Then she hurried from the office.

Angie had to all but run down the sidewalk to keep up with Paavo as he marched toward his car. Yosh stayed behind her. Paavo reached the car and unlocked it.

"Are you okay?" she asked, her hands on his car door, as she gasped to catch her breath.

"Who me? I'm just great! How the hell do I look? And what business is it of yours anyway?" he bit out savagely.

She stepped back, stricken.

"Damn it, Angie when the hell are you going to learn to keep out of my business? You've got no right to go running around to places like this, with me or Yosh or anyone else. Is that clear? Can you understand me?"

"Yes, but—"

"But nothing! You don't belong. Keep the hell away from me and my job!" Paavo got in his car, slammed the door shut, and drove off.

Angie and Yosh stared after him until finally they went to Angie's car, Yosh's face filled with concerned. She drove him back to Homicide without speaking while Yosh prattled on about the case.

Angie wasn't able to think about it. She was still trying to get over the shock of seeing Paavo and Klaw pointing guns at each other. Ready to shoot. Ready to die. She'd thought her heart would stop. How could Paavo show such careless disregard for his own life? Damn him, why was he that way?

Angie dropped Yosh off at the Hall of Justice, and didn't

bother to get out of the car. No sense going upstairs. Paavo wouldn't want to see her. Not now, and the way he spoke to her, probably not ever.

She drove back to her apartment, no longer worrying about its safety. Klaw, she had the definite impression, wasn't going to go looking for her anytime soon.

Seated on the Hepplewhite chair, she sipped hot tea. The "classic" pornographic movies she'd purchased sat atop her DVD player. She took them into the kitchen and put them in a brown paper bag.

"Mrs. Calamatti, are you down there?" she called into the garbage chute.

No answer. Even Mrs. Calamatti had abandoned her. "Look out below!" she called and dropped the movies. That was the best place for them. She felt all right throwing them out because Mrs. Calamatti didn't own a DVD player.

Angie curled up in front of her bay windows. It was soon dark enough that she could see the beacon from Alcatraz illuminate the bay every nine seconds. At least some things never changed.

But she had. Her radio job was gone, and Paavo had withdrawn even further from her life. At one time, she'd wished he'd give up being a cop. But that was childish, she realized. He'd never give it up, definitely not for her, and especially not when he was close to getting the man he believed responsible for his sister's death.

Paavo had always been there when she needed him, but other than that he was never there for the two of them to simply enjoy being together. He couldn't accept what she had to offer, and he couldn't or wouldn't, let them have the togetherness she needed in a relationship.

Angie leaned forward, holding her head, her elbows on her knees. She hadn't truly understood, before encountering Axel Klaw, just how ugly Paavo's world could be. While she recognized the greed and desire to "make it big" that could corrupt a basically good man like Karl Wielund; the mistaken pride that would allow Lacy Latour to be used by a man like Klaw, causing her to commit murder and be blackmailed for it; and even the wrongheaded ambition of a man like Mark Dustman; she had never before encountered anyone with the complete lack of morals of the degenerate creature known as Axel Klaw.

As much as Klaw had held his gun emotionlessly on Paavo, so too had Paavo held his gun on Klaw. She covered her eyes, trying not to relive the horror of that scene. But no matter how hard she tried, she couldn't get it out of her mind. And the thought... if they had both fired...

She had seen Paavo shot once and still had nightmares about it. She never wanted to go through anything like that again.

Her father wanted her and Paavo to stop seeing each other, to not let this attraction they felt grow and become more serious. So did her sisters. So did Calderon, and possibly Yoshiwara as well. Maybe all those people did know what was best for her as well as Paavo. Suddenly, she felt too tired to fight them any longer, too tired to go on caring too much.

The Alcatraz beacon shimmered and grew misty as she blinked away foolish tears.

40

Paavo had to admit to more than a little trepidation as he knocked on the door of Angie's apartment. For sure, she'd be angry after the way he'd treated her the day before in Berkeley. Being unable to arrest Axel Klaw or even to search his premises, had put him in no mood to be civil with anyone, and he'd taken his frustration and anger out on her. He'd lost control, badly, and it had been wrong of him.

He still wasn't sure how his gun duel would have played out had he and Klaw not been interrupted. A stupid stunt, yet at the time, holding that gun on Klaw had felt beyond good. He almost hated to admit to himself just how good, especially since a part of him suspected that if they hadn't been stopped, they might easily have killed each other. Hell, they might still.

All the more reason, he thought, to apologize to Angie. That was the only reason he'd come here this afternoon, to apologize. It was only natural to shower and wear clean clothes, along with the after shave she liked. He couldn't apologize properly if he looked scruffy. Same with the bouquet of red roses he held. So what that he could have eaten for a week on what they'd cost him. He couldn't imagine giving her anything less.

Maybe it was stupid to be here. But the guilt he felt had only deepened when Yosh told him that she was the one who realized he must be headed for Berkeley, and why. She understood a lot more than he imagined. And she deserved to be told that. As well as to be told he was fifty kinds of idiot for hurting her—a hard-headed fool who didn't deserve her.

And to ask her to forgive him.

He knocked again. Was she just being slow to answer, or had she gone out?

He knocked once more, feeling more foolish with each passing minute he stood there.

A door opened across the hallway. A head peeped out. "She's not home," Stan Bonnette said with immense satisfaction.

"Do you know when she'll be back?" Paavo asked, much as he hated to ask Stan anything about Angie.

"Maybe never."

Paavo turned cold. "What do you mean?"

"She packed a suitcase this morning, then gave me her key and said she'd send some movers over to pack up the rest of her clothes and her computer files."

Movers?! No, she couldn't... "Where are the movers supposed to deliver her things?"

"She didn't tell me."

Maybe Stan was just lying, wanting to annoy him... the way Stan always did. His heart began to drum. "What's the name of the moving company?"

"I don't know."

Paavo grew more and more agitated with each smug, annoying non-answer. "What about her furniture, her cooking stuff?"

"Listen, Inspector, this isn't one of your cases. I'm just helping out my neighbor, okay?"

Paavo fought the urge to put this hands around the little twerp's skinny neck and make him answer. "Fine! Good neighbor Stan. *That doesn't answer the question!*"

Stan sighed. "They'll stay here, I guess, until she decides if she's coming back or not."

"Did she drive?"

Stan shrugged. "She didn't leave me the key to her car. But then, she never did let me drive it."

Paavo felt beyond lost. His voice dropped, low and soft. "Any message for anyone? For me?"

Stan's lips curved into a contented smile. "Not a single word."

Paavo got off the elevator on the third floor, walked to apartment 301 and knocked on the door.

Mrs. Calamatti opened it. "Oh, hello. You're Angie's young man, aren't you? I can't remember your name—something foreign as I recall. The old brain isn't as sharp as it once was."

"I thought you might like these flowers, Mrs. Calamatti," he said.

Her eyes lit up with pleasure and she opened her arms to receive the bouquet. "Why, thank you. What a lovely surprise. I can't remember the last time a young man brought me flowers, and such beautiful ones, too."

He was glad she liked them. "Just promise me you'll never get into a dumpster again."

Her lips downturned. "Never?"

He took out his badge and held it before her. "Never. You could get hurt. You never know what strange things people will throw away, including broken glass."

She sighed. "I see. All right... never."

"Good. Well, goodbye." He put the badge away and headed back toward the elevator.

"Oh, young man?"

He stopped and turned.

"Could you take a moment to help me, please? My son and daughter-in-law gave me a DVD player some years ago. I put it away in the closet and never hooked it up because I didn't have anything to watch. But now...." She abruptly stopped her explanation. "Anyway, could you hook it up to the TV for me?"

"Sure," he said. "I'd be glad to."

41

Once home, Paavo fed Hercules then called the special directory assistance number the force used and found out Sal Amalfi's unlisted phone number in Hillsborough, a tiny, exclusive enclave nestled among the hills on the San Francisco peninsula.

The maid answered his call.

"This is Inspector Paavo Smith," he said, "San Francisco Police Department. I'm calling to speak to Miss Angelina Amalfi."

"I'm sorry, but she isn't here."

His heart sank. He'd been sure she'd gone back to her parents' home. Now what? "Do you know where I can reach her?"

"No, sir. But she's expected back this evening."

It actually took a moment for him to realize what the maid has just said. If she'd been there, he would have kissed her. "This evening, you said? Thank you."

As evening approached, he left the house, got into his car, and put the key in the ignition. Instead of turning the key, though, he folded his arms over the steering wheel, staring straight ahead.

Why was he planning to rush off to Hillsborough? She'd left without telling him, without leaving him any kind of message. Shouldn't he be glad? After all his backing away, telling her it'd never work between the two of them, and her insisting that it would, he'd finally won. It was what he wanted.

She was gone. It was over. *Let it be, Smith!*

Back in the house, Paavo walked straight through the living room and into his large, thoroughly empty kitchen.

He opened the refrigerator, and saw what remained of the eggs and bacon and such that Angie had bought to make him a big breakfast the other day. He shut the door again.

He sat in the living room. It was absolutely quiet. No Angie to ask him to light the fireplace, to talk to him, to quiz him about his cases, or badger him by asking if he'd thought about this or that. Hell, he should be happy she wasn't here. Now he could have a little peace in his life again. And he could forget all about her.

But he probably never would forget the first time he ever saw her, a pretty little thing trying to act sophisticated and tough even though a dishwasher had just exploded and could have killed her. Or even the way she'd stood up for him when Yosh went to his house to take him to a press conference and she felt he needed to stay home and rest. He couldn't remember anyone but Aulis, when he was a kid, doing anything like that for him.

He'd never forget the way she could brighten his day with a simple smile, or tell crazy stories to make him laugh. She could be whimsical or wild, starry-eyed or passionate.

He shouldn't think this way. Hadn't his friends encouraged him to find a woman like Rebecca? It'd never work out with someone who didn't understand police work, they said. Look at

Calderon. Fifteen years with a woman, and then she'd walked out on him.

Fifteen years....

He wondered what it'd be like to spend fifteen years with Angie. It wouldn't be dull, that was for sure. Open, joyful and trusting... everything he wasn't.

Everything he needed...

Thinking this way was nonsense. He should go to bed. Why not have a long, peaceful night's sleep?

But in bed, it was only worse. He lay there staring at the darkened ceiling, and feeling as if what little light there had been in his life had gone out of it completely.

42

Two days later, after meeting with an assistant district attorney about Lacy LaTour's case, Paavo was called into Chief Hollins' office.

"I just got a call from the chief of police over in Berkeley," Hollins said. "He began by apologizing that one of his men believed Axel Klaw was nothing but a producer who made movies—not great movies, but also not illegal. They think now they were wrong about him."

Paavo nodded, anxious about what was to come.

Hollins continued. "Apparently, Klaw's porno studio was cleaned out the day after you met with him. Not even a fingerprint was left behind. Klaw seems to have vanished into thin air."

Paavo shut his eyes. This news only confirmed what he'd expected—that Klaw had connections, big ones, and that the seedy little porn studio was nothing but a front. But he also told himself Klaw would turn up again in time. Klaw had too much invested, too many connections, in this area to leave it completely.

Paavo opened his eyes to see the Hollins watching him intently.

"I'd like the rest of the day off," he said.

Hollins nodded. "Have patience, Smith." He pointed the unlit cigar at him. "And be careful."

Paavo left Homicide. He hated the fact that Klaw had slipped underground. He hadn't expected anything less. But now that he knew what alias Clausen was using, and the business he was into, tracking him down would no longer be the mystery it had been for years. Klaw would lie low for a while, but eventually he would come back. Men like him always did.

And then, Paavo would be waiting.

Which meant that, right now, Axel Klaw wasn't his most pressing problem.

Instead of heading across the city toward home, Paavo headed south, towards Hillsborough. He didn't allow himself even to think about what he was doing as he turned onto the brick driveway that made a half-circle in front of the white mansion that was the Amalfi family home. He rang the doorbell, and the maid opened the door.

"Paavo Smith. I'm here to see Miss Amalfi."

"Won't you come in, Mr. Smith?" The maid led him across the marble-floored entry to the library. "I'll see if Miss Amalfi is available."

Paavo had been to the house only once before, but he hadn't forgotten the vaulted ceilings, the tapestries, the heavy mahogany furniture that made the house look more like an expensive villa on the Mediterranean than a home in California. He crossed the library with its leather-upholstered furniture and book-lined walls to the French doors looking out onto manicured lawns that would have made a golf course gardener jealous.

A man's slightly accented voice said, "Inspector Smith."

Paavo turned to see Sal Amalfi enter the room. "Mr. Amalfi." Paavo walked toward Sal and extended his hand. The older man gripped it in a strong, quick handshake.

"I want to talk to you..., Paavo."

Paavo eyed him, trying to figure out what was going on. Was Angie's father here to throw him out without seeing her, or what? "Sure..., Sal."

Sal's eyes narrowed ever so slightly. "I know there was some kind of trouble, but Angie won't tell me about it, and not even Commissioner Barcelli will say."

Paavo lifted his chin. "Maybe there's nothing to tell."

"There was something." Sal's eyes sharpened. "Now, though, she says she doesn't even want to think about it anymore."

Paavo's brow furrowed. "All I want to do is apologize to her about the other day."

"I don't think she needs your apology," Sal said. "I think she needs time to forget."

Although he understood the fatherly concern, Paavo spoke with all the sincerity and conviction he possessed. "I need to know what Angie thinks, not you."

"So that you can *apologize* to her?"

At Sal's badgering question, Paavo was forced to face the fact that while he wanted to apologize, he also wanted much more. And he recognized that Sal had been purposefully misunderstanding him, purposefully pressing him to explain.

Paavo wasn't one to bare his feelings to anyone, not even the few people he'd ever loved. But he knew he had to let Sal know just how special Angie was to him, and that whatever it was he felt for her was real and deep. Yet, when he looked at Sal and tried to explain, all he could say was, "To tell her... how much I miss her."

Sal nodded thoughtfully, his expression penetrating, as if taking in the full measure of the tough, close-mouthed policeman. "You care about her a lot, don't you?"

Paavo drew in a deep breath. "Yes. More than I ever imagined was possible."

Troubled concern warred with resignation as Sal studied Paavo. Finally, he gave a defeated sigh. "Serafina's got a keen eye, and she says you're okay. I have my doubts. And I don't like you seeing my daughter." He walked over to a world globe and spun it, watching the blue ocean merge with colorful countries as the world spun round and round. He slid his hands into his trouser pockets and, as the globe slowed down, he faced Paavo once more. "But I can't fight all three of you. Angelina's miserable. It's like living with a rain cloud inside the house. Do what you have to do. But be sure. And *go slow*."

Paavo's spirits leaped. "I will."

"Good, because Angelina won't!" Sal shook his head. "I'll get her." He left the room.

Despite how good he felt at having overcome the first hurdle, Paavo braced himself to face Angie, knowing how distressed she must be. The thought of seeing her upset with him was making him, a hardened police veteran, break out in a sweat.

He waited a full fifteen minutes before he heard the click-click of her high heels on the marble entry hall. She appeared in the doorway. He slowly stood, holding his breath, unsure what to expect.

She didn't look upset at all. Instead, she looked dazzling in a red silk dress with black trim and jet buttons. Her hair didn't have a strand out of place, elegantly swept back off her face, with more blond highlights than he remembered. Her make-up was flawless, her eyes clear and sparkling, and her lipstick and long, long fingernails matched her cherry-colored dress.

"Hello. How nice to see you." She sounded as if she were meeting a lady friend at an afternoon tea. Then she crossed the room to him. The tantalizing scent of tea roses wafted to his nose and did crazy things to his heartbeat. "Won't you sit down?" She gestured toward the sofa and chairs.

Speechless, he sat on a sofa. She sat on a chair, catty corner to him.

"You look very nice," he said, once he'd found his voice. Nice, hell, she looked beautiful. Gorgeous, even.

"Thank you."

"I wanted to apologize for the last time I saw you." He drew in his breath. Apologies didn't come easy to him, and this one, he absolutely had to get right. "I was so angry with Klaw, it was all I could think about."

Angie lifted an eyebrow, and then, nonchalantly, she shrugged. "I understand perfectly."

"Good. I'm sorry, Angie."

She gave a swift nod, and said nothing more.

He cleared his throat. "I heard you've packed up your clothes and might leave your apartment. Your neighbor, Bonnette, told me."

She stood and walked behind the chair she'd sat on, running her finger along the piping on the headrest. "I felt I needed a change."

"Do you need... *much* of a change, Angie?"

Her eyes met his and held. He stood, ready to step closer to her.

Abruptly, she turned her back on him, running her finger now along the spines of books in a case. "I came here to find out," she said.

"Angie, I miss you. I... I think I'd like to see you again. Soon."

She slowly turned, glaring at him as she all but whispered, "You *what?*"

He wondered if she hadn't heard him, and repeated, "I think I'd like to see you again."

She gripped a hardback novel as he watched her face redden and her eyes blaze. "You *think?*"

He stared, not sure what to say.

Her hands tightened on the book and he was half-way sure she was about to throw it at him. Instead she put it down.

"Angie, what—?"

Her voice was low, cutting, and beyond angry. "I don't care what you *think*, Paavo! Or what your so-called buddies think!" She drew in her breath.

"Angie, please."

"If you ever *know* how you feel about me, then I just might *think* about changing my mind about you!"

He strode toward her. "I'm not here to upset you. I've gone about this all wrong."

"Have you?" She flung her arms wide and moved away from him. "I can't take this, Paavo. Whenever I thought I'd gotten close to you, you'd shut down, turn me away, and then leave! I can't live like that. And since, after all this, you still don't know how you feel, I can't see you anymore. It's simply too hard."

The finality of her words crushed him.

The low roar of a sports car approaching the house filled the room and Angie's attention turned to the window. A new, green Jaguar pulled to a stop in the driveway in front of Paavo's old Mustang.

"You must excuse me," she said, her bottom lip trembling as she smoothed her dress, "but Joey Marcuccio is here. My date."

He couldn't believe any of this. "The kid who used to rub pie in your face?"

"That was when we were *little.*" She heard the car engine

shut off. "He'll be in here any second. Come on." She looped her arm in Paavo's and led him out of the library.

"What are you doing?" he asked as she hurried him into the kitchen.

She opened the back door and pushed him out into the garden. "As soon as Joey and I leave, you can slip out the side gate. Goodbye."

Before he could get over his stunned shock, she slammed the door shut. The loud 'click' of the dead bolt that followed sounded as final as her words back in the house. Paavo found himself gaping at a closed door, not believing what had just happened.

It was over. She'd said it more than once. She'd left him no doubt.

And she'd explained exactly why.

***

"Joey, how nice," Angie said as she opened the front door.

"Are you having some work done on the house?" he asked. "There's some old, battered car in your driveway—"

"Ignore it. Let's go." She took hold of his arm and hurried him from the house.

She was almost at Joey's Jaguar when she heard Paavo calling her name. Joey continued to his car and got in as she turned around.

Paavo ran to her, faced her.

"Don't go," he said.

She waited.

"I hate the idea of you going off on a date with someone else. I can't stand it, in fact."

She couldn't believe what she was hearing. "Oh?"

He seemed to hesitate a moment, and then confessed, "I

want to be with you. I *know* I do. I've never been more sure of anything."

She could scarcely believe he was admitting that to her. "But you're the one who told me to stay away."

"I was wrong. Completely, stupidly wrong. I can only hope someday you'll forgive me."

She searched his face a long time, and then nodded. "Of course, I will. It was only because you acted as if you didn't ever want to see me, or—"

He stepped closer and placed his hands against her hair. She stopped speaking. Looking into his eyes, she saw desire and need, and knew the same was reflected in her gaze at him. Ever so slowly, he bent his head toward her. And finally, their lips met.

She felt as if a tremor rocked her as she kissed the lips that had so often spoken words that went straight to her heart.

He didn't put his arms around her, didn't hold her. Only their lips met.

Then he lifted his head as his gaze met hers. "Damn," he whispered.

She couldn't help but hold her breath. Despite him saying words she'd long wanted to hear, would he walk away again, as he had in the past, fearing their closeness? She waited, wondering.

His hands went to her waist, drawing her closer. Her body swayed toward his, and then his lips found hers once more with a fire and urgency far beyond her expectations. He held her tight as her arms circled his neck and she returned his kisses, kisses that sent sparks of desire through her body that left her breathless.

Kissing him, rather than releasing the tension that had pulsated through her around him for so long, only increased it. The way she felt about him was both wonderful and frightening in its strength, its need, yet, in her heart, she'd always known it would be this way between them, it would feel as if—

"Ah, *excuse me! Excuse me, Angelina! Hey there! Angie! Angie?*"

Slowly, the voice calling her cut through to her, and she pulled back from Paavo. They stared at each other as if a little stunned by what had just happened, and by the intensity of their feelings.

"Angie. Yoo-hoo?"

She turned to see Joey Marcuccio leaning across the white leather seats of his Jaguar and peering out at them through the open passenger-side window. "Does this mean you don't want to go out with me tonight?"

She glanced at Paavo and smiled. "I'm afraid not, Joey. I believe I'll be busy moving back to my apartment in the city."

Paavo smiled back at her and nodded. "That sounds like a fine idea."

She realized, and knew he probably did as well, that her parents were very likely watching everything that had just happened. And she didn't care in the slightest.

"I guess I should go inside," she said, her eyes searching Paavo's face. "I'll have some explaining and packing to do. Do you want to come with me?"

"Of course."

She smiled. "Good. But first, I need one more thing from you."

He looked at her with curiosity. "Anything."

She put her arms around him, holding him as if she never wanted to let him go. "Another kiss."

He happily complied.

I hope you enjoyed this Cook and Inspector Mystery. Continue to follow Angie and Paavo's story with **The Marinara Murders.**

ABOUT THE AUTHOR

Joanne Pence was born and raised in northern California and now lives in Idaho. She has been an award-winning, *USA Today* best-selling author of mysteries for many years, but she has also written historical fiction, contemporary romance, romantic suspense, a fantasy, and supernatural suspense. All of her books are now available as ebooks and in print, and most are also offered in special large print editions. Joanne hopes you'll enjoy her books, which present a variety of times, places, and reading experiences, from mysterious to thrilling, emotional to lightly humorous, as well as powerful tales of times long past.

Visit her at www.joannepence.com and be sure to sign up for Joanne's mailing list to hear about new books.

www.ingramcontent.com/pod-product-compliance
Lightning Source LLC
Chambersburg PA
CBHW020917060726
47591CB00004B/1280